I0575141

STONEFALL

Stonefall Book One

————————————

AVERY BLAKE

DAVID W. WRIGHT

STERLING & STONE

The authors greatly appreciate you taking the time to read our work. Please consider leaving a review wherever you bought the book, or telling your friends about it, to help us spread the word.

Thank you for supporting our work.

STONEFALL

Chapter One

SOMETIMES MONEY COSTS TOO DAMNED much.

The thought kept looping in Eamon's head, over and over as he sat in the passenger seat of Felony's ancient Mustang, the pair of them on their way to something only one of them wanted to do.

This was why Eamon left and swore he'd never be where he was right now. He loathed this part of his family. Loathed himself even more. By contrast, violence was in Felony's blood. Always had been. Before that fateful day when Liam first brought him home, after he came back from the Middle East and a sea of legal machine guns, then every day since. Born Franklin Washington — *"Two white presidents, and ain't that some shit?"* — Eamon knew him for years before he ever heard the name Franklin. He'd introduced himself as Felony, a nickname he chose for himself at a time when he could only be tried as a minor, no matter how awful the crime.

They were almost there. Eamon was working his nerves, steeling himself for what was coming. Felony was making it harder, eyeing him at every red light. He was the only person Eamon knew who still *chose* to manually drive a car, no matter the roads or their condition, and not because the engine deserved it. Just because he wanted to.

The old Mustang had never been outfitted with auto-drive, but that was intentional. Even if they'd been driving the brand new Blacklander, Felony would still have his hands at ten and two, eyes on the windshield like the glass was a target.

Eamon could no longer take it. "You want to tell me why you're staring at me like that?"

The light turned green.

Felony looked back at the road, turning away from Eamon as he accelerated. "Just curious …"

"Curious about whether you should've brought me along? Curious if my father's lost his shit for making you? Curious to see if—"

"I'm curious why you're back, seeing as how you never had the stomach."

"Who cares if I have the stomach?" Eamon said. "I have the aptitude."

"The *aptitude?*" Felony smiled like that was a punchline. "We ain't talking cognitive ability or inductive reasoning or any such shit. This kind of work *lives* in the gut. You either have it or you don't."

"And you're not sure I do."

"I guess if I'm being generous." Felony swung a right and the Tinker Town sign came into view. "You've never wanted anything to do with any of this, so why are you here?"

Eamon had heard more stories about Felony than he wanted to. The man never flinched when pulling the trigger, but he also didn't give a shit what anyone thought of him. So this could go either way. He might be chiding

Eamon or questioning his strength. And in the way he always had, not quite like an uncle or a brother but a little of both, he might have been disappointed, thinking Eamon could do better, that he'd gotten out of this life for a reason and for good.

"I need the money."

Felony nodded. "You sure do."

Eamon flinched.

Fuck you, Felony.

He'd never wanted to be here and had naively believed he could escape the violence of his childhood while still providing a life for his family. The good kind, keeping them safe and happy. But Eamon was raised by wolves and was never allowed to enjoy the quiet like a sheep. He was born with little capacity for violence, always longing for exploration. Instead, he was taught to quell the empathy he felt for his friends and fellow humans. Only the family mattered, including the killers his father called kin, even without any blood between them.

Jack Quinn taught his son to fight. To use his fists like bludgeons. Taught him to kill in close quarters. Showed him as a boy how he could be the kind of man who walked into the heart of darkness, then left unscathed.

Turned him into a wolf before he had hair on his balls. Yet inside his son was still a lamb.

It had taken a long while for Eamon to learn who he was — neither the wolf nor the lamb, Eamon was the sheepdog. Unlike the innocents, he had seen the wolves. Lived his life close enough to smell them. So, he could never think like a sheep. They lived pretending the wolves would never come, while the sheepdog spent his life waiting for the inevitable day when the wolf would come to rip the unsuspecting sheep to pieces.

Poppy was the sweetest sort of sheep there was, the

kind Eamon could love forever. But that asshole at her work was a wolf for sure. It was his fault all of this happened. He shouldn't have been harassing her. If he'd kept to himself, Poppy would still have a job and Eamon would be anywhere but here, hating himself more than he had in a long time, since before the first time she kissed him, less than a week after showing up at Liam's and begging his brother for help.

Eamon couldn't let pride get in the way. Not with Poppy eight months pregnant.

He still hadn't responded to Felony. Now it was too late.

They pulled into the Tinker Town parking lot.

Felony killed the engine. Then he took his hands off the wheel and turned to Eamon. "You ready for this?"

"Of course I am." But he was only as much ready as he wasn't.

They entered in perfect step, strides harmonized despite Felony's six extra inches and his being raised feral and allergic to the leash. They stopped at the counter and a twenty-something clerk croaked a few words that resembled, *Can I help you?*

But he knew why they were there.

"Runyon."

Felony peered at the clerk. He didn't need another word. The kid scampered off, leaving the bruisers to look around the room.

Eamon wished they were there for a different reason. He'd love to investigate. Jacob Runyon ran Tinker Town, a collective of makers who created crazy shit to sell in-house and online. A lot of tech and 3-D printing. Runyon only had the one physical location, but online sales were global and steady. Like a lot of people who made a lot of money for the first time in their lives, Runyon didn't know what to do with his. So, like some of those people, he gambled.

He came out to greet Eamon and Felony at the counter. His wide smile suggested he wasn't in deep enough with the Quinns for the bubbles to tickle his nose. He nervously tugged on a beard that looked like molting birds.

"Hey guys!"

"Time's up," Felony said.

"Wait a minute …" Runyon started.

"You hear what I just said?" Felony waited a beat, glaring at Runyon to get the man in a sweat. "Ain't no more time. You're outta days. Same for your hours and minutes. We've come to collect."

Another tug on his beard, then Runyon crossed his arms and stood straighter. "What happens if you can't?"

Eamon wanted to get the hell out of there. This was supposed to simple.

He wasn't that late. This was a warning, and Eamon was backup. Everyone knew the rules. It wasn't like Runyon would have to surrender the whole amount. Just enough to make Jack happy. They would come back for more.

But it looked like Runyon wanted to hold his ground, and that meant that Eamon was at bat.

Tinkerers emerged from the shadows, gathering around them to make Eamon acutely aware of how oblivious he'd been.

But Felony wasn't surprised. Fists at his side, studying the room. His gaze like a gunslinger, eyes peeled for an agitation of movement or more. "You paying, or what?"

Arms still crossed. "I'll pay you every cent I owe you the minute I can afford to. I'm good for my debts. Always have been. I don't need you coming in here to threaten me. Or bringing the boss's son with you."

He dared a glance at Eamon, then turned back to Felony.

The closest tinkerer stepped forward. He had a face like faded denim. "You need anything, boss?"

"No. These gentlemen were just leaving. They're planning to come back this time next week, when we're more prepared for their company."

Eamon wanted to close his eyes but couldn't put his fear on display.

Felony shook his head and for a second like he almost looked sorry, but then he was grabbing Runyon by the shoulders, lifting him up and tossing the man onto his side of the counter. His fists were immediate, pistons on Runyon's pigheaded face. Something crunched. Blood went flying. Runyon's men sprang into action.

There were five. Runyon would have made an even six, but he wouldn't be going anywhere for a while.

Felony stood as a trio of assailants crowded around him, the other two making their way toward Eamon.

That math felt about right.

Eamon turned to Faded Denim and a ginger with mustard-colored teeth.

Denim swung first, but his fist was unpracticed and wild. Despite his size there was little behind it, and Eamon caught the wayward punch in his left open palm. He squeezed hard, surprising the man, before blinding him with a flat handed thrust to the bridge of his nose.

Denim staggered back and Ginger took his place, hands high to keep Eamon from hitting his nose.

But that was an idiot's move. Eamon's first punch landed full in Ginger's stomach, stealing most of his air and making him choke for the few remaining gasps. The second punch went right to the kidneys, followed by a hard stomp on the man's knee to get his lips kissing the ground.

Both assholes bounced back up and came charging at Eamon. He stole a glance at Felony to make sure he was okay — one of his attackers was down, another was limping, and the last looked scared out of his gourd — then turned back to Denim and Ginger.

"You really want to do this?"

The men stopped. They looked over to their two friends, about to get pounded. Then the foursome backed away, leaving three limp bodies and a pool of blood on the ground.

"We'll be back tomorrow for our money, and we expect things will go better than this." Felony stared them down, making sure each man flinched before moving on to the next. Then he trashed a few displays on his way out of the shop.

Eamon felt worse with every crash on the floor.

Back in the Denali, Felony said, "That was some damn fine fighting …"

He didn't finish, though there was clearly more to the sentence.

"But?" Eamon prompted.

"But I'm not sure you would've been ready if I hadn't been there to make sure we were."

Eamon stared at the window, because fuck Felony.

"You can't afford to flinch. The second you do, your enemy will see your hesitation."

Eamon had grown up with Jack Quinn as his father. There wasn't a thing Felony could possibly say that Eamon hadn't already heard, countless times, whether he wanted to or not.

But Eamon was even more annoyed at himself. It was his *first* job and the violent impulses were right there on the surface. He didn't have to dive deep like he told himself he would.

"You didn't see me flinch. Because I don't."

And Felony laughed. "Alrighty, Simba. We'll see."

Chapter Two

HOME WAS the last place Eamon wanted to go, despite it being pretty much the only place he ever wanted to be.

Poppy would know something was wrong the second he stepped through the door. She always did. But this time he had a rip on his collar and scuffed knuckles to finish the story.

Eamon would rather peel off all five of his fingernails than lie to her, but that's what he'd have to do because even though prying off his nails would leave him in a separate hell, it wouldn't keep Poppy from asking her questions.

"I'm home," he called, looking in the mirror. His cheek was swelling from a punch he didn't realize he'd taken and hadn't seen the last time he checked himself in the car.

Poppy walked in from the kitchen, but whimpered when she saw him as the smile fell from her face.

"What happened?"

Eamon held his arms open and Poppy ran over. He expected her to collapse into them. Instead she grabbed them both, just above the elbows, and stared into his eyes. "Tell me the truth."

And even though he desperately wanted to, Eamon went ahead and lied. "I got jumped."

It was a while before she blinked. Then she narrowed her eyes. "Where did you get jumped?"

"I was making a sales call, over behind the Target on Bench."

Her face didn't relax, but it did shift into something different. "That's dangerous, Eamon. Why would you do that?"

"People in terrible neighborhoods need the most insurance. Tommy told me he *killed it* in that neighborhood."

"Yeah, well, Tommy says a lot of things."

Poppy might not like the idea of his working with Tommy, idiot that he was, but selling insurance was a legitimate gig and kept her from asking too many questions. Unfortunately, it didn't keep Eamon from feeling like shit every time he left the house, knowing he'd always return with his time full of lies.

But they needed the money. The alternative was a brick wall and a ring of fire around it.

Eamon couldn't tell her he was working for his father. He swore he'd never take his family's filthy money. He'd sold himself that story his entire life, but it wasn't until Eamon saw her smiling from across a crowded campus when he finally believed he had a chance.

Poppy was a kind-hearted soul, and strong enough to hold his moral center. Eamon set himself on the right path, but she kept him there. Or at least she had, until he started to lie.

He would get them out of this, then close the door and never open it — or look behind him — again.

"Maybe you should get a different job."

"What sort of job?" Eamon asked. "It's not like anyone is beating down our door and throwing me offers."

"No one's going to beat down your door, but that doesn't mean you're not worth hiring."

"This is the best money I can make right now. At least we have *something* coming in."

Eamon took Poppy's hand and led her to the couch. They sat facing each other, their knees touching. He planted his palm on her belly and slowly started to rub it.

"I don't want you going door to door anymore, Eamon. It's dangerous. And you can do better."

"I'll do anything, so tell me — *How are we supposed to raise a child without any insurance?*"

Poppy made a face. And in the silence, he heard her bellowing thoughts.

This was all his fault. She'd made good money before he lost his temper and cost her her job. A helluva lot more than he ever made as a maintenance man.

They didn't need a lot. They had each other and plenty to live on. Her job had benefits, including a generous maternity package. But when Professor Graubner began to harass her — before and after nearly every class, finding every excuse to be around, despite her constant refusal — Eamon could only take it so long.

Unfortunately, Eamon took care of things with more color than the situation warranted. The professor didn't press charges, but that didn't stop either Eamon or Poppy from losing their jobs.

"Neither one of us should have to be looking door-to-door right now," she finally said.

"What, was I supposed to let that asshole sexually harass you?"

"There are proper procedures for that kind of stuff. But you ignored them all, and now here we are."

"I said I was sorry."

"A bunch of times. Every time we discuss it. And I

always say, 'That's okay, honey. I forgive you.' Then half the time, we have sex. But not now, Eamon. And not just because I'm tired and sore. You can do better than this."

"I was only trying to protect you." Then, though it was petulant and unnecessary, he added, "And Graubner was a dick."

She looked at him, almost admonishingly. He had to blink, looking away as Poppy spoke. "We're lucky he didn't sue you for having his jaw wired shut. Yes, he's a royal asshole. But he obviously felt guilty, or he wouldn't have dropped it."

Eamon couldn't tell her the real reason the asshole dropped it because that would've made everything so much worse than it already was. Like everything else about this situation, Eamon had driven them in without meaning to and would now do anything possible to get things back to where they were, including the personal nightmare of going to Liam for help.

Poppy took his hands. "I'm not mad at you."

"I know."

"But I do want you to get another job. One that's not going door-to-door after dark in Billing's worst neighborhoods."

"It wasn't dark when it happened."

Eamon was angry and getting angrier. A seed of wrath slowly warming. Soon it would crack through its shell, reaching past the soil for sunlight that promised its growth. Unless he quelled it.

For most of his life he'd been unable to throttle the worst of his urges. It's what always kept him in trouble, despite his best intentions. He was better now, thanks mostly to Poppy.

He had learned to think before speaking. Exercised more, ate better than ever before, and became a solution finder. He never wanted to hurt Poppy or let her see the worst of him.

"You're right. Just give me another week, and then I'll find something else. Okay?"

"Sure."

"I promise."

"I know."

Then, silence stretched between them. Liam insisted his first few paychecks would be used to cover the cost of setting things right with Graubner. He said it would make the position feel real, earned rather than given. But so far it only made Eamon hate his brother even more than he already did.

"Any leads on your end?" Words were like barbs in his throat.

"It's still coming in," Poppy said. "Today I got a gig writing some bullshit copy for some bullshit company, where I have to ignore everything I know just to finish the job. But it pays decent."

"How decent?"

"Not nearly enough." She smiled, rubbing the top of Eamon's hand. "But everything will work out."

Then, as if to prove the truth to them both, Poppy leaned forward and planted a wet and lingering kiss on his cheek. "I love you more than anything in this world. And I trust you."

Eamon smiled, swallowing bile as it rose in his throat. "I love you, too. Thanks for believing in me."

"I've always believed in you."

Eamon leaned back, and Poppy rested her head on his chest.

They *would* be okay, and both of them knew it, though for very different reasons.

Jack Quinn owned half the politicians in Billings, so no

matter what happened, his son would stay out of trouble. In the meantime, Eamon would figure something out. Make a plan to get them stable so he could stop working for his old family and take care of his new one. He didn't need much, just a few thousand dollars, enough to get them settled in a new place.

If he could get them out of the city, Poppy could land another job somewhere else.

Starting over would be easy.

He pledged a year with his family in exchange for landing a high paying union gig in sanitation, but there was zero chance he'd make it that long. Eamon was doing everything he could to free himself from their grip and planned to be well on his way to freedom before the next month was over.

Eamon put his hand back on her belly and slowly rubbed it.

Soon, the two of them were sleeping.

Chapter Three

GLEESON CROWE LOOKED AROUND STONEFALL, wondering how long it would take to break out.

They put him in a place with sky high walls specifically because he'd proven himself rather magical when it came to disappearing from one side of a prison wall and reappearing on the other. He was fifty-five now, and there was zero chance he was going to serve fifteen years in this place, stuck in the middle of nowhere, a hundred or so miles from Yellowstone, trapped and forgotten in a blight on Montana cast in concrete and steel.

Idiotically, drugs were still illegal in this country. And while that afforded men like Gleeson ample opportunities, it also meant they would have to relocate behind bars if they got caught operating outside the law. He got snagged red-handed, and that put him in prison the first time. He escaped, easily enough. Most people thought movies made escaping look easier than it really was, but Gleeson thought the opposite.

Next time he got sent behind bars was for armed robbery. He escaped again, and despite getting arrested less than a year later, he was roughed up enough when they dragged him in that a slick lawyer got Gleeson right back out, like the two times he'd escaped before didn't even matter.

The timing was perfect. He had a daughter to get acquainted with and nearly a decade to do it before he got picked up again. For assault, despite all three of those Mexicans getting exactly what they deserved. Back into prison he went, where he stayed for five long years before finally disappearing.

Gleeson eventually got picked up after a bar fight. The place was surrounded before he could leave, even though the fight had just ended. He was shoved into the cruiser with chunks of glass in his bloody knuckles. The prosecuting attorney was almost comically incompetent, but the judge was a hardass, and Gleeson's rap sheet was far from sympathetic, so off to Stonefall he went.

The first day was always the hardest. Not because the reality set in, but because Gleeson was forced into surrender.

He signed in, signing away his autonomy. Freedom and possessions now things of the past.

And it was always the same. Through Receiving and Discharge where Gleeson could say his final goodbyes — to no one this time, as Angel hadn't wanted anything to do with him in forever — before he was handed his prison clothes, then photographed, fingerprinted, and given his prison ID.

Gleeson was led into his cell by his CO, a black man named Percy. "Do you feel suicidal or like you might want to hurt yourself?" Then he stood on the other side of the bars, awaiting an answer.

"Not in the least," Gleeson grinned. "Though I'd love to put a hurting on you."

He always said things like that, especially on the first day. Helped him to parse the guards, to figure out who was crazy and who might be cool. Allies were scarce. Guards came in mostly two types — opportunists and crusaders. The latter had something to prove or were looking for someone to punish. Stonefall seemed to have more than its share of crusaders.

Gleeson kept his head down in the dining hall, same for everywhere else. By the second day, it seemed staying invisible would be harder than he had imagined. He was a mountain of a man with a face the size of a prize-winning pumpkin. But also, this supermax facility was nothing like he expected. He had imagined solitary, but this was more like a regular prison, albeit with higher walls climbing eighteen feet into the sky, and nothing but nothing for a hundred miles in every direction.

He was glad to be outside and away from his cellmate, Roy. The man didn't know how to shut up, and Gleeson worried he'd end up murdering the bastard mid-sentence and get years added to his sentence. He surveyed the yard, seeing his ultimate destination wasn't much of a choice. There were two weight benches and work out areas, one used by the skinheads and the other by the blacks and everyone else.

One of the men — big as Gleeson, despite that being such an unlikely rarity — sidled up without hesitation. Gleeson had been watching him since yesterday, pegged the man as one of the higher ups among Stonefall's population of Nazis.

"I'm Walter." He held out a beefy paw.

Gleeson took it, gave it a firm shake. No reason to make an enemy on his second day. "Gleeson."

"Where you from?"

Walter didn't give a shit where Gleeson was born, or

where he'd been living when Johnny Law threw him into Stonefall. He wanted to know who he was affiliated with, and if they might be friends or foes.

"I'm not from anywhere." Gleeson stared straight ahead rather than giving his eyes to Walter.

"Maybe you should reconsider."

"Maybe I prefer keeping to myself."

"Makes sense." Walter nodded. "A lot of guys feel that way. But then they get to reading all the statistics about how loneliness leads to an earlier death, especially in prison, and then they start reconsidering things like alliances."

Walter let that sink in, taking the moment to eye all the blacks and Hispanics. Then he continued.

"You know, guys like you and me need to stick together. Fucking mongrels and monkeys might be taking over the world out there" — Walter jerked a thumb behind him, presumably at the eighteen feet of concrete and the cursed world beyond it — "but in here, *we* run things. Just as it should be."

He fell quiet again, giving Gleeson ample time to see the error in his ways.

But Gleeson wasn't in a hurry to talk. In a situation like this, it was a lot easier to say the wrong things than it was to land on the right ones. For better or worse, this conversation was setting a precedent, and he was smart enough not to piss Walter off. Sure, Gleeson had his own problems with blacks, Mexicans, and any of the other lower classes constantly taking more than they gave from a country that used to stand head and shoulders above the rest of the world, but that hardly made him a Nazi.

"Good luck keeping them in line."

Walter laughed. "That your way of saying you don't give a shit what happens to you in here?"

"Not at all. But I've never been interested in politics, religion, or anything else. Not inside or outside. I'm here to do my time, then get back to my family. If it's all the same to you."

Walter wasn't about to challenge Gleeson right there in the open. The brawl would come later, in an empty hallway, shower, or laundry room. Surely with a small army of Aryans behind him, considering Gleeson's ample size.

But for now, the lie would have to serve him. Help him tread water until he deciphered his surroundings. Knew who was who, and how to get by.

"Things change fast," Walter said, offering him another chance.

But Gleeson had no intention of taking it. "A snake'll die if it can't shed its skin."

There was commotion over in the second yard, a crowd of blacks getting into it with a handful of Mexicans. Walter had one eye on the brewing tussle and the other on Gleeson. "What's that supposed to mean?"

"That I ain't afraid of change, but I decide when I'm ready."

Walter was about to respond, and Gleeson had a feeling that he probably wasn't going to like what the skin-head had to say, but the Nazi never got a chance. A commotion exploded over in the opposite yard.

They both looked over to a flurry of swinging fists.

COs scrambled out from the edges, racing into the fray to break up the brawl before it blew out of control.

He should turn around. Get out of the way of what-ever this was.

But Walter ran toward the fracas with a wide smile and murderous eyes, and Gleeson had never turned from a fight in his life. If he fled the scene now, he'd be branded a coward. And prison only had a couple labels worse than that.

The scuffle was brutal. But it didn't last long, with the officers doing a decent job of quickly quelling the violence. Percy set the tone, using the necessary physical force but never getting anywhere near out of control.

The CO didn't see Walter coming up from behind, nor the shiv in his hand.

But Gleeson did and acted fast.

He approached Walter from behind. Grabbed his wrist on its downward arc, hard but not hard enough to break it, less than a second before the shiv would've bitten into the Percy's skin.

The shiv dropped to the concrete — a toothbrush filed down into a gnarled plastic fang.

Walter turned around, instinctively grabbing at his wrist while glaring at Gleeson.

"The fuck are you thinking?" he growled.

Gleeson had no idea. He'd never done anything like that in his life. Never saved anyone from anything. Never even wanted to. Walter could have stabbed Percy — what the hell did he care?

He didn't know the man or give a shit about him. If the CO had a family who would grieve the loss at home, Gleeson had no idea, and until a moment ago would have sworn he couldn't care less.

The only thing that made sense in a situation like this was keeping his head down and getting away from the fight. And yet, Gleeson had entered it anyway, telling himself he had no other choice, even though he *always* had a choice.

"You're gonna pay for that," Walter warned him.

Gleeson knew he was right. Didn't even try to fight

either one of the COs approaching from behind and knocking them both to the ground.

He had made an enemy in Stonewall on his second day inside, and it might as well have been the devil himself.

Yet, even sprawled on the stained concrete, Gleeson held his head high, choosing to look past the concrete walls, into the sky and the sprawl of gray clouds above them.

Chapter Four

Gleeson expected solitary after that scuffle in the yard. Might've even preferred it to being trapped in a one-sided conversation with his twitchy cellmate, Roy Oversham. The man shouldn't be in Stonefall. He belonged in a loony bin with all the other nuts, not in Stonefall with all these hardened criminals.

Gleeson lay on his bunk, eyes closed, pretending to sleep so he wouldn't accidentally grab Roy by his skinny throat and throttle him until he cracked the nut from its shell.

"You don't have to say anything. I know you're listening, brother."

Roy wasn't his brother, but the man refused to call Gleeson anything else. Yet another reason he needed to keep his eyes closed and choke his murderous urges.

"The end is coming. This time right now. These are our final days."

Gleeson finally spoke, though he didn't open his eyes. "Shame I'm in here sharing them with you, then."

"There he is!" Roy laughed. "I knew you were in there somewhere."

Gleeson ignored him, wishing he hadn't lost his resolve.

"The Lord loves you, brother," Roy reminded him yet again. The sixth or seventh time in the two days they'd known each other. That was the best evidence yet that the guy was crazy.

No one loved Gleeson Crowe, especially God.

Again, he lost the battle with himself. "If there is a God, I doubt he knows I exist."

"Are you kidding me?" Roy laughed louder. "He spoke through you today. What happened out there, it wasn't an accident. Not with the end times so close. They are coming, you know."

"I think you might have mentioned that." Then, again losing the battle with himself and knowing he'd regret the question the second it came out, Gleeson asked, "What makes you so sure?"

"Visions," Roy said, surprising Gleeson with what sounded like a dial tone of truth.

"What kind of visions?"

"All kinds. Angels and demons descending upon us all. Passing judgement. The breaking of the Seven Seals."

"What's that?" Gleeson asked, annoyed by his curiosity.

Instead of giving him an answer, Roy responded with a Bible verse. It was far from the first time.

"And I saw in the right hand of Him who sat on the throne a scroll written inside and on the back, sealed with seven seals."

"I don't know what that means," Gleeson admitted.

"It's Revelation 5:1. It means the breaking of each seal signifies an increase in war. Famine and natural disasters are coming, but that's just the start, brother. The breaking of the seals is the first stage in the Great Tribulation, this time of turmoil and distress to signify the end times. The Millennium is coming."

"The Millennium came a while ago." Gleeson finally opened his eyes and sat up. Looked over at Roy, who was shaking his head.

"Not that Millennium. *The Millennium.*"

"I still don't know what you're talking about."

"I'm talking about The Millennium that comes after the blowing of the Seven Trumpets and the emptying of the Seven Bowls. I'm talking about the Second Coming of Jesus."

"Oh, got it. Thanks for clearing that up."

"Then the Lord will go forth and fight. He'll banish Satan to the Lake of Fire and begin his reign for a thousand years while we wait for Final Judgement and Eternity. Do you hear me, brother?"

"I wish I couldn't."

But Roy only smiled. "I understand why you would say that, brother. But you should know that Gleeson Crowe will be among the saved."

Despite his cellmate being crazy, that caught Gleeson's attention. It was the way he said it, with the certainty so thick in his voice. "I'm long past saving."

"No. I saw what you did out there today. So did the Lord. You could have let Walter kill Percy, but you intervened. Why did you do that, brother?"

"I'm not your brother."

"Why did you do it? Deny Cain and go with Abel like you did?"

He honestly had no idea. "I don't know," Gleeson finally said, shaking his head in what felt like defeat.

"I think you do. Go ahead, brother, take your time. Think about it."

Now he was talking to Gleeson like a kindergarten teacher.

"I guess I'm tired of all the violence."

"No," Roy said, eyeing Gleeson and lightly shaking his head. "That's not why."

"What do you know? You some sort of shrink before you went nuts?"

"God acted through you, man. He——"

Roy started rattling where stood, a second before he fell on the ground to finish it there. He was shaking and mumbling, though Gleeson couldn't tell what. It happened so fast, and he was sure his cellmate had to be faking.

Gleeson looked out past the bars, hoping to see a passing CO because he sure as hell didn't want to call out for one.

But he wouldn't need to. Roy suddenly stopped shaking and slowly gathered his feet.

He looked at Gleeson with a quarter smile, only there at the corners. "It's okay. I forgive what you're going to do."

The show was ridiculous. He was trapped with a lunatic man-child with a flair for theatrics. Gleeson closed his eyes. "Go to sleep."

Roy started talking again, reciting verses, both about the end of the world. But he didn't have much of an audience because by the second verse, his cellmate was sleeping.

Gleeson slept like a happy death, but when he woke up, Roy was already back to reciting.

"Then I saw a new Heaven and a new Earth; for the first Heaven and the first Earth passed away, and there is no longer any sea." Then he saw Gleeson looking at him and added, "Good morning, brother. It will happen, you know."

"Do you ever shut up?"

"I make sure to deliver what the Good Lord puts in my mouth. That's the promise we've made to each other."

It was a marathon of a day. Thanks to the exchange of blows, nobody from their housing unit was allowed any yard time. That meant he was trapped in his cell with Roy all day, except for meal times, where the man still stuck to Gleeson like stink on shit, unable or unwilling to take a goddamned hint.

Breakfast was miserable — a glop of inexplicably gray oatmeal. Gleeson spent every minute on edge. In addition to Roy's incessant chatter, he had his eye out for Walter and his brotherhood.

They would be coming. That was a *when*, and nowhere near an *if*.

Gleeson hadn't even shoveled the first of his lunch slop into his mouth, and Roy was already yapping.

"But you are not in darkness, brother, for that day to surprise you like a thief. For you are a child of light, a child of the day. We are not of the night or of the darkness." Roy stopped, grazed, chewed and swallowed. "That's Thessalonians 5:1-5. I'm telling you all this because if you know the signs, you can be prepared. This isn't horizon pie. I'm talking about imminent shit … what? What is it, brother?"

Gleeson was looking across the cafeteria at a blond man. Legal drinking age, give or take a year. A steroid case staring him dead in the eye. An *I Kill Niggers* tattoo on one forearm and a bright red swastika on the other. He was big, but Gleeson could still turn his head into a broken bottle of strawberry jam if he wanted.

Maybe that was the plan, Walter sending someone to take the fall. To show Gleeson how expendable his men were, just to teach him a lesson. Getting him sent to solitary or worse.

Maybe there were more in waiting, and the one eyeing Gleeson was only meant to draw his attention.

"He can't hurt you. You have protection no one in here has." Roy looked up to the ceiling then back at Gleeson. "God saw what you did yesterday, and he isn't about to forget it."

Roy was a delusional idiot. Gleeson's strength didn't matter. He was new and Walter entrenched. He'd made an unnecessary enemy, and God wasn't going to protect him. The same for everyone else. He needed to steer clear of any confrontation with the Aryan eyeing him from across the cafeteria and make peace with the assholes.

But that was the rub. How was Gleeson supposed to do that? He didn't want to be any part of their group, and they probably wouldn't take him now, even if he wanted to join them.

Maybe he could tell Walter he was only looking out for him. There were too many people around and Gleeson didn't want to see him get caught. Sure, he could play that angle, beg to join the group, then seed a disease from the inside once there. Manipulation was easy enough, once you knew the players as pieces and had access to the board.

Eventually, Gleeson could be the new Walter. If that was what he wanted.

But it wasn't, and it was hard to think his way out of this with Roy prattling on.

"I know how hard it is coming to this place, especially when on that very same day you arrive, you also discover the truth about the end of the world. But remember, Jesus overcame and so can you. He will come back for His people, and count you among them."

Gleeson clenched and unclenched his fists. It was

getting harder and harder not to use them as battering rams on his cellmate's skull. Especially after Nazi Bolt tried to start shit, shoving him on his way out of the cafeteria. But Gleeson played Gandhi and walked right by the guy.

The only thing that got him through the moment was picturing himself palming Roy's head like a basketball then slamming it into their shared wall over and over and over.

Back in their cell, he kept on talking, this time going on and on about his newest vision. Gleeson was tuning him out, barely listening until his "vision" got a little too personal.

"She'll need you after The Fall, brother. You'll need to be ready to see her then, even if you aren't now. Angel, I mean. She—"

"What do you know about my daughter?"

Gleeson was off of his bed and inches from Roy, his big right hand around the asshole's skinny little throat.

Roy was choking too much for an answer, so Gleeson relaxed his grip and waited.

"It was a vision," he finally sputtered.

"Wrong answer." He squeezed hard, willing to go all the way. Since Gleeson didn't believe in visions, his cell-mate was a snitch or connected to one of his enemies.

"Tell me right now or I'll kill you," Gleeson growled, squeezing again, fingers deep in the impostor's flesh, loosening up enough to let the man answer.

And with pleading but unapologetic eyes Roy said, "I told you, brother. It was a vis—"

His body started twitching, sending a current through Gleeson that he could no longer doubt. But it startled him, and as he released Roy, he flew into a rage, wrapping both hands around the man's head and hurling him down onto the toilet.

Blood pooled into a river on the floor.

Gleeson started to panic. Roy was bleeding out fast. "Guards!"

Roy looked up and met his eyes with a smile. "It's okay. I forgive you. God has plans for you, Gleeson. Be open to his message."

It was the first time Roy had said his name.

The last thing he said before the COs came in to drag his brother to The Hole.

Chapter Five

EAMON'S PHONE buzzed three times before he finally turned it to *Do Not Disturb*.

Poppy asked him who it was every time. Not because she was nosy, Poppy just always cared. He lied, twice saying he was getting spammed by political campaigns and the last time shrugging and muttering something about the number being unlisted.

It took Eamon an hour before he could get outside to call his brother back without arousing suspicion. And even then, he was half-sure he'd walk back in to find Poppy yelling, demanding to know what he was really doing during the day and who he was talking to at night.

Eamon swiped for his brother, knowing he'd be a prick before the second ring.

And sure enough, he was. "What took you so long?"

"I had things to take care of."

"And I'm sure you don't want those things to know you're on the phone with me right now."

"What do you want, Liam?"

"For you to have more respect for your family."

"I have plenty of respect for my family. I'm working, aren't I?"

"Sure you are. And not because we were your last result."

"What difference does it make, so long as I'm back?"

"Why don't you ask Pop," Liam said. "He wants to see you. Tonight."

"I can't tonight. I've got obligations."

"Tell your obligations you'll be home late. You have an unexpected sales call, or whatever other bullshit you need to plop on your bedroom floor."

"That's a lot to ask."

"It's not. And even if it is, you've asked a lot."

"You're not even going to tell me what it's about?" Eamon hated the pleading he heard in his voice.

"You can find out in an hour."

And then the line went dead.

Eamon needed a moment. He couldn't go back inside. Not before he processed what happened and conjured a lie to tell Poppy. It hurt to know his wheels were already turning.

His father and brother lived their lives without remorse. Their world view was a disease. And contagious. Eamon hated himself for letting the poison leak back inside him. His needed amends were mounting, but he'd pay them off, every one.

He just had to get through this.

Meeting his father wouldn't be pleasant. Jack Quinn would only want to see his second son if he had the chance to gloat. He knew exactly what Eamon thought of the family business, and the man who ran it, because he'd been free with his tongue for years.

Eamon didn't know how to hold back, starting in his late teens when the violence shook him the hardest, inside and out, enough to finally speak up. Still, he stayed for a couple of years as a world war raged inside him, pounding the pavement with bodies, therapy by way of his knuckles.

Until Eamon could no longer take it. He left. Swore he'd never be back.

But now he had begged his brother for help. And though Liam had let him back in, Eamon still hadn't spoken to their father. Not in the three years since he walked out. He hadn't even gone home for the holidays. Part of him missed it, but most of him didn't. Their lavish life was only possible through ill-gotten means, and the guilt for Eamon was always greater than the pleasure.

Now he faced the agony of his swallowed pride, and swelling deception.

But for now, Eamon needed to stretch the truth and beg the future to forgive him.

"Who was it?" Poppy asked when he came back inside.

He was sure she'd be lying down in the living room, so he had slipped in through the back. But it was hard to know these days. Pregnancy made Poppy nomadic.

"It was Tommy."

"Tommy?" It was like his wife had a mouthful of fish. "What did he want?"

"He had some crazy idea … that might actually be worth something."

Pure suspicion laced her words. "What do you mean?"

"I'm not dumb. I get that this is Tommy. But he had a crazy idea that might work."

Poppy drummed her fingers on the counter. "Might work to do what?"

"Make some money."

"Ah." False understanding crossed her face. "A get rich quick scheme. That sounds great. Please, tell me more."

"It's not a get rich quick scheme. It's about selling

discount policies to this group of guys he met while drinking."

"Why is that a crazy idea? I thought that's exactly what you were supposed to do."

"It's the way he wants to get the discount. He was trying to explain it, but I want him to show me. I need to see it."

"Why the urgency?" Poppy asked.

"He wrangled them into meeting tomorrow morning. So, it's now or never. Our needing the money makes it now." Eamon smiled. "I'm sorry."

"Before dinner?"

Eamon shrugged and gave her an apologetic look. "Yeah. Sorry."

"It's fine. But seriously, make sure Tommy isn't doing anything stupid. If you so much as—"

"Smell something wrong, I'll make a one-eighty and walk the other way. Promise."

A quick kiss, then he was out of there, lying down in the car as the auto drive took him to meet his father.

Al Dente. The restaurant had barely changed, not in Eamon's entire life. Not the menu, not the quality, and not the ambiance. There were no wearables allowed inside. The place still smelled like basil, and there was still a carafe of olive oil atop every table.

The car stopped about twenty minutes after it started, and after a ten second rest, the door whispered open.

"Not yet," Eamon said, and the door slid closed.

His heart was beating absurdly hard. This shouldn't be difficult. He was here for dinner with his father and brother, plus whoever else might suddenly appear like the darkest of tricks. But none of them had any true power over him. Power only came in the moment, and Eamon had control over every one of those.

He told the car to open, then stepped out and made the short walk into Al Dente.

"Welcome back, Mr. Quinn," Fausto said as he entered.

"I'm assuming I'm the last to arrive?"

"Right this way, Mr. Quinn."

Eamon followed Fausto to the back of the restaurant, where he was sat at a small table, despite the abundance of empties and Jack's owning the place. Liam sat on the opposite side of their father, forcing his brother into a supplicant's seat, making him feel like he was waiting to get called into the principal's office.

"Good to see you," Jack said, staring at Eamon and clearly not meaning a word.

"You, too." Eamon grabbed the water in front of him, grateful for its presence. He looked at the empty table, all glasses and no plates. "Are we eating?"

And Liam said, "We already ate."

Jack smiled and took a sip of his wine while Eamon boiled inside.

"So, Liam tells me you're back."

"For now," Eamon said.

"Why so glum?" Jack asked, taking a long moment to study his son. "You don't look very happy to see me."

"What do you want me to say, Pop?"

He answered without hesitation. "That you're sorry for turning your back on this family. Which is the only thing I've ever forbidden you to do."

That was total bullshit. There were plenty of things Eamon grew up being forbidden to do. But this wasn't the time for that conversation.

He didn't respond. Liam's smirking face made it hard to think of the right words. Or any words.

"So then, no apology," Jack said, still smiling into

another sip of wine. "Would you like some dessert? Maybe a little sugar to sweeten the mood? If you're planning to stay, we could order a soufflé."

"I haven't eaten … and I'd like to go home whenever you're finished with me here."

"Of course you would." His father's smile had thinned. Liam's had widened.

"Can one of you please tell me why I'm here?"

"I told you his girl helped him with the manners," Liam said.

Eamon clenched and unclenched his fists under the table.

Jack took another sip, this time he finished the glass. "I want you, Liam, and Felony to handle something big for me."

"Big?" Eamon repeated, hating the way his father just said that.

"Huge, really." He cleared his throat. "Seems we caught ourselves a crooked cop. He's been working for the Tomlinsons, and we've had our eye on him. Today he was skulking around Climax, and one of our guys saw him."

"Well, he did more than see him," Liam interrupted.

"Right." Jack nodded. "And that brings us to you."

"And where is he now?" Eamon asked.

Liam answered for their father. "He's drugged, cuffed, and waiting for us at the club."

"And what do you want us to do?" Eamon swallowed.

"I want you to question him. Things aren't going as smoothly as we would like them to around here lately, and we'll be taking some more decisive action. The three of you will convince our new friend to help us. Safehouses, various resources, plans, hidden allies — whatever that cop knows, I expect we'll know it soon, too."

"And what happens after he spills his guts? I don't suppose we're going to let him go."

Jack laughed, not even bothering to answer.

"I can't do this." Eamon shook his head. "You'll have to find someone else."

"Told you," Liam said to their father, not sounding at all disappointed.

Jack stared, unblinking, waiting for Eamon to flinch like he always did, using this task as a tool to test his loyalty, to get his buy-in with the family business. Finally, he said, "You can take our money, but you're too good to do any of the work that makes us that money. Is that correct?"

"No, Pop. I'm happy to help. That's why I'm here. But I'll do my best job if you put me in places where I can excel, instead of—"

"*Put you in places where you can excel?*" Jack laughed louder and harder. "This isn't an internship at some sweet little startup, son. This is our business, and you're either in or out. You want money for your girl and for your new little life, fine, I'm happy to take care of you. That's what family does. But it goes both ways, and it's time you started giving more of yourself."

"Fine," Eamon said, his wheels already turning, thinking of a way he might be able to get out of this. Not show up in the morning. Confess to Poppy and come up with some other plan before this one went too far. "Just tell me what to do."

But Eamon knew his father better than that and shouldn't have made such a rookie mistake.

"Great." Jack slapped his palms on the table. "Liam will take you now. Felony's already waiting outside."

Chapter Six

"YOU STILL THINK you have the aptitude for this?" Felony asked, pulling the van into the street, driving manual like always.

"To conquer oneself is a greater victory than to conquer thousands in a battle," Eamon said.

"The fuck does that mean?"

"Nothing," Eamon answered, his brother smirking beside him.

Climax was only a few minutes away, so shit was getting real, fast. The Quinns owned three strip clubs in a twenty-block radius, but Climax was the biggest among them, and the one where much of the family's planning went down. A place where people had disappeared before.

Eamon's body was tense. Everything about the situation felt wrong. The fact that he was here, that he hadn't stood up for himself, that he'd allowed himself to be so easily led down a road he swore he'd never set foot on.

Poppy conquered his every thought. He couldn't stop thinking about her and how much he was letting her down just by sitting in the van on his way to do something unthinkable, anticipating the stew of anger and rage and guilt that was sure to follow his bloody knuckles and worse.

Liam hadn't lost his smirk. Eamon imagined himself punching it permanently off of his brother's face.

The car pulled up to the curb outside of Climax. Liam handed Eamon a gun. "Here ya go, baby brother."

Eamon took the weapon because he had no other choice. Maybe this was a trap. He'd heard stories. It wasn't easy to believe his father would want to get rid of him, even after everything between them. But it wasn't impossible, and that by itself was a knife in his stomach.

Climax wasn't just the biggest of the family's three strip clubs, it was the best. The building was the newest. Same for the paint and everything else. It was the cleanest, the most elegantly lit, and the one where every stripper in Billings wanted to work. Drinks were more expensive, ditto for the dances. Almost obnoxiously so.

It was also a de facto headquarters, complete with a safe room where Jack held a safe containing a veritable fortune.

Jack Quinn wasn't just ruthless, he was a smart businessman. It was one of the things that pissed Eamon off most about his father. He didn't have to be a criminal. It would be one thing if he grew up in the business, though Eamon barely saw that as an excuse, or if he had to build it from nothing with no other choice. But Jack Quinn behaved like a monster because he enjoyed it. Destroyed lives for a living because he thought it was fun. Lied and cheated and stole — surely murdered, though he never said that one out loud — simply because he could.

Climax was a price anchor. It was the best, so those customers who were willing to pay refused to go anywhere else. And the sky-high prices at Climax worked to justify the much lower but still higher than the national average prices in the other two. That set the city's rates. Eamon's father would never have bought a single strip club. He needed all three for his idea to work. Americans were in love with *small, medium,* and *large.* Had been since the 1950s.

Eamon glanced at the stage, a step behind Liam and Felony on their way to the back. A brunette graced the stage. She had a perfect body, no doubt, but the best thing by far was her smile. She clearly wanted to be there, unlike most of the girls at Kinky Kitty Kat, Bottom's UP, or any of the other nine clubs in the city outside of the Quinn's well-branded stable. The girl had to be making a fortune, and no one made it at Climax without enjoying it. The well-mannered patrons expected nothing less and paid well for the pleasure. The stage was littered with tens and twenties. Eamon saw a pair of Grants and a Benjamin, but not one single. Strip clubs were one of the few places around where a person could still expect to see a lot of cash, but what he saw at Climax was ridiculous.

Eamon looked away, shaking his head, thinking of Poppy amid a flood of guilt for the eyeful.

Felony opened the office door, waited for the brothers to enter, then closed them inside.

His heart sank, seeing the man strapped to the chair. The cop wouldn't be leaving this room alive. That truth had already darkened his eyes.

Eamon wondered how many men had died in this place. And women. There were probably a few of them, too. His father was a pig, and so were many of the men who worked for him. Some of the women who ended up stripping were light on people to wonder where they might've run off to. Easy to imagine Jack's men occasionally getting carried away, then having to clean up.

The prisoner was strong in the shoulder and jaw. His stubble was thick, a couple of week's worth, dirty blond like his hair. His shirt was ripped at the collar and again on the bottom. A long gash snaked across his cheek, and blood caked his face in a pair of matching drips like fangs. His skin was ashen yet waxy. The wet spot was drying between his legs, but the reek of human shit was still ripe inside the room.

He took the three newcomers in, then snarled.

Benni — one of his father's pigs — was sitting behind the cop, in the corner, staring down at his tablet. Eamon would have bet both of his balls it was porn, and probably not the legal stuff.

"He give you any trouble?" Liam asked.

Benni stood from his seat with an obvious bulge. "Nah. He got so scared he shit himself, but other than that he's been a sniveling little bitch."

"You wouldn't let me use the bathroom," the prisoner said.

Felony turned to Benni. "You really want to smell that? Because now we have to. The fuck is wrong with you?"

"I told you," Benni said. "He was scared."

Another growl. "I wasn't scared."

Liam said to Benni, "We've got it from here."

"Sure thing," said the thug, with a wink to the prisoner on his way out.

Liam went to the freshly emptied chair then dragged it across the floor until it was directly in front of the cop. He sat, looked him in the eyes, and spoke in a perfectly reasonable voice.

"There's no reason to make this painful. You've heard enough stories, seen enough movies, or have a vivid enough imagination to know exactly what the stakes are here. The odds of you surviving this are slim, but not nonexistent. You want to live, you'll tell us every little thing we wanna know. Enough so you'll never *ever* consider going back to the Tomlinsons, knowing they'll kill you, and we'll be the only safe harbor for the rest of your life."

Liam took a breath and let the first part of his message settle. He waited three beats, then continued.

"That's one end of the spectrum. The preferred one for all of us. The other end is a lot uglier. That's where you die, holding out all the way until the end. You would only do something stupid like that because of some misplaced sense of honor, but you should know, *the Tomlinson's would never do that for you.* You might also do it to feel like a man, but that's pointless. You'll surrender in the end. There's no way you're the first one to be as strong as he thinks. You'll give up and spill it all eventually, after your body's unnecessarily suffered all the cuts and lashes, all the punches and kicks, the—"

"He's got it."

Eamon couldn't help himself.

Liam turned around and gave his brother a long glare before finally turning back to the prisoner.

"What is it you want to know?"

Eamon wasn't sure if the cop was playing ball or buying time.

"You tell me," Liam said. "What *do* I want to know?"

He opened his mouth, but was interrupted by a knock, then the door opened before anyone answered.

"What is it?" Felony asked Benni, now back inside.

"Somebody's in here looking for him." He glanced at the prisoner, then looked at Liam with an expression that said, *What do I do?*

"Fuck," Liam said.

"Should I go out there?" Felony asked.

"Goddammit, yes. Both of you. Eamon, you stay here with me." Liam was biting his bottom lip, clearly irritated.

"You got it," Felony said, then opened the door and

clapped Benni on the shoulder, the gesture an obvious 'you first.'

The door closed, and Liam looked at Eamon.

"What the hell are you smiling about?"

Eamon swallowed hard, feeling caught. That was a stupid mistake, allowing Liam to see his relief. "I'm not smiling."

"You sure the fuck are. So you better either let me in on the joke, or otherwise convince me you're not delighted that there's a Tweedle-Dum out there looking for Tweedle-Dee in here." Liam pulled a gun out of nowhere and aimed it at the prisoner before waving it in a lazy line toward Eamon. "I'm serious, Eamon. Tell me why you're smiling."

"I'm nervous." It wasn't a lie, or anywhere near the truth. He changed the subject. "So, what do we do now?"

Instead of answering, Liam went to a desk in the corner, opposite of the one where Benni was watching porn on his tablet, and studied a small bank of monitors. Without looking up he said, "We've got trouble."

"What kind of trouble?" Eamon asked.

"What kind do you think? The kind that isn't getting slowed down by Felony or Benni. The kind that's on its way in here."

"The door's locked."

"It sure is," Liam agreed, "that gets us a delay if we're lucky. He's a cop. Same as this asshole. He can come back with a warrant at any time."

"How do you know he's a cop?"

Liam looked at Eamon as though his brother were stupid. "Because we pay attention. Come on, we're getting him out of here. Let's head out the back."

Liam checked the monitors again, announced they were all clear, then jerked their prisoner out of his seat, shoving him toward the back door as a fist pounded on the one behind them.

"They're here," Eamon announced.

"Thanks for the update," Liam said, already on the other side of the door.

The cop bellowed, "It's Richard! I'm in here!"

Liam yelled at Eamon to *Shut him the fuck up*, but he already had a hand over Richard's mouth as he nudged their prisoner toward the now open door.

There was loud muttering from the other side. Benni, Felony, and a third, unfamiliar voice. The sound of possible salvation.

"You think Santa Clause is coming?" Liam said, yanking Richard outside.

A car came screaming into the alley.

Liam shoved them both back into the office and slammed the door behind him.

"FUCK!" Liam yelled, then turned to his brother. "Did you do this? Did you call him in here? I saw you fucking with your phone in the car! What were you doing?"

"Nothing! I wasn't even fucking with my phone."

"Like hell you weren't," Liam said, looking unsure.

There were pounding fists and kicking behind both closed doors. The brothers were trapped with their prisoner without any hope of escape, and one of them was in the wrong place at the wrong goddamned time.

A pair of gunshots, then the back door exploded open.

An armed man marched inside, pointing his gun at Liam.

Seconds from death, Eamon couldn't help but thinking of Poppy and the child he'd be leaving behind. So little as he wanted to do it, his gun was out and he had one arm around Richard's throat.

"I'm not supposed to be here," Eamon said.

"But you are." The man pulled out his gun and aimed it at Eamon's head.

But he never got a chance to fire. Liam had always been fast, and this time it wasn't even close.

The bullet wasn't big, just large enough to leave a cigarette burn sized hole in the center of their enemy's head, drooling sticky red syrup as he collapsed to the floor. Except the man was never supposed to be his enemy.

The other door swung open. Three men spilled inside, with Felony and Benni a step behind their intruder.

The man saw one compadre lying on the floor, and the other restrained. The pair of guys behind him had drawn their weapons, and the second pair in the room were already holding.

Doing the math killed that light in his eyes.

Liam and Felony opened fire and eliminated the threat.

Then Liam leaned into Eamon's ear and whispered, "Go with Felony. Pick up your girl, and get out of town. Have him take you to the Cottage. Now."

Eamon hated to take anything from his brother, but this time he took it and *ran*.

Chapter Seven

"Stop looking at me like that," Eamon told Felony. Again.

"What do you want me to do, man? We've been sitting here for five minutes. Liam wants you out of town. We need to get this show on the goddamned road."

"Fuck Liam."

"Don't say that. Your brother wants to keep you safe."

"Bullshit. He wants to know where I am because he thinks I had something to do with what went down at the club, but I didn't have—"

"I know you didn't, and your brother doesn't think you did, either. Don't be stupid."

"Don't call me stupid," Eamon wasn't dumb and hated being treated like the village idiot half the time.

"Then stop acting like an imbecile. Come on, we have to get in and get out of here."

"She's going to kill me."

"Tell her to hurry." Felony pointed at the door, ajar since their arrival.

"It's the middle of the night."

"Not yet. It's just late. Be gentle when you wake her."
Felony shoved Eamon on the shoulder. "Giddyap, little
doggie."

Eamon mumbled something unintelligible on his way
out of the car. He skulked up the drive, déjà vu on his way,
hoping Poppy wasn't in the kitchen this time, because he
really needed her to be sleeping. Even waking her up
would be better than having her waiting and pacing and
angry.

He closed the kitchen door behind him. The room was
dark. Same for the entire house it seemed, except for the
living room where Poppy had left a lamp on — for him.
She was obviously in bed.

Eamon made his way down the hallway, his heart
pounding like there was an intruder waiting to slay him.
He wished there was. That would be easier to deal with.
He'd snap the asshole's neck and be a hero. Poppy
wouldn't care if they had to get the hell out of Dodge if
she was still swooning from his saving her life.

He opened the bedroom door with a whisper. Poppy
used to be a heavy sleeper. She could even sleep through
the neighbor a few doors away keeping his motorcycle
roaring while he worked out. But pregnancy changed that.
In the last couple months, Poppy could be woken by
someone sneezing in China.

Eamon listened to her breathing, beautiful and spare,
striking him like a familiar song, two chords on an acoustic
guitar or an old chair rocking back and forth on an even
older porch.

He somehow made it to the edge of Poppy's bed
without disturbing her. Got on one knee and put a gentle
hand on her shoulder, aware of the ticking clock and
Felony waiting outside.

Eamon softly shook her shoulder and gave Poppy a kiss on her cheek. "Wake up, sweetheart."

It took a her a moment, then she was blinking up at him. His eyes had almost adjusted. Hers would likely be trying for a while. "What is it?"

"We have to go."

Poppy sat straight up, an awkward move as out of balance as she was, suddenly fully awake. "What do you mean *we have to go*. Where? What's happening?"

Eamon swallowed hard and reminded himself that he had no other choice. He'd fucked up a few times already and was only making it worse with every second he kept the truth to himself.

"I've been working with my family. We—"

"WHAT?" It wasn't a yell but was full bodied and ready for blood.

"It hasn't been long, but the insurance thing with Tommy wasn't panning out and we needed money, so—"

"How long?" Her bottom lip was quivering. Despite the dark, Eamon couldn't have missed it.

"A couple of days. Less than a week."

"You're being vague," she said. "Why should I trust you?"

"Because I never lie to you."

"Except for this time."

"I'm telling the truth now. And I'm sorry it took me so long. The last few days have been a fog. I called Liam, then I had to deal with him and some initiation shit. Today was my first real day. I went on a job this morning, then my dad made me go down to the club tonight—"

"The *strip* club?"

"Yes, and shit went bad when we were there. Now we need to split. Felony's waiting outside. He'll take us to my family's Cottage. It's hidden away in the woods, has solar

47

powered everything, and supplies to last us as long as we need to hide out. We'll be safe there."

"Why do we need to be safe, Eamon?" Poppy was losing it. "Tell me what happened."

"On the way, I promise. But we've gotta go. And we need to be fast. Felony is waiting and I—"

"I don't give a shit about Felony! What the fuck?"

She shook her head, no longer in waking disbelief so much as dripping with ire. A single word would send her over the edge, so Eamon said nothing, waiting for Poppy to finally finish.

Then she did, but it wasn't what he expected.

Poppy started to cry. Deep, heaving sobs, gushing from her eyes, soaking her face. Shoulders shaking and swollen breasts trembling.

Eamon tried to put his arm around her, but she swatted it away.

He waited a few moments, tried again, and got hit even harder.

Then he wondered about Felony, the time, and what he should do.

"We need to go," Eamon gently reminded her, careful to keep his voice clear of impatience and heavy with concern.

But Poppy, normally verbose and a little too colorful to ever be called direct said, "I've never been angrier with you, Eamon."

He didn't know what to do with a jab like that. Straight to the gut. It could've been worse. Poppy could have said she hated him, or ordered Eamon to get the hell out of the house. She needed sleep and so did the baby. Eamon could fend for himself. Her thought seemed unfinished. Those words could still be coming.

"How could you do this to us?"

"I was trying to do the right thing, I swear," Eamon said, feeling lost without any idea of what to do with his hands.

"But you didn't. You did the wrong thing. The *really wrong thing.* Then you lied about it, which makes everything so much …"

Poppy couldn't finish. Her sentence dangled like the end of Eamon's rope.

"I'm going to make it right," he promised.

"You better." Her voice was still furious. She looked down at her belly and added, "You owe it to both of us."

They heard a loud bang, like the front door slamming closed, then Eamon managed to get *I know* out of his mouth before Felony was in their bedroom.

"We need to go!" He stared at them from the doorway.

"We were on our way," Eamon said.

"Looks like it." Felony flipped on a light. "You've got five minutes, and you'll both need to give me your phones."

"No way," Poppy said. She had met Felony twice and hadn't cared for him either time.

But Eamon was already handing his over. He knew the drill and there wouldn't be any arguing their way out of it. "They can be traced to us," he told Poppy. "Even if you turn off GPS, the phone is still tracking us wherever we go. He's right."

Poppy glared at him. He'd never seen her so angry. Not even close.

She went slowly over to her dresser, yanked the phone from its charger, and pretended to read from the screen. "Nope. No texts saying you're working for your asshole family or we'll be fleeing from our home like criminals in the middle of the night … *while I'm eight months pregnant!*"

Eamon swallowed and tried to gobble a breath. But he didn't dare speak.

She thrust out her phone. He took it, handed it over to Felony, and watched as he smashed them both with three firm stomps of his heel on the glass.

"That oughtta do it," he said, kicking the remains into the corner.

Felony reached into his pocket and produced a new pair of phones. He handed one to each of them.

"You carry around a bunch of phones, just in case?" Poppy smirked at Felony, proving she wasn't afraid.

"I keep them in the car."

"My contacts are all in my old phone. I don't know anyone's number."

"Shame it ain't the old days."

"Seriously. How am I supposed to contact anyone I care about?"

"You don't," he told her. "At least not for now. You'll be able to sync things eventually. Right now, we're running late to our funerals, so I'd appreciate it if we could get going."

"*Eventually?* How long do you expect me to stay at that cabin? I'm about to have a baby!"

"*We're* about to have a baby," Eamon said, even though he shouldn't have.

Poppy whipped toward him. "What did you say?"

Felony answered, "He said it's time to get the fuck out of here."

"He's right, we need to go," Eamon said. "You can hate me forever, but that's not going to stop me from keeping the two of you safe. Let's pack fast. You have every right to be mad at me, and whether or not we sort this out later, I need you to realize that we're on the same side now."

"Sure, Eamon. It really feels like it."

But still, they packed together, and now she was hustling. Eamon kept reminding himself that he could only live in the present and that he had to go with the flow because that was the only way he could ever be happy.

Poppy whispered, "Why do we need to go with him? Can't we just go somewhere together?"

Eamon hated not having an answer. Or at least not anything better than, *Because I don't have a plan and am ill-equipped to take care of you and our child.*

They finished packing, then followed Felony outside.

Despite Poppy's furious quiet, Eamon felt sure of her thoughts. Same as his. Both of them wondering if they'd ever see their place again, with a growing worm of doubt that of course they would not.

It was like driving in a coffin, with the looming silence among them.

But it stopped when they arrived at the Cottage. It was light outside, mid- to late-morning already, Eamon wasn't sure.

Felony stood, got out of the car, stretched. Then he checked his phone.

Eamon was watching, mostly because he was waiting for Poppy to make the first move.

Felony's face strobed in alarm, and Eamon feared the worst — a worst that might end up being the best. His brother or his father dead. Maybe both of them.

But it wasn't anything like that.

Felony couldn't speak.

Poppy must've been watching, too. "What is it? Are you okay?"

He cleared his throat and licked his lips, then Felony drew a ninety-pound breath, glanced at his phone again, as if double checking his sanity, and looked like a ghost as he answered. "Aliens or something."

The look on his face kept them from laughing.

"What are you talking about?" Poppy asked.

"Check your Astral app if you have it. If you don't, it's too late. We don't have service out here. Everything I saw was from before we lost service. So my last update was about an hour ago."

"And what did it say?" Eamon asked.

"That the aliens or whatever will be here in less than a week."

Chapter Eight

GLEESON LOOKED up to the black sky as it suddenly opened, and the torrent came in full.

Demons descending, their wings of leather and membrane flapping as they shot toward their targets.

The humans on the ground weren't ready. Not even close. And so they perished *en masse*. Some of them licked by fire and others rendered to shredded meat by the gnashing teeth of the devil's minions.

He was safe, high on a plateau, watching. The demons would be coming for him soon. Until then, Gleeson would watch the carnage below. But a scampering behind him wrenched his attention — a furious gallop and the skittering of rocks.

Gleeson turned, his eyes widening at the sight of Roy racing toward him, mere feet from a demon giving chase and closing the distance. "Please, Gleeson!" Roy was screaming. "You've gotta help me!"

He stared at the man, no idea what to do, and indecision like concrete, anyway.

"Angels and demons!" Roy roared, no longer asking for

help. "Come down to pass judgment on us all. It's the breaking of the Seven Seals!"

He had to help his friend. Gleeson reached out a hand as Roy continued to rant.

"Then I saw a new Heaven and a new Earth; for the first Heaven and the first Earth passed, and there is no longer any sea."

Gleeson reached out for Roy, but the man seemed to be running in place.

It will happen, you know.

"I'll help you," Gleeson promised.

But he wasn't fast enough. A demon's hooked tail punctured Roy through the back and erupted through the front of his chest, spilling blood like lava from the lip of a volcano, with pieces of his—

Gleeson woke up drenched in sweat, still in his tiny cell in solitary confinement. A different hell with an equally insidious architect. Humans instead of the devil, though without much division between them.

Solitary was the bleeding asshole of prison — a system designed to break a man's will to live. A dehumanizing zoo where guards were spectators. Sixty square feet and four walls that felt coffin narrow. Cinderblocks buried some of the screaming, but nowhere near all of it, and Gleeson still heard plenty.

A cold egg and a biscuit for breakfast, along with an expired carton of milk. Lunch that wasn't fit for the filthiest three-legged mutt, and a dinner that was worse more often than not. The place played tricks on your mind by bleaching the soul of all positive contact.

Solitary even ruined the innocents. Gleeson had seen it for himself. Enough time inside, which really wasn't all that long, and even the most unimpeachable man would live up to society's rotten expectations. With a starving soul and pillaged memories of what it means to be human, the same thing could happen to anyone.

Worse than the solitary was the way Gleeson kept wrestling with what happened to Roy. What he had *done* to Roy. It was affecting his dreams. He couldn't remember his nightmare, but the feeling of letting Roy down was still heavy like a blanket around him.

It was an accident, and yet Gleeson felt a deeper breed of guilt than he'd ever felt before. Solitary gave him plenty of time to think about it, but his thoughts weren't circling the usual drain. Instead of wondering when he would be brought to court for his latest infraction, or getting fixed on the time that might be added to his sentence, he found himself wondering things like whether the man had family, or if there was a morsel of truth in the things he'd been saying before Gleeson ended his life.

The regular thoughts were there. Of course he wondered about his extra time, and when he would be held accountable, but those musings were like a breeze before the storm. He was getting older, so maybe that was it. Maybe Gleeson was thinking about Roy more than himself because he'd finally reached the age where time would always take more than it gave, and repenting was the only thing that would give any worth to what he had left.

Gleeson was picking at fragments of his nightmare when the cell door opened and Percy stepped inside. What felt so vivid in his first second of waking was now like a three-year-old fog. There might have been demons or something like that, but there was fire for sure. Gleeson could still imagine it burning his skin.

"Morning," the CO said.

Gleeson nodded, saying nothing.

He didn't understand the stalemate sitting between them. While Gleeson had ended Roy's life, he had saved

Percy's — an act that didn't make sense even to the man who did it, and probably not to anyone else.

Now there was this weird energy passing between them. A current Gleeson couldn't deny or ignore. Still it confused him. Percy too, judging by the way he was always looking at the prisoner, like something better than an animal.

He set Gleeson's biscuit and egg on the ground, along with the carton of milk, then stepped back outside of the cell. He didn't have to come in at all. Gleeson wondered why he bothered.

He started to close the door, then put an end to their stalemate instead. "Why'd you do it?"

"Do what?"

"Stop Walter … and save my life."

Gleeson was glad he asked and had been waiting for a chance like this. But the moment was there, and his answer wasn't around like he thought it would be.

"I don't know," he shrugged. "Guess I'm just tired of all the violence."

But that was a bullshit answer and both of them knew it. There was more to it than that, and Gleeson could feel it. Same for Percy. Otherwise he wouldn't be inside the cell, looking at him like that.

Gleeson wasn't even sure what his own angle was, but he was always playing one, so surely he was now.

What did his answer mean? Was he trying to sound better than he was? Play on Percy's sympathies and maybe find a friend among the guards? Saying nonsense out loud so he could figure things out for himself?

After a long silence Percy finally said, "Thank you."

And Gleeson answered, "Of course."

Then the CO stood there, as though leaving Gleeson's cell was the last thing he wanted to do.

He flinched to leave, but Gleeson didn't want that to happen. "Wait."

"Yeah?" Percy turned back with the hint of a happy surprise on his face.

"I was wondering if you could do me a favor."

Percy looked unsure, but still he said, "If it's legal and in my power, just tell me what I can do."

"It's legal and you'll like it." Gleeson paused, barely able to believe what he was asking. "I was wondering if you could bring me a Bible."

Percy's face exploded in a smile. "Of course I can bring you a Bible. Should have thought of it myself. I guess at first you didn't strike me as a man of scripture."

"No hurry. Just whenever you can."

But the CO was still smiling. "Ask and ye shall receive."

Gleeson was only alone with his thoughts for another hour or so before the cell door opened again and Percy came back holding a Bible, black and battered to shit. The Good Book looked like it had been read by every prisoner twice.

"Sorry that took so long," Percy said, handing the Bible to Gleeson.

"Seemed fast to me."

"I had to finish my rounds, then get this from my locker."

Gleeson looked from the Bible to Percy. "This is yours? I figured you would get me one from the library or something. Maybe by the end of the week."

"The Good Lord should never wait." Percy set a hand on Gleeson's shoulder. It was almost too much. "And it just seemed right ... that I should give you mine."

And as he said that, Gleeson thought he felt something go from the Bible and into his hands. More of that current he'd felt between himself and the CO, only now with a tangible object he could clutch to his chest, soon as Percy was out of his cell.

He stopped at the door. "Need anything else?"

"Is there a best way to read it?"

"No." Another smile. "Just get started and you already got it right."

Then the door closed and left Gleeson and God to themselves.

The Bible was a balm, words like the touch of a lover. It had been so long since he'd read, but as a boy he devoured books like meat from a bone. Philosophy and lots of theology. Things he didn't understand all that much at the time, though it stoked his curiosity. He had forgotten how to look, or how good it felt. Maybe it was the isolation, and the lack of alternatives, but he didn't think so. There was something special about what Gleeson was reading right now, the ancient sentences stirring something inside him.

Percy showed up again for lunch. Gleeson looked up from his reading.

"So where did you start?"

"In the beginning," Gleeson said. "Just like God would have wanted me to."

"And what do you think?"

"That men are monsters. That there's no hope. That we're all going to burn. And that either way, it doesn't even matter."

"What makes you say that?" Percy asked.

"If the moon slammed into the Earth tomorrow and killed everything on the planet, so what? How does it matter to the universe? We're gone in a blink. Probably one species in a billion or more."

"That doesn't make it meaningless. God has a purpose,

even when you can't understand it or see the whole picture."

"God would be too busy to manage a planet, let alone trillions of them. *We* give meaning to the universe. It isn't the other way around."

"Saying nothing has meaning is another way of giving meaning to nothing. You're right, our planet might be inconsequential in the eyes of the universe, but to the people who live here, humans are everything. If my woman were to be taken from this Earth, that would destroy me, with or without the universe caring."

"What makes you think God cares — about you, your woman, or any of it?"

Percy shrugged. "I'm not sure He does, but I can't let that uncertainty dictate the way I live my life. I have to believe He cares about me."

"Why?"

"Because then no matter what, even if I lose my wife, I won't be alone."

"What makes you have faith that there even is a God?" Gleeson asked.

"I choose to believe because it's better than not. And if something is deemed worth doing, then I'm not about to start doing it with half of my heart. The Bible's survived for thousands of years. People have done their best to destroy it, and yet the Good Book lives on, giving us glimpses into our past and hints as to what might be coming. Is there anything better than that?"

"Of course there is. Humans are a lot smarter now than they were thousands of years ago."

"Oh, I don't know about that," Percy said. "More tools for sure, but raw intelligence … I'd argue that men had to fight a lot harder thousands of years ago for all that they had or didn't have."

And again, Gleeson found himself smiling. "Fair enough."

"Keep reading. It gets better."

"What's better than Creation?"

"Resurrection," Percy promised before closing Gleeson's door.

Chapter Nine

SHERRY WAS TIRED OF WAITING, but what could she do?

She'd been killing time while hoping Bickford would show for the last seventeen minutes now. She didn't mind hanging around, but not if she was waiting for nothing. Sherry had been wondering if Bickford would start losing interest then just not show up one day. He'd been punctual every time. A down-to-the-minute sort of guy. Never early or late.

So yeah, this was weird.

Sherry rubbed her belly, sick of being pregnant. It hadn't gotten any easier, not since the first time she threw up and stole a few tests. Every day seemed harder than the one before it. For eight months she'd barely slept, and last night might have been the worst. Awful dreams she couldn't remember, though they were nightmares for sure, she knew it because of the way her skin still itched after she opened her eyes.

She thought about turning on the TV, maybe watching something from Fable. But the remote was on the other side of the room, and the voice activation hadn't been working right in a while and never did all that well to begin with. Probably because her mom always bought knock-offs.

Sherry wanted to look busy when Bickford finally showed up, so he knew her time was valuable. But it's not like having the TV on in the background would help her to tell that particular story.

She met Bickford in a chat room two months ago. The back and forth was easy, so soon enough they went from talking with their fingers to looking at each other through an open window on LiveLyfe. He was older than her, mid-twenties, maybe even late, and about as awkward as anyone named Bickford would be. He wasn't ugly, at least not totally, but no one would ever call the man attractive. But Sherry figured he was handsome enough, if Bickford was also her way out. He only lived two states away and she thought running off to live with him every time they talked, along with a lot of times when they didn't.

Unfortunately, they had been talking face-to-face for six weeks now and Bickford hadn't so much as said a single dirty word, at least not directed toward Sherry in the way that she wanted. He hadn't even asked her to show him her tits. And guys always wanted you to show them your tits.

Her computer made a little *plink* sound, then a video box popped onto the screen. A second later Bickford appeared, but he didn't look happy to see her. He didn't seem happy at all, about anything. Bickford looked scared, and maybe like he had just shit his pants.

"What is it?" Sherry asked. "Are you okay? Why were you late?"

"You haven't seen the news?"

"No. What is it? More of that stuff about the royal wedding?"

"No." Bickford shook his head, visibly upset. "Turn on

the TV. You should see this for yourself. You wouldn't believe me if I told you, anyway."

"Okay," Sherry said, slowly standing with one hand on her belly and the other held out for balance, easing herself out of the chair so she could make her way to the remote. Halfway there she turned back toward the screen and said, "What channel?"

"Any of them," Bickford said.

Dread overwhelmed her. At the back of her mind, something began to furiously itch. She longed to scratch it, digging deep enough to claw her metaphorical mind to ribbons if promised the answer. Something had been nagging at Sherry since she woke up, but now she was stewing in it. Familiarity striking her body like lightning.

Had she lived through this before?

Did she know that something like this — whatever it was — would happen?

Why did she feel horrified, yet not entirely surprised?

Sherry grabbed the remote, returned to her chair, sat with a plop, then aimed it at the TV. She clicked and:

—*Are now reporting that the incoming objects are at a trajectory that puts them approximately six days away.*

"What's six days away?"

"Keep watching," Bickford said.

Sherry did, and got some more of those terrifying yet not altogether surprising answers.

Aliens were coming, and if she was to believe the nonsense leaving the anchorwoman's lips — the nonsense that Sherry had zero difficulty believing at all — the world as they knew it would be history in less than a week.

Or, Sherry supposed, it already was.

"Do you think it's real?" Bickford asked.

"Of course it's real."

"What makes you so sure?"

"Why would they lie?"

"Are you kidding me?" Bickford said. "The media lies all the time. It's what they do for a living."

"Well, not exactly."

"Why are you acting like this isn't a big deal?"

Sherry shrugged for the camera. "The universe is a big place. Guess it seems that something like this is sort of inevitable."

It was a weird thing to say. Sherry thought so, too, and was surprised to hear herself say it.

"But here?" Bickford protested, shaking his head, having a much more difficult time then his newest online friend. "And now?"

"I've gotta go."

"You've gotta go?" Bickford repeated. "What do you mean, you've gotta go? Aliens are coming! What else do you possibly have to do?"

"You know what time it is. And you know what time my mom comes home. It's not my fault you were late."

"It's not my fault aliens showed up on the Astral app this morning," Bickford said, sounding insolent.

"We can talk tomorrow."

"Who knows if there'll even be a tomorrow!"

Sherry said, "There might not be another next week, but there will definitely be a tomorrow."

"You don't sound like yourself."

"I don't feel like myself." She waited a beat then reminded him, "I've gotta go."

That time Sherry didn't wait for Bickford's protest, closing the window then the lid to her ancient laptop. Piece of shit was the perfect metaphor for her life. It barely worked and was a miserable experience, but still better than nothing.

Sherry had to make sure she was off with Bickford before her mom got home. She was due any minute, and she was a raging bitch even without the news. Sherry usually got flirty before hanging up, hoping he'd linger and ask her to say or do something dirty because then it could lead to something bigger and better, maybe with more responsibility on his part. But if Sherry's mom saw her, she'd take it the wrong way. Like always. She wouldn't see it as her daughter trying to be responsible. She'd call her a whore, several times.

Mom wasn't as punctual as Bickford, but she usually walked in within the same ten-minute window. Today was no exception. She stormed in like normal, reeking of cigarettes and misery. Threw her purse on the counter without looking at Sherry and said, "You didn't have time to clean this place up?"

"I don't feel well."

"Looks like you felt well enough to shower off."

"Cleaning up helped me feel better." She shouldn't have to explain this.

Her mother muttered something then turned away.

She must not have heard the news, and Sherry wasn't sure she wanted to inform her.

"How was your shift?"

"How do you think it was? Same as always, total bullshit. Too much hard work and not enough reward, with the few scraps I get always going to you. Not that you ever appreciate it."

"I do appreciate it, Mom. You —"

"More bullshit. You're an entitled child. Always have been. You don't know *how* to work hard or do more than your share. It's one of the reasons you're worthless."

"You promised you'd stop saying that."

"I worked up through the day you fell out of me, then I

was back at it two days later. I sure as shit didn't have anyone helping *me* out. Life sucks, so get used to it."

Feeling awful was the default whenever Sherry had one of these little talks her mother. But this was still worse than usual. Even if the world wasn't ending, it was changing for sure. If there had ever been a time for the two of them to start coming together, it was definitely now.

"Did you hear the news?"

She scoffed. "You mean the aliens? That's a heaping pile."

"But it's all over the news."

"It's a hoax. Probably trying to get us all to buy more bottled water or something." She wasn't looking at Sherry. Her mom was digging into the cupboard, pulling out a bottle of Smirnoff. "Long shift. I'm sleeping it off."

Unless Sherry's math was off, her mother's shift was the same length it always was.

"Good morning and good night," Sherry said as her mother walked away.

She turned back with one foot in the hallway. "Clean this place up. It looks like a couple of pigs live here."

Because they do.

Sherry waited to hear her mother's door swing shut, but instead of cleaning anything up, she downloaded the Astral app. The world was in love with the thing for some reason she never understood. It seemed stupid to her. So what? They put a giant telescope on the dark side of the moon and it stared into space. There was enough to worry about on this planet without looking out into nothing and wondering about all the other ones.

But now she had a reason, and felt almost breathless as the thing was loading onto her phone. Slowly. You usually clicked on the app you wanted and it was just there on your phone. This one seemed to be taking its time. Maybe because all the bandwagon riders like her were downloading it this morning, to see what the aliens were up to.

She laughed out loud. The whole thing was so ridiculous. But not.

Sherry went over to her computer and tried to get ahold of Bickford, but he wasn't around. She pinged him in the two ways she knew, first on LiveLyfe and then on Twitter, only realizing then that he'd never given her his number and she had no way of getting a hold of him unless he wanted to be reached.

Were they even really friends?

The rest of Sherry's day was miserable. Her mom drank herself to sleep, probably to numb herself for the aliens she knew were real but had to tell herself were bullshit to keep from going batshit or worse. She went to bed early, a bit before her mother was likely to get up.

She lay in bed, rubbing her belly and thinking about what kind of mom she would be.

The child inside her was Sherry's only comfort. Life had wronged her in many ways, she would make it right with her child. She wasn't sure how, but Sherry knew she would always do whatever it took to make sure her daughter always felt loved, taken care of, and supported — no matter what. Even if she had to get three jobs and sleep four hours a day. She would be the kind of mother her daughter could count on.

Sherry fell slowly to sleep, rubbing her belly, and saying, "I love you, Chelsea" until the day was behind her and last night's nightmares were back.

A cavernous space with inexplicable lights. A domed ceiling that seemed as high as the heavens themselves. Her consciousness nowhere and everywhere, shared with so many others. Her body poked and prodded, though that was better than what was happening to her mind.

And to her baby.

Sherry woke up screaming. Red blood on her white sheets.

She threw the covers off of her bed, then made her way to her mother's room, sobbing, hoping she could get help without begging.

"What is it?" Her mom's groggy eyes were widening as she slowly woke and saw the horror on Sherry's face. "What happened? Is it that thing with the Astral app?"

"No." Sherry shook her head, tears streaming down her cheeks. "But I need you to take me to the hospital. *Now.*"

Chapter Ten

No one had spoken for what might have been the longest ten minutes of Sherry's life.

Her mother was even colder than normal, and at a time when Sherry had never needed more of her warmth, suffering from a vacuum of emotion after being so emptied out. Losing all that blood, then her baby, watching them pull the lifeless body out of her, only letting her hold it for what felt like a minute. Then every drop of hope for some sort of an escape to a better future was suddenly gone.

None of the doctors or nurses had it in them to worry about a thing like bedside manner with aliens on the way. They figured Sherry should feel grateful they even showed up to work, and the hell of it all was they were probably right. But at least her mother could've said something to ease Sherry's pain.

Sherry had been born into misery, but this last year had been her worst by far. The assault that put a baby inside her, and the way her mother — an awful ally, but still her only one — was on her the second she found out what happened, as if it was somehow Sherry's fault.

And now aliens were apparently coming. It made her want to laugh, or cry, maybe shake her head with a knowing understanding, because as surprising as all of this was, she wasn't shocked at all.

"So, are you going to say anything?" Sherry finally asked.

Her mother never drove with her hands at ten and two, but this was worse than usual. She had her right hand at the bottom of the wheel, barely keeping the car steady, sucking on a cigarette in her left hand and blowing smoke out the window. One of the few concessions she made for Sherry during her "abortion waiting to happen."

"What do you want me to say?" She blew another plume of acrid smoke out the window.

"I don't know … anything … maybe something comforting?"

"You should already have all the comfort you need. That thing's finally gone, and now you don't have to deal with it. Sometimes the blessings are hard to recognize at first, but this will end up being the best thing that could have happened to us. You'll see."

Sherry didn't want to respond, because any possible answer would only trigger another big fight. It was hard to hear her mother's words, since she understood them for what they were. A condemnation on Sherry being the biggest mistake of *her* life. The one thing that ruined everything else. The error that held her back. Destroyed her dreams like rain pounding down on a mountain of sugar.

"I didn't want to lose the baby, Mom. This isn't a good thing. I was ready for Chelsea."

It was so hard not to cry, and her mother wasn't making it any easier.

"Well, you should've wanted to lose that thing, and you sure as hell weren't ready to have it. We both know you were only being stubborn and would've been bored with the whole situation before your titties ran out of milk. Now you don't have to raise your rapist's baby. Why you would even want a reminder of the darkest night of your life is beyond me."

Another drag. More smoke out the window.

Sherry said, "The darkest days are the ones that change you. Hard stuff makes us grow, isn't that what you're always telling me whenever I complain about anything, no matter how much I just need you to hear me? Well, that was the hardest thing in my life. But a baby was still made, and as torn up as I was, something healed inside me. Chelsea saved me by giving me a reason to hope. I wouldn't have been raising a rapist's baby, Mom. I would have been raising *my* baby."

"It was a reminder of something awful."

"She is a reminder of how wrong I can be."

"I know it might not seem like it now, but this really is the best thing that could've happened. You should have gotten the abortion instead of crying out loud when I took you. Maybe this is the Lord's way of teaching you to listen. You decided to carry this out despite my warning, insisting you had to see it through to the end. You had to do it your way, like always. Now you get to see exactly what that's brought you. Was there any purpose? Did you accomplish anything? No, you didn't. You wasted a lot of our time and our money, taking vitamins you didn't need and staycations away from work you felt you were too good to do."

Another drag, followed by another reeking exhale. "Sometimes I think you enjoy inflicting your pain on me. Just to see me upset. Like we need another mouth to feed or any more shit to worry about. I did an awful job teaching you to think about anyone other than yourself."

Sherry had never hated her mother more than she did

in that moment, and that was saying a lot, but the last thing she wanted to do was show it by crying.

"I still don't understand what you're so upset about."

And Sherry bellowed, "That's exactly the problem! You don't understand me at all!"

"What is there to understand? You're a spoiled child who's never done her share. You came into my life unwanted and unannounced, and after waiting through all of these long years to finally be finished with all of this shit, you're repeating history but making it even worse because this time, your problem is now my problem. We should be celebrating that we unclogged the crapper, not —"

"You're making this all about you. You make everything all about you!"

"This *is* about me, Sherry. You might've been carrying that child, but I would've raised it. Are you really telling me that you were planning on doing all the work?"

"Not all of it, no. But my share and probably some of yours. Just like now."

Sherry shouldn't have added that last part. Her mother's hands tightened on the wheel. If she hadn't just lost a child, her left cheek would be stinging from a swift and vicious slap.

"You wouldn't know how to do your share if it was paint by numbers," her mother said.

Sherry didn't know what that meant, but wasn't about to ask, content to travel the rest of their way in quiet misery.

There wasn't any comfort at home. Sherry's mom grabbed another bottle from the cupboard and disappeared into her room. Sherry did the same, sans bottle.

She lay in bed, crying softly, feeling alone and thinking about aliens. An odd reality to be wrestling all of a sudden. At least it kept her mind off of all she lost. Sherry kept thinking of her Chelsea. Every time the name flitted into her brain was like barbs dragged across her flesh.

The rest of that afternoon passed as though Sherry were moving through it with a bucket of sand strapped to each foot. Her mom didn't go to work, only left the house to refill her bottles. Same for the next day.

On the third afternoon after the balls were spotted near Jupiter, Sherry turned off the news — apparently Austin, Texas was going to shit — and wondered if Bickford was around. It was nowhere near their usual time, and she hadn't been able to get him the day before or so far today. And she'd tried plenty. But she was desperate to talk and would even do it on video because who cared what Mom would have to say about her now? The bitch could call her a whore all she wanted.

Sherry logged on to LiveLyfe and tried again. Sent a message to Bickford then waited.

But this time he was online and responded immediately.

What's up? Are you getting ready for the invasion?

Are you around? Sherry typed. *Can you talk?*

Sherry's heart beat harder while waiting for Bickford to finish typing.

Sure. Video? Then the part that took the longest. *Is everything okay?*

Yes, I just don't want to be alone right now.

The video screen appeared without any sound. Sherry realized it was mute and turned it up, wiping her eyes, thinking about how awful she must look.

Bickford seemed alarmed. "What happened?"

Her voice hitched and the words came out like vomit. "I lost the baby."

Then Bickford said something that surprised the hell right out of her, even when an alien invasion hadn't.

"I wish I could hold you."

Sherry didn't know what to say because there wasn't an answer for something like that. Bickford had never said anything affectionate before, even though she would've like that, and even tried to encourage it in her own way.

"I'm sorry," he finally said. "I hope that was okay."

"Of course it was. I just didn't expect it."

"How is your mom? She at least being nice to you now?"

"Hardly." Sherry wanted to laugh, but her throat was burning up like the rest of her body. "She's in bed with another bottle."

"Is there anything I can do for you?" Bickford asked.

"You already did it." Sherry gave him the first smile her face had seen all day. "Thank you."

They talked about life, her lost child, and a little about the aliens. Bickford wasn't scared so much as he was excited.

By the time they finally hung up, Sherry was surprised to find herself feeling slightly better. Good enough to get the seed of an idea.

What if he could hold her? She still had his address from that poem she sent him. She could go to him. Two states away wasn't that far. He had his own place. And Sherry would be eighteen in two months.

She packed in a hurry. There wasn't much in the house worth caring about, or taking with her. The thing she wanted most had died in her sleep, then was taken out of her body like garbage on trash day.

The next part was harder. Sherry had to convince herself that she wasn't doing the wrong thing, first by taking everything of value from her mother's purse, then scouring their shack in search of dollars but settling for dimes.

The last part was hardest, even though her mom was a monster who couldn't have given less of a shit about her. Sherry knew it was wrong to leave the woman stranded, especially with all the Astral app was reporting. She would have to figure it out for a few shifts at most. Take public transportation, ask for a ride from their neighbor Mr. Bilson.

Whatever. It wasn't Sherry's problem and wouldn't matter long. Even if she tried to do the right thing, her mother would only call her worthless or entitled or worse.

She needed a car to get to Bickford's. She opened the old Nissan door, climbed behind the wheel, and turned the engine, glad that she'd learned to drive even though more than two thirds of the cars on the road were now fully automated.

Sherry plugged Bickford's GPS coordinates into her phone and drove without thinking.

Chapter Eleven

SOMETHING HAD CHANGED, and Gleeson could smell it.

And not just because he'd started reading the Bible. The air was different. Solitary somehow felt even more remote than normal, with him severed from the population and having to guess at everything. He hadn't seen Percy in a couple of days and was dying to ask him about what he was feeling. None of the other guards would answer him if he asked or could even get the right question out of him, seeing as he wasn't exactly sure of what it was.

Gleeson also wanted to tell Percy about his nightmares. Because now he was starting to remember them. More than that, or *worse* than that, now he couldn't forget if he wanted to. They were seared onto his vision. And thanks to solitary, they were just about all he could see. At least a rat in a cage could look through its bars.

Maybe if Gleeson could have an hour outside he might stop seeing the demons. Maybe the horrible crunching of bones would finally fade away. Maybe he wouldn't feel the need to start slamming his head against the wall until he broke it open and was smearing the wall with his brains.

Percy's old Bible was the only thing keeping him sane, and he didn't know what to think of that.

The door opened, and the CO appeared like an angel.

"Where've you been?" Gleeson asked, as though he had any right to know.

"It's been busy out there." Percy's face was grave and ashen. Sorrow lit his eyes, the kind that reminded Gleeson not of what happened but more of what was sure to be coming.

"What is it?"

Percy shook his head. He opened his mouth but a little laugh gurgled right out. It sounded like an accident, and it was, because a tear immediately followed. He stopped shaking his head and wiped it away. "I don't know how to tell you."

"Tell me what?"

Gleeson should have been scared. His body wanted him to follow Percy's instructions, the posture telling him that something unbelievable or terrible or probably both had happened. Maybe the country was on fire. Or worse.

"I'm not about to be fooling with you," Percy said.

"I know."

He drew a breath, then exhaled into his answer. It came out fast, like liquid from a tipped over bottle.

"Aliens are coming. The prisoners in general are losing their shit. Hell, so is half the world."

"Aliens?" Gleeson was repeating the word, almost as if to be polite. But for some reason, he had no trouble believing what Percy was saying at all. If anything, it sounded familiar. Maybe like the breaking of those Seven Seals.

"That's what they're saying. You know the Astral app?"

"Of course."

"It spotted them around Jupiter. A bunch of giant

spheres. NASA's saying we have six days, but that was three days ago."

"Just NASA?"

"Well, everybody."

"What's happening?" Gleeson asked.

"Where do you mean?"

"Anywhere. Everywhere."

"It's what you would imagine, everything from people preparing for the rapture to other folks thinking it's a hoax. There was a record number of homicides, but barely a blip in suicides for some reason. A dip, actually. Surprised the hell out of the media."

"It gave them something to live for," Gleeson said, smiling. "Something to see."

"I suppose." Percy shook his head and looked behind him. "There's gonna be a riot in here, it's only a matter of when. And we're not getting any help. The world is waist deep in its own shit right now. No one cares about what's happening in a Montana prison."

"Why are you telling me this?"

"Because the end times are here."

"What do you think is coming?" Gleeson asked, mostly because of the look in Percy's eyes.

"Intervention from a higher species, maybe, since we sure as hell aren't doing well enough on our own. But whatever is coming, God sent it to us."

"He's destroyed the world before. Maybe he's doing it again."

"Like I said. The end times."

"Be careful what you wish for," Gleeson said. "This might have nothing to do with your God, and if there's a higher species coming, they'll likely see us as the vermin we are. And you know what happens to roaches."

"Maybe they're not sinners, so they won't know who to kill."

"What if that's exactly what they are, and it's all they know how to do?"

"Then we will go home to the Lord."

"You and Melinda."

"Yes. Me and Melinda. Maybe you, too. God can see inside your heart, Gleeson. And He knows what you did for me." Percy clapped him on the shoulder. "I've been gone too long. I hope to see you later. Maybe for dinner."

But Gleeson didn't see him for dinner, getting a guard who clearly belonged to the Aryan Brotherhood despite his uniform instead. A man he'd heard guards call Damian.

The door swung open then the Nazi sauntered inside. He dropped a tray on the ground with a smirk. No cold eggs or biscuit. It wasn't even food, at least not for a human. "What? You don't like rat."

Gleeson didn't answer. Damian continued to stare.

"You better watch your back," he finally said.

"Walter sent you."

"He sure did."

Gleeson stared right into his soul. "What kind of man are you, siding with some Aryan shithead over your own co-worker? You pretend you're on the law's side, but Percy's a good man, and you're hitching your wagon to a murdering lifer. How do you explain that?"

"Easiest thing in the world," Damian replied without flinching. "It doesn't matter what Walter did or didn't do on the outside. He's in here now, and smart enough to know that the only good nigger is a dead nigger."

Gleeson had heard such vitriol before, even from relatives and back before he would have called it out. But right now, he wanted to grab the Nazi's head and do to it what he never should have done to Roy's.

Still staring into his soul, Gleeson imagined his casket. "You best hope you're making the right choices, brother, because the Seven Seals have been broken, so angels and demons will be descending."

He smiled at the CO's confusion then added, "They're coming to judge us."

Chapter Twelve

POPPY HAD NEVER BEEN angrier at Eamon, but her rage was finally waning.

This was their third night stuck in the Cottage, waiting for intermittent calls from Liam and unpacking and repacking everything they did and didn't know. There was a speck of the first and a spill of the second. Poppy could go into labor any day now, if the baby came just a little early, and with all the stress that might be a possibility. But she was stuck out here in the middle of nowhere, thanks to Eamon. Suffering from the arrogant decisions made without her inclusion and the consequences that naturally followed.

The longest conversation with Liam had lasted for only ten minutes, and the asshole's usual rancor was gone. Felony put him on speaker every time, and Poppy was surprised at his even tone, considering that the world was apparently going to seed in every major city. Three days and things were already falling apart. It felt like an episode of Black Mirror or Version Control. Vegas had burned and Texas had — no joke — seceded from the rest of the

Country. For the first two days Poppy thought she would do anything to get back to Billings, now she wondered how much longer there would be anything for them to get back to.

Poppy was sitting in the picture window, reading a tattered old book that was already there, faded by the sun and sitting on the bench. She could barely follow the plot and didn't really care. Technically, she wasn't even reading. Just fixing her eyes on a paragraph here and there, occasionally turning the page and making sure to look transfixed enough by the words that Eamon would leave her alone in this last couple of hours before bedtime. The strategy had worked well for the last two days, but she'd been seeing diminishing returns, and it now looked like her operation was broken.

"Please," Eamon begged her again. "Can we just talk?"

"We were just talking. Now I want to read." Poppy shifted on the bench, trying to get comfortable despite that being impossible.

"That wasn't talking. I mean you and me."

Eamon was right. It wasn't even close to talking, or at least not in the way that he meant. Their only conversations since getting to the Cottage had been the ones where all three of them were discussing Liam's calls, usually for a couple of hours after each one. But Poppy refused to talk with him alone. And for the last two nights, he'd slept on the couch.

Guilt and disappointment had settled hard onto his shoulders, warping his posture and making Poppy feel bad when she shouldn't. Because fuck Eamon for all of this. He deserved to stew in the juices he brewed for himself. He had broken every promise, and though Poppy was loyal for better or worse, she was also very, very pregnant. So unfair or not, every new stabbing pain in her body was yet another reminder of what he had done.

"We don't have anything to talk about, Eamon. You want to apologize, and I don't want to accept it yet. That puts us at an impasse."

"I understand that. And you're right to be upset with me. But how long do you think this impasse is going to last?"

"I'm glad I have your permission to be upset. That makes all of this so much easier."

"We're going to make up eventually," Eamon said, his voice still patient. "I'm just asking if we can please do it earlier. Especially with everything that's happening."

A single sentence shouldn't have been strong enough to crumble Poppy's walls, but those final five words were battering rams against them. Eamon was right. If aliens were coming, then that made all of this petty. But she couldn't just ignore it, either. Sure, this might be a hoax, or something everyone was in a tizzy about even though it didn't really mean anything, like what her parents told her about that whole Y2K thing. But even in the aftermath of an alien invasion the two of them would have to stay alive and hopefully raise their child together. So she had to trust him, but their old bond had been broken, or damaged at least, and Poppy couldn't start forming a new one until she wasn't so royally pissed.

"Even if the sky is full of Klingons tomorrow, that doesn't change what you did."

"I know, and I'm sorry."

Poppy looked up into Eamon's eyes. Seeing how much he meant it rattled her insides. She needed him, too. She wanted to receive and relieve him. Center them both by kissing him deeply. Wrap her hand around his hardening cock and empty him out so he could finally feel full again.

But no, she wasn't ready for that.

"I know you're sorry … I'm just still really pissed at you."

"You have every right to be. We can talk about it now or later. But we need to be together."

He touched her and she let him, his hand on top of hers, their eyes finally fixed on each other's.

"You're right," she said, finally broken and feeling better already. "But I still want to talk about it later."

Eamon leaned back and Poppy put her head on his chest. He petted her for several minutes before either of them spoke.

She was first to break their silence. "I'm trying not to freak out."

"I know. Me, too. But everything will be okay."

"How do you know that?"

"Because it has to be. There's nothing we can to do change things, so we have to accept that this might be the end."

"That's not what I need from you right now, Eamon."

"What do you need?"

"A plan. Or at least I need to know you're capable of making one."

"How can we have a plan for the unexpected and the unexplainable? We don't have any idea what's going to happen when those ships or whatever get here. How can we possibly prepare for something like that?"

"I don't know," Poppy said. "But do you really think waiting around in the middle of the forest is the best thing for us to be doing?"

"Maybe. What if this is exactly where we're supposed to be? Maybe the universe is looking out for us. Everything for a reason … like you always say."

"Maybe." She wanted to believe it. "I hope so."

They lay in silence for an hour or so after that, both of them feeling a bit more stitched together.

"Can we go to bed?" Eamon asked as their bodies parted.

"Not yet. Maybe tomorrow."

"Okay."

He kissed her on the cheek, and she kissed him back on the lips. "I love you."

"I love you, too," he said.

Then Poppy went into her room, closed the door, and collapsed on her bed, trying not to think about things getting worse, or wondering if life as they knew it was over, but failing to bar either thought from her brain.

It didn't take long to fall asleep, though she was wide awake in her dream, and it felt like she was there for an eon or many. There was a circle of rocks, terrestrial yet otherworldly — a wide circle waiting for worship. And maybe a place that Poppy had been before. She didn't exactly remember ever having seen it, yet it felt as familiar as the child inside her.

The rocks were a reminder of how beautiful the world already was and what it was still waiting to be. What it might become, now that it had the chance and the stars had finally come home.

Poppy didn't know what that meant, but she looked up into the black sky hoping to find out. Sure enough, it was like billions of diamonds dropped onto pressed velvet. Any one of them had the answers, and maybe all of them did.

She closed her eyes to keep the tears from falling. The stars were stunning, and Poppy felt powerless while standing under their awe. Besides, with her eyes closed she could hear the rocks humming their secrets, whispers and treasures meant only for her, inviting her to visit, begging her to come, to bring Eamon and their child.

Poppy studied her surroundings, knowing even in the thick of her dream that she'd have to remember what she saw now back in her waking life.

"I will find you," she said to the rocks and the stars.

They answered, *I know,* then Poppy opened her eyes to fresh sunlight pouring through the window.

She didn't wake slowly. Less than a minute after opening her eyes and Poppy was already emptying her bladder. She flushed, then went to find Eamon.

"I had a dream," she told him.

There was the lightest sparkle in his eyes, reminding Poppy of just how long it had been since she'd seen it.

"Oh?" He raised his eyebrows. "What kind of dream?"

Poppy had never been shy about sharing her dreams with Eamon. At his best he was the purest of listeners, and throughout their years together he had learned to trust her intuition. It wasn't flawless, but Poppy was right a lot more often than she was wrong, and with a sixth sense born from her depths, even the most discordant of her instincts felt honest.

"I dreamed about a place."

"What kind of place?" Eamon asked.

"The place where I think we should go."

"And where is that?"

"I don't know," Poppy admitted. "But it isn't here."

"You've gotta give me more than that."

"It looked like Stonehenge."

"Stonehenge? In England?"

"Yes," she nodded, "but it wasn't Stonehenge. It was here … and not too far from where we are now."

Eamon looked confused. Maybe incredulous, even though he was obviously trying to believe. "So how are we supposed to find it?"

"I'm not sure. But we need to get out of here. Start driving."

"That's awfully specific … and simultaneously vague."

"I know." Poppy laughed. The sound had become unfamiliar and now felt welcome on her lips.

"What do we do now?"

"How hard do you think it will be to convince Felony we need to leave?"

"I don't think it's going to be easy."

But Eamon was wrong about that. Felony appeared less than a minute later, barely a moment into the crafting of their plan. "Liam says we've gotta get out of here. Things are going to shit in Billings. He says our cover is blown and it probably doesn't matter, but he's suggesting we leave the Cottage, anyway."

Eamon and Poppy traded a look.

Then Eamon said, "Where does he want us to go?"

"He didn't say," Felony answered.

"Where do you think we should go?" Poppy's question sounded like a test.

Felony shrugged and shook his head. "I have no idea."

"I do," Poppy said.

Felony looked curious. "Okay, where?"

She looked at Eamon, then turned back to Felony. "To our future."

Chapter Thirteen

THE NISSAN WAS GIVING Sherry some trouble, making noises she didn't understand and lurching suddenly forward every handful of miles. She kept telling herself not to worry, the thing was almost as old as her mother. Sherry was pretty sure her mom gave their neighbor hand jobs to keep it running. Charlie lived two doors down and had sort of implied the situation while leering at Sherry in a *the price might be going up* sort of way.

The check engine light had been on for a while, and there was nothing Sherry could do. There weren't a lot of Charlies around. She'd be happy to give a hand job if it would help her get to Bickford. Even if Charlie was gross, but that wasn't a big deal. She knew how to get it done fast. Where to spit, what to say, and how to move her hand.

But that wasn't likely out here. Sherry was driving the backroads because all the apps agreed traffic was fucked. The Astral app showed a heat map of cars across the planet. It looked like a billion ants descending upon a cake that had fallen to the ground and crumbled in wedges. The few cars Sherry had seen on the tiny little strip of dirt had either raced right by her Nissan or had their auto-drives making obnoxious noises, trying to communicate with an old piece of shit that didn't speak its language. Or any language for that matter.

There was a second light brightening her dim and ancient dashboard. And that one was a hell of a fucker.

Modern cars burned fuel like the striking of a lighter, a spark to get the fire burning. Sherry's crappy metal box was more like a match, and the engine was striking it over and over and over and over, until the box was finally emptied.

If she didn't get to a gas station soon, she would be stuck out in the middle of nowhere.

Raped then murdered, this time without any baby to follow.

The end of the world would give her attacker every excuse.

But that could't happen. She had to reach the stones.

Sherry shook her head. *Bickford.* She had to reach Bickford.

She checked her phone. Nine miles to the nearest station. It could be worse, but this was an inch from disaster already. The car burned fast at the end, calling to mind more bad memories over the desperation of her current situation. Sherry had run out of gas with her mother four or five times — she wasn't sure since shit with her mom sort of always ran together. She never missed a shift at work but fell short of most things beyond being a barely competent waitress in a crappy unintentionally retro dive.

The next nine miles were hell. The road got worse and the car worked harder. Another light came on, but it looked like a box with an X and that didn't mean shit to Sherry. She started to bleed. First a little between her legs and then all over the seat. She was drenched in sweat, and her entire body was vibrating from the steering wheel throwing jolts into her hands and up through her shoulders, down Sherry's spine before leaking into everywhere else. She tasted the blood as it spilled between her legs, hanging in the air like an inescapable reek. Too afraid to roll down the window for air, she choked on the coppery fumes, terrified her car might have to work that much harder.

Maybe the rocks would save her. Not that Sherry had any idea what that meant. Smaller rocks than the ones she kept thinking about for some reason seemed to be fucking up some major shit up on the underside of her carriage.

Sherry swung off the dirt cut and onto a real road. Then she slammed into traffic.

The gas station was only a couple of miles away, but it was bumper to bumper all the way there, and she wondered if there would even be any gas by the time it was her turn. Did it take extra gas to start a car? Was she better off killing the engine and restarting it each time?

This was impossible.

Sherry thought again about Charlie, and some of the other ways he helped her mom out. Having no friends and a horrible mother didn't make a person ugly. She was a pretty girl, hungry for someone to love her. That's why she was so good at the hand jobs, plus the blowjobs and everything else. Even on the worst night of her life, Sherry managed to sort of disappear inside herself until the horror was over. Pretended it was something it wasn't because that was a bit like cutting her trauma in two.

Maybe she could find herself a Charlie. If that was what would happen anyway, she might as well start looking. Make it her choice rather than his.

She got out of the car, looking down at her yellow skirt,

a red pool the size of a birthday cake covering the crotch. She looked at her reflection in the filthy window. Awful, of course. Even worse than expected. She fluffed her hair and wiped her brow, acknowledged that it changed nothing, and started her trek toward the station.

Sherry felt every stare through her very long walk, ending with her about to pass out, aghast that not a single person had stopped to help or ask her if she was okay. Maybe offer her water or anything else.

Her head swam as hard as her stomach by the time she reached the station. She needed to lie down and vomit, the order didn't matter. The place had been ransacked. Sherry was hoping for some food, and definitely water, but there wasn't any of either. The station was automated. Most in the city were, but out here in the sticks it was slightly surprising.

She didn't know what to do. There weren't any gas cans, but there were plenty of people looking for them, and three days after the Astral announcement, that apparently came with a lot of pushing and shoving.

Sherry stepped outside and saw the flashing of cop cars, looked down at her crotch again as if she needed the reminder, then ducked back into the station, immediately heading toward the bathroom.

Sure enough, there was a window, and sick as she was, Sherry was climbing onto the just tall enough garbage can to scramble out of it.

She cut across the road and ran back into the forest. Maybe not the smartest move, Sherry realized after about fifteen minutes of walking, when she checked the GPS and discovered she didn't have any signal. She had no idea where she was, and no ability to navigate her space. In seventeen years, she'd never even once used a map. GPS didn't count because it made the world revolve around you.

She didn't want to be worried, but darkness was coming. All the things she was scared of in the daylight were a thin sheet to the heavy blanket that covered her once it was time for the moon, whether it was waning or not.

Sherry kept walking until she couldn't. Then she sat for a while, longer than she wanted, then a lot longer after that.

She wanted to surprise Bickford and show up unannounced, but Sherry might die if she stuck to that plan. So she took out her phone and messaged him, then wanted to hurl it against the nearest tree after the thing betrayed her yet again. Finally, she walked over to that trunk, planted her back against it, sank to the dirt floor, then started to cry.

This was her bottom. The most awful it had ever been. Even worse than that terrible night.

Maybe she should just go home. Bickford couldn't save her. Sherry's life was over.

She'd lost her baby, and her existence was now an ugly echo of her unfortunate mother's. White trash in a trailer, looking for a Charlie or ten to pave her survival with favors for sex.

It was strange for her hope to circle the drain like that. A few hours ago, she was on her way to Bickford's, picturing a future that promised to be so much better than her past, whatever that meant. But some of Sherry died with the car. A part she needed to keep her faith in if she expected the fuel to keep going. Now there were vapors in her tank, same as the Nissan, and Sherry wasn't sure she could even go on. Or more importantly, if she wanted to.

Maybe she had been arrogant to believe that escaping hell was a choice. That she was better than where she came from. That this reality wasn't both her bloodline and birthright. Maybe this was what fate had in mind all along, and God was just setting her up for the longest laugh. Toying with her the way those boys had, taking turns and yelling terrible things. Using Sherry like a posable doll.

It wasn't even fucking. Just six monsters using her body to masturbate themselves to a finish.

She had been bullied and bullied, but nobody cared. Gang raped, and it was a joke. There was a video on FuckIt, and probably a ton of other apps, but that was the one she'd seen linked all over social media, and always with the most vile comments. The headline on the video hurt her the most.

Slutty Whore Begs to Get Pregnant While Six Studs Cum Inside Her!

That wasn't true. She never said that in the video, or in real life. They asked her if she was on the pill and she said yes. Partly because she was scared, and partly because she did the math and figured she was safe enough. Most guys liked to finish on her body, anyway.

Her mother didn't even care. Because the camera kept her face out of the picture, and her assailants were all wearing masks, there was nothing anyone could do, and it was easy for her mom to pretend it wasn't the soul-destroying horror it was.

Sherry started walking again, but it wasn't long before she found herself stopping in the center of a short bridge with a long drop onto sharp rocks below. The moon illuminated the crags, promising instant death for a brave girl who had given up on life enough to take the plunge.

Climbing up onto the railing, Sherry decided she was exactly that type of girl.

Her hands were out at her sides, both feet on a narrow beam of wood. A breeze might blow her over, a gust would end things for sure. She had only one reason to live, to see the arrival.

The rocks were also calling her name. Not the ones waiting below. The other ones, the ones from her dreams.

So that gave Sherry two reasons to stay.

But good things came in threes. And she was having an impossible time finding a third. She was dying, and the world was too frantic to help her.

Ending things would be easy.

All she had to do was let go.

And so she—

Sherry stopped. Looked over at the high beams of a car somehow lurching to the perfect stop. Urgent, but aware. Careful to not startle her.

The car door opened and a woman stepped onto the road. Even in the dark, Sherry could see she was beautiful. Long ringlets of blonde hair, and a tentative smile brightened by the high beams. And very, very pregnant.

"Please don't," the woman said.

"I wasn't going to."

"Yes. You were. But it's okay. I'm going to come over there, okay?"

Sherry nodded. Even that pregnant, the woman was graceful.

At the railing she held her hand out for Sherry, then helped her down from the railing after she took it.

"Everything will be okay." The woman's words sounded like a pledge. "Nothing is this bad."

"Thank you," Sherry choked.

"You can cry. You probably need to."

She did, sobbing against the angel's chest, just above her baby. That made Sherry sob even harder, thinking about Chelsea, her hands going down to rub her own barren belly as she cried.

"I'm Poppy."

"I'm Chelsea."

"It's nice to meet you, Chelsea. Can we offer you a ride?"

"Where are you going?" Poppy looked behind her at the quietly humming car. Two men sat inside it. Sherry couldn't see them well, but both appeared to be patiently waiting. "That's my husband and my friend. I think we're going to see the aliens." She laughed from what looked like the embarrassed side of a shrug.

"Why do you think that?"

Still shrugging, Poppy looked like she was about to tell Sherry a secret. Then in a whisper, she did. "I had a dream about these rocks."

Poppy saying that was like a light bulb going bright inside Sherry. It made sense.

"I know the rocks." It felt like confession. "I think I had the dream, too."

Poppy didn't seem surprised. "Come with us."

Sherry shook her head. "I can't. I'm going to meet my boyfriend, Bickford."

"It doesn't look that way." Poppy glanced at the bridge.

"I didn't mean that. I just couldn't walk anymore. I'll wait around and hitch a ride to someone heading his way."

"How do you know we're not? Where does Bickford live?"

"Nowhere near the rocks." Sherry said it like a fact. Because she knew where they were, same as Poppy.

"We'll take you to Bickford after ... whatever happens at the rocks. I promise."

The tears were coming again. "Can I sleep in your car?"

"We have plenty of room." Poppy took Sherry's hand then tucked her into the back seat.

Chapter Fourteen

DESPITE BEING IN SOLITARY, Gleeson finally had a cellmate. An old one made new again.

It had been days. Maybe three, but really, he had no idea. Gleeson was dreaming of Roy whenever he closed his eyes and still seeing him once they were back open. Gleeson was still aware enough to realize that solitary did things like that to a man, but he hadn't been inside long enough for the insanity to kick in. Not like this. Roy existed somewhere, and his unsettled energy was speaking to Gleeson. He had something to tell him and wasn't going to leave until he felt both heard and understood.

Messages came in metaphor, allegory, and simple fact. Roy wanted him to know a singular thing but didn't believe he got it.

But he did.

It was Gleeson's time. Judgment was coming. He had to keep his mind open to the truth. He was bound to be part of whatever was going to happen — a hammer and saw to build the new world.

"Do you see it, brother?" Roy pointed at the burning cities below. "And do you understand your part?"

"I do." Gleeson nodded, desperate for Roy to believe him this time. He was ready, had been for a while.

Roy raised his gaze to the heavens, to the giant balls of electric life, each one several stadiums wide, and more than Gleeson could count. "They're here. Are you ready?"

"I am." Gleeson nodded again, then the world around him filled with —

He opened his eyes, gasping.

A klaxon punched him in the ear. The horn was loud enough to fill the middle of his bones. He vibrated everywhere as he stood from the bed and stared at his open cell door in disbelief.

Gleeson had no idea why his door was open or who had opened it, but he wasn't about to squander opportunity. He was out of his cell in a second, looking both ways as he crossed the threshold. His heel pounded the latticed metal scaffolding.

Hell was visible at the edges. He couldn't see much, but there was no looking away from the two fallen guards on the ground or the five Nazis fronted by Walter all headed his way. It was a safe bet they were the ones who opened Gleeson's door to freedom, then execution, spaced just seconds apart.

Nowhere to run. Gleeson's cell was at the end of a second-floor hallway, and the stairs were on the opposite side of his enemies. They were here to end things, planning to make him suffer hard enough to wish for a death they would take too long to grant. And Gleeson was a big guy. Not quite a giant, but close. He could endure, so this could last a while.

Walter only stopped walking once within striking distance. Gleeson should have seen it coming, a failure on his part. He expected a monologue but got a swift fist instead.

Right to the jaw, but he didn't go down. Not until all five of them were on him, pulling him to the ground. Then two of them held him there while Walter and another Aryan with bloodshot eyes began to kick him over and over.

Walter stepped on his throat. "Do you like that?"

Gleeson choked and tried to spit, but the foot on his neck made him swallow.

"Hey, Kirk," Walter said to the Aryan beside him. The guy with the charming tattoos.

"Yeah?"

"You remember the last time we had to deal with a nigger lover?"

Kirk answered, though there was something unsteady in his voice. "The time we kept shoving the broom up his ass until it and the stick were both covered in blood?"

"That's the time," Walter agreed, still looking down at Gleeson. "You thinking what I'm thinking?"

A gunshot tore through the air, deafening as it echoed against a world full of metal.

The Aryans looked behind them and saw Percy holding his firearm.

"Break it up," he said, coming closer.

The Nazis let Gleeson go. Hard to argue with a loaded gun and a pending apocalypse.

Percy held his aim, approaching the horde. "Nobody move."

But the rats were out of their cage with nothing to lose.

Percy was too close. His gun was aimed right at Kirk's face, but he was too damned close for his own good. How could he not see it?

Kirk was a current, reaching out and grabbing the

weapon right from Percy's hand in a flinch. He could've pulled the trigger, but instead crushed Percy's face with the butt. It echoed like a sound effect, the crunch of his nose somehow worse than the bone-smashing clatter of his knees hitting the metal grating. Or the plink of a single tooth a second later.

Kirk and Walter dragged Percy over to the corner, but only Walter was laughing. He held his hand out expectantly, then his subordinate filled it with the gun.

They came for Gleeson next. It took all five of them to get him into the corner with Percy, and he was sure at least two of the assholes were terrified he might rip them apart with his bare hands the second he got a chance, despite their strength in numbers and Walter's gun.

Four of them kept holding Gleeson, forcing him to his knees. That was the only thing keeping them alive. He could take a few bullets. Had before. His body was practically built for it. A human tank, he kept aiming his eyes at Walter like a cannon, letting him know every time he looked that he better pray for missed opportunities, pray Gleeson got sloppy. Because he only needed one, then Walter would be no more. Gleeson would get the gun and empty it into everyone except Percy.

Walter kept slapping the CO, rousing him back to consciousness while Gleeson was being held to the ground. A stupid move. His men were getting tired while Gleeson got a rest. He'd turn the tables and crush that fucker's head.

Walter turned to Gleeson. "We're patient." Then he turned back to Percy and slapped him hard.

The CO opened his eyes, choking. Then his body snapped his body to attention, and he went rigid on his knees.

"Oh, good. He's up." Walter smiled and scratched his

head with the barrel of his gun. He turned to his men. "I'm not sure what's worse. A nigger, or a nigger lover. Any of you have opinions on that?"

"I'd say a nigger," said Aryan One.

"Nigger lover for me," said Aryan Two.

"Definitely nigger," said Aryan Three.

Still no smile from Kirk. "I'd say they're equal."

"Much as I hate a sympathizer," Walter said, his voice suddenly serious, "I hate the enemy more. Definitely nigger. But that ain't necessarily the order of operations."

He turned to Gleeson. "Open your mouth."

"No." He stared up at Walter.

"Here's the deal, Mongo. You don't open that giant hatch of yours, I'm going to blow the nigger's brains out, and I'm gonna do it on his left side so you'll get doused with blood and nuggets like a coat of paint before it's your turn. I'll make it so the bullet misses you when it comes out the other end. Only spatter for the nigger lover. Until it's your turn."

Gleeson was safe. If Walter wanted to kill him, he would put the gun to his forehead and pull the trigger. The fucker wanted to play with him first. Bought time, so far as Gleeson was concerned.

He opened his mouth and Walter smiled.

Then he shoved the gun into Gleeson's mouth, taking a tooth on its way.

He winced but tried not to show it. Needed to look anywhere other than up at Walter, at least for a moment. Looked over and caught Kirk's expression. The man was surprised. He flinched and looked away, but Gleeson still saw it. The trapped animal behind the monster. A kid eager to prove himself because that was the best way to keep breathing in a place like this. But he wasn't a masochist and didn't revel in it like Walter.

Gleeson understood him. Maybe even felt sorry for him. Seemed a reasonable thing to feel on his way out.

Walter pushed the gun in farther. Gleeson was wrong. This was the end. The big Aryan wasn't going to toy with him — he just wanted to end it his way, with a metal cock between a nigger lover's whore lips.

"Any last words?"

Gleeson said nothing. He'd find Walter in hell and skull fuck his mother in front of him.

"Kinda hard to talk with a gun in your mouth, though."

Gleeson stared up at Walter, unafraid to die.

And Walter glared back, ready to end him.

But then there was a sudden explosion of light, and the opposite happened.

Chapter Fifteen

Percy was knocked to the ground.

But so was everyone else. The light was too much. As though God himself had opened his robe to the world.

Time stopped, and he disappeared. Left Earth behind, trading it for something ethereal and better. Altered him on a cellular level. Because there he was, floating in the heavens and watching the world from above.

He could see Gleeson. Hovering over the ground, a bit below Percy, as though he jumped from the plane just moments ahead and opened his parachute early.

By the time Percy was back on the ground, his head was filled with too many memories, most of them new and only a few even made any sense. The world was more of a mystery than ever, and yet it also made sense. Or at least it could start to, now that Percy was being returned from a place he wasn't sure he had ever really gone off to.

Then the light was gone, and Percy was back on the ground. Dazed and disoriented, but nowhere near defeated. In some ways, stronger than ever. Ready to help Gleeson, which was the very thing he'd come down this hallway to do. Percy had to protect him. That duty burned in his blood.

But it might not be necessary.

He looked over at Gleeson in disbelief. There was a reason no one was paying attention to Percy. All six of the Aryans were working on the big man, but they weren't beating him into paste like Percy expected. Gleeson was holding his own. None of them were touching him, and even though they had their prey backed against a wall with a half-dozen enemies in a semi-circle around him, Gleeson was grinning as if he was the predator.

The moment was ten months pregnant, overdue to deliver, with no one willing to move.

But then the skinhead in the middle flinched. Gleeson must have taken that as an invitation. He charged for the guy, wrapping both arms around him as he ran past, then hefting him up onto his shoulder before hurling him over the railing down onto the second floor.

It wasn't a big enough drop to kill him, but the landing could break a limb or two, and judging by the wailing that followed his crash, it had.

With one down and five to go, the predator was still smiling, and Percy was wondering if Gleeson needed his help. Walter drew his pistol, as if only now remembering he had it, and aimed it between his enemy's eyes.

Gleeson kept grinning. "You better not miss."

"I won't," Walter promised, then steadied his aim to pull the trigger.

But God had poured lightning into Gleeson. The man moved like illumination itself. First standing a few feet away from Walter, right in the weapon's line of fire, then the next second diving toward his ankles and under the breadth of his shot.

Walter went down and Gleeson grabbed the gun, snapping his wrist without effort.

The other four were already on him, or trying to be, but Gleeson shrugged them off like losing a shirt on his way to the shower. He pulled the trigger three times in a staccato of shots. Sent one bullet into a forehead, another into a throat, and the last like a bullseye into an Aryan's heart.

Three bodies clattered to the floor, leaving only Walter and Kirk still able to fight.

The two men were on their knees, just like Percy and Gleeson had been before the light. Before the Lord came to save them. They were both looking up and into their assailant's eyes, staring with terror.

"You got anything to say?" Gleeson asked Walter.

"I hope you burn with the niggers."

Gleeson put the gun into his waistband, then kneeled toward Walter and pulled him into what appeared to be an embrace. But it wasn't. Percy heard a sickening snap, then watched as Walter's bent neck sent his head lolling to the side, bulging his eyes before bringing him death.

Gleeson let the body fall then turned to Kirk, pulling the gun back out of his pants.

He pressed it to Kirk's forehead. "Do you repent for your sins?"

There was a softness to Gleeson's voice that Percy had never heard.

Kirk nodded, fast enough that Percy wondered if his head might snap.

"Then bow and repent," Gleeson commanded.

Kirk did, then when he looked up, Gleeson offered his hand. "Do you swear to only fight for God from now on?"

Another nod.

"Then you are forgiven, brother."

Percy kept staring, astonished. There was something different about Gleeson. Like maybe everything. Looking at the man was a religious experience, reminding Percy of the first time he felt the Lord. He'd been young, standing in one of the back pews in between his parents. He didn't feel the presence during the service itself. Only afterwards, when his parents were talking to the pastor. He had a fistful of his mother's skirt and remembered looking up, feeling a presence from this man that made every hair on his body stand on end.

He didn't remember a single thing the man said, but Percy didn't need to. The feeling mattered, and that same sensation was like a halo around him now. He was too young to understand it then, though he asked his parents, and his Mama told him he'd felt the Holy Spirit.

Percy believed it then, and had zero doubt now.

Gleeson ordered Kirk to stand, then came over to Percy. He offered his hand and helped him to his feet.

"You okay?"

"What happened?" Percy asked instead of giving Gleeson an answer.

He smiled. "I saw God. He spoke to me."

"What did He say?" Percy whispered in awe, desperate to hear it.

"Later," Gleeson said. "Right now, we have to go. I'll need you to lead the way."

"Of course."

Percy led the prisoner turned prophet into the bright light then to freedom outside. The sky was littered with what had to be alien drones, small ships like ball bearings buzzing overhead. Guards and prisoners ran about, screaming. Bullets screamed, too. And blasts from the bellies of those drones, like great beams of lights.

A few of them landed, opened up, then dropped aliens

onto the ground. Reptilian insects pulsing blue lightning from their throats ripped into humans indiscriminately.

But that wasn't exactly true. Everyone was dying, but Gleeson and Percy passed through Stonefall as though walking across burning coals. Same for Kirk right behind them. Danger was omnipresent and underfoot, but steady grace under fire kept them all safe.

"Where to now?" Percy asked once they had made it to relative safety and the three of them were sitting in his car.

"Your wife," Gleeson said. "She'll need our help, and you need her."

Percy looked at Kirk. "Not with him. He stays."

Kirk said nothing.

Gleeson turned to the man, then to Percy. "He's repented. He's no threat."

And, for some weird reason, it made sense. Percy let his doubts about the racist asshole murderer fade away. Whatever light had touched Gleeson was so bright, his words almost felt as if they were coming from inside Percy's own mind. And he believed that yes, Kirk had changed in an instant.

"My place it is," Percy said.

His car already knew where to go.

Chapter Sixteen

THE GIRL SEEMED NICE ENOUGH, but Eamon was unnerved by her presence.

He was trying not to take it personally and didn't want to come off as sounding jealous, especially to Poppy, but it had been days and she was still acting like he was the enemy. They hadn't made up. Not like they needed to. And here she was, offering her affections to a stranger. Starving him of the thing he needed most but giving the girl a generous pour, as though it came from a bottomless pitcher.

If she was going to ignore him because of what he did, fine. Eamon deserved it and they would figure it out eventually, but in the meantime, she could at least tell him more about wherever it was they were supposedly going. She was the one having dreams. Eamon was willing to trust her visions or whatever they were, but she should have been more willing to let him in. Not tit for tat; both were true.

Saying that she couldn't explain it was no longer acceptable. She had a responsibility to tell them as much as she could. But so far, all she had done was describe something that sounded an awful lot like Stonehenge, except in southern Montana. None of it gave them a compass or made any sense.

Also, Poppy hadn't been surprised by the sight of Sherry standing on the bridge. She said that the girl was probably on her way to the rocks, too. But then she couldn't elaborate or explain why she thought that.

Weird thing was, Poppy wasn't the only one who knew about the rocks. They had to leave the Cottage, with nowhere else to go. So why not head down to the rocks?

Their cabin had been quiet for a while. After the first few hours of intermittent whispering between Poppy and Sherry after they left that bridge days ago, a mostly broken conversation that left Eamon and Felony on the sidelines in silence, the van fell into a rumbling quiet. The roads were getting worse, and they were getting closer to their destination.

But once their phones were back to getting intermittent signals and they could get radio in the van, they started hearing the rumors. Not many, but they were there, and the three of them hunted for nuggets like treasure.

The world was falling apart. It was one thing to hear Liam's reports while they were stuck at the cabin. Quite another to hear it on the news.

Montana was free of the problems that much of the country seemed to be having. Nothing like what was still happening in Austin. The place was a war zone already and the aliens hadn't even landed. No riots around these parts, but Eamon was pretty sure that Felony had killed someone for gas. He was grateful for the fuel, and even more so that Poppy was nowhere around when it happened, but the guilt still twisted him, and he didn't want to ask about the incident and have Felony confirm it. Better to pretend it didn't exist.

They'd been traveling for three long days. Stopping a lot since gas was so precious, and it was worth it whenever they saw a gathering, because information was everything. Time was running out. They were near the rocks, the people who could feel them all seemed to agree about that. Eamon kept asking himself why Felony was sticking around.

Eventually Poppy claimed they were close enough and she could feel their way there. Felony looked dubious but drove anyway.

"Do you feel them?" Poppy asked into the quiet.

And Sherry said, "Yes."

They had been driving in varying circles for days and weren't all that far from the Cottage, midway between a place called Carson's Neck, where there was a prison Poppy said the energy was *brutal,* and the edges of Yellowstone.

They arrived at the mile-long line leading to the rocks about an hour and a half after reports of the first official sightings in Earth's night sky.

"We're here," Felony said, as the van came to a full stop behind the last car. "I'll be right back. I wanna talk to some folks."

"I'll come with you," Eamon said. Anything was better than being in the car.

They divided and conquered, each of them spreading out to query the various clusters of hopefuls standing around their cars alongside the many migrants abandoning their vehicles to approach the rocks on foot.

Religious nuts and crazy new agers. Rumor said Stonehenge was a landing site for flying saucers thousands of years ago when the Druids or whoever built it. Some rich guy paid to have one built out here in the middle of nowhere in the hopes that it would draw aliens right to him. Supposedly, that guy was in the crowd. Even so, that wouldn't explain how people were supposed to just know it was there, then actually did.

"I say we walk the rest of the way," Eamon said back at the car.

Felony shook his head. "Man, I don't think your girl *can* walk."

"Then maybe we can carry her."

"Shit, I don't need your help. I can carry her."

"Why are you still here, Felony?" Eamon finally asked. "You could've left us at any time."

He shrugged. "Where else am I going to go?"

They helped the girls out of the van, but Poppy insisted she could walk and preferred it to being carried.

Felony stayed ahead with Sherry while Eamon and Poppy kept pace behind them in silence. She took his hand, and he was filled with relief. Everything would be okay.

And then she said it out loud. "Everything will be fine."

"You seem so strong."

"I feel strong." She patted her stomach. "I've gotta stay strong for another couple of weeks or whatever."

The moment turned heavy. Their child finally had a name. Sweet William, though Poppy promised they could call him William, or Will, and pretend the *Sweet* wasn't part of his name. But it was, seeing as she wanted their son to have a flower name like her, but all of them felt too girly to him. Just yesterday she suggested Sweet William, and Eamon didn't want to refuse, especially being so close to the other side of that conversation — what would happen once Poppy's water broke.

Eamon smiled, cooled by Poppy's warmth as lights appeared in the sky, moving slowly.

All of them gasped. Eamon's came from someplace

deep. Maybe bottomless. He felt one with the universe in a way he never had, but it was only for a second and left him terrified that he'd never feel it again.

He needed more of that light.

Longed to be near it.

Instantly, he understood what Poppy couldn't articulate and what had driven them all to the rocks.

There was a mess of people. It looked like half of Montana. Eamon had never seen so many all in one place, and he had no idea where they all came from.

They crested the ridge, another four gasps in the wind.

"There they are," Poppy said in a whisper.

"You mean the rocks or the people?" Felony asked.

"All of it," Poppy answered.

"We need to get closer," Sherry said. "I can walk. Even run if we need to. But we have to get there."

Felony looked from all the people to Sherry. "It's crowded, meaning it's more dangerous up close."

"She's right," Poppy said with the strangest look in her eyes. "We need to be closer. We're *supposed* to be closer."

"What do you mean *supposed to be*?" Felony asked. "How can you know something like that?"

Poppy and Sherry spoke as one. "Because it is true."

Then Sherry was walking fast, with Poppy right beside her.

Crowds were clustered away from the rocks, giving the small circle of boulders a safe and almost reverent distance. A few were huddled up front, like patrons near the pole.

A light appeared in the center of the circle. A bead then a bowling ball before it became a wide beam, the size of a small swimming pool, bleeding light onto the ground, rising like a pillar into the sky then inside the belly of a hamlet-sized sphere. Humming a wonderful song. Whirring in the air. Waiting.

An animal bellow rented the air, then a tall man ran out from the crowd, galloping, past the rocks and into the circle where no other person had apparently dared to go, stomping on hallowed ground, kicking up dirt and getting swallowed by dust before the light finally found him.

It made him beautiful, then it made him disappear.

The crowd was *oohing* and *aahing*, masses now rushing toward the light, every person in the crowd either wanting to be taken next or be there to see it happen again.

Chaos erupted around them. Humans gone feral in anticipation and everything else, no one willing to miss their chance at transcendence, hovering above them.

There was yelling and crying, though all of it sounded frantically happy.

But then the mass became too much, and Eamon found himself swimming in a sea of people. He couldn't find Poppy or Felony. Not even Sherry.

He fell. Got tromped on by boot heels and arches. Nobody stopped. Nobody cared. How could they think about anything else when that millennial light was shining right there in front of them?

Eamon battled his way back and earned both of his feet, but he was still freaking out, afraid that Poppy could be getting trampled. Or their unborn child.

A scream cut through the cacophony, sharper than anything else. Violence getting volcanic as the skirmish inched closer and closer to the circle's beating heart.

There was another detonation of light, but this time rocks around the perimeter exploded. Maybe four of them, like directions on a compass, blasting inward, containing the strike in the belly of the circle itself.

There was a terrible sound, hateful and piercing. Enough to make Eamon wonder if he might have permanent damage. Not that it mattered. He was seconds away from nothing mattering, not ever again.

Something hit him hard, knocked him down to the ground. Broke his shoulder in at least two places. Knew it the second he heard the sound and felt the snap.

He managed to stand again, stomping away from the chaos, drawn toward a light in the distance and calling out for his Poppy.

Then he found her and wished he hadn't — her half naked body, bathed in light, buried under an unforgiving wedge of alien rock.

Dead forever, no chance at ascension.

Everything broke inside Eamon.

His body was in shock. Couldn't stand, just wobbled in place for half a minute before finally shaking the jelly away from his legs and running to his fallen lover.

He fell to his knees, pulled her empty husk into his arms, then cradled her back and forth, petting her hair and listening to her cries.

Except they didn't belong to Poppy.

Those were the shrill and insistent cries of a baby.

His heart pounded, and even though Eamon couldn't believe his eyes, the reality was lying right there on the ground. His newborn child, forced out of Poppy, pushed out from under her dress. Also bathed in a faint white light.

His shoulder was hellfire, so every step over to the baby was worse than excruciating, but thoroughly worth it. Eamon picked up his newborn and cradled him close. His shoulder felt warm, warmer, then normal after that. Healed, impossible as it was.

The only thing not healed was the scar across Sweet William's right cheek, two parallel lines that slanted down diagonally. Not cuts. There was no blood. Instead, the scars glowed faintly white, like the light that had bathed him and his mother, even as those lights were now faded.

Glowing scars?

He didn't understand what was happening, or need to. Poppy was gone, and that would have killed him for sure, but now with their child in his arms, Eamon had purpose and would do anything in his power to protect him.

The baby cried louder. Maybe he was hungry. But Eamon didn't know how he would feed him.

Sherry appeared like an angel from nowhere. Unbuttoned her shirt and showed Eamon her swollen breasts. It took him a moment to get it. Once he did, Eamon handed his newborn to Sherry, and she used her body to keep his son from starving.

Chapter Seventeen

THE WORLD CHANGED on Astral Day, then for the next six months kept on changing. Eamon was still getting used to it.

The government breakdown wasn't immediate, and no one seemed to know when it actually collapsed or if there were even still remnants of what it once was. True information had become scarce. Internet and radio were spotty, and there were rumors that the aliens were controlling, monitoring, or even creating the news. No one knew what to believe.

Vail, Colorado had turned into some sort of Mecca, with an endless slew of people starting to migrate there. The place had power, and tons of it. On the road, it was practically all Eamon heard anyone talking about. Like Poppy talking about the rocks, except this was with everyone. You didn't have to be special or spiritually touched to know about Heaven's Veil. Some famous movie guy named Meyer Dempsey was taken from the spot and hadn't been returned. One of nine such cases in the world, if Eamon believed that particular set of rumors.

The world had collapsed. Felony had stayed with Eamon and Sherry after Poppy's death, promising to help with the baby, again insisting he had nowhere else to go — especially since their van had been taken one night a month into their stay at the Cottage, even though it had been well-hidden beneath a tarp in a copse of trees a half-mile from their hideaway.

Every day was difficult. Even though there were other cars to be found, they were more hassle than they were worth because gas was at such a premium and cars made their passengers a target of both road bandits and aliens. So everything had to be done on foot. And as the weather turned bad and the snow began to make travel difficult, getting supplies became a struggle.

But at least they were safe in the Cottage so long as nobody happened upon it.

Eamon and Felony were on a supply run, looking for anything, but especially food. Sherry was a Godsend. William would be dead without her. They supplemented with whatever baby food or formula they managed to scrounge, but there wasn't much, and Sherry's milk kept flowing like the miracle it was.

Like the miracle William might be.

It was hard to ignore his specialness, or even articulate what it was. From being born early, yet already large, to growing fast despite having so little and suffering trauma at birth, William was special.

But the rest of them required a lot more than that to survive, so it was the men's job to make sure the four of them had what they needed. The trips took them farther and farther from the Cottage, each one riskier than the last. This one looked like it might be their suicide.

"Are you sure about this?" Eamon asked.

Felony shook his head. "No, but I'm also not sure we have a choice."

A group of bandits stood between them and a small and newer looking residential development they'd been hitting for their last several runs. A place called The Oaks. There were enough houses to give them a reasonable shot at finding some much-needed supplies, even if most of the homes had been looted.

Most of the outlaws they had encountered were simple robbers and raiders. Solo marauders had apparently all died off, but there were many duos and trios, plus a lot of small gangs. But those groups were growing, from a cluster to a crowd to a swarm. This mass was one of the latter, with nineteen trucks by Felony's count, before Eamon spotted a twentieth far to the side, a second before lowering his binoculars.

It still felt like suicide. "And you really think our best bet is walking right in?"

"I think it's our *only* bet," Felony said. "The only good thing about a group that size is that it had to be assembled in pieces, meaning a lot of the guys are new and don't really know each other. So we waltz in like we have every right to be there, and I bet no one says shit."

"What if they do?"

"Then we got a problem. But doing nothing might be a bigger one."

Despite the loose-fitting logic, Eamon didn't believe it would work. But Felony was right, and getting through the gates really was as simple as the two of them keeping their artificial conversation in motion, easily passing through their enemies in the absence of any official guard at the gate, then immediately looking for a home to plunder once inside.

"How about that one?" Eamon pointed to a modest

sized house, painted white with green trim. One of the smaller homes on a tidy lot. The sort that was easy to ignore in favor of larger estates.

"Looks good to me," Felony agreed.

They knocked and waited, but there wasn't any answer. That didn't mean that the home was empty. Eamon knocked again and they waited even longer. Still, no answer.

So Felony wrapped his sweater around his fist, punched through the back door window, then released the lock.

It was colder inside than Eamon imagined. His bones needed warming.

"It doesn't look like the place has been touched," Felony said.

And it didn't. The home was full of supplies. But, as they found out after heading upstairs, the house was also holding an old man, his old lady, and a shotgun aimed at Eamon when he opened their bedroom door.

Felony's gun was out. The old guy didn't want to shoot, Eamon could see it in his placid eyes. He seemed patient. More than anything. Same for the woman beside him. He wasn't smiling, nor was he scared.

Felony was smart enough to aim at the woman instead of the man as he entered. So there they were in a good old-fashioned Mexican standoff.

"You can leave now," said the old man. "Your choice, but it would be better for all of us."

"We just need a few things," Felony said.

"I'm sure you'll take what you need."

"Give us ten minutes and we'll be gone," Felony tried again, not sure if the old man was making a threat.

"No. We're not going to take anything," Eamon said. "My friend and I are sorry for bothering you. We thought the house was empty. We'll be on our way."

The man nodded and gave them a friendly smile. The woman did the same.

Eamon backed out of the room. Felony followed, closing the door before turning around.

They made their way down the stairs, then left the house without taking a thing or breaking Eamon's word. But as expected, Felony chastised him outside.

"You know, sooner or later we're gonna need to find some folks you're willing to rob."

"Were you really willing to kill those people?"

Eamon knew the answer. If he hadn't been there, Felony would have ended them both, emptied the house, and come home with a story about how he found this sad old couple dead — murder/suicide, marauders, or both. If he approached the truth, it would only be in saying he had to defend himself because the old man had a shotgun, and it was him or them.

"I wasn't gonna kill no one, but we could at least have taken some stuff."

"They were still alive, so that makes it stealing. Why take from them if we already have to look for something else? We'll have to load up wherever we go, so we shouldn't leave them with anything less."

"Ain't my baby or lady back home needing food."

"Stop calling her that. Sherry isn't my lady, and she's only a kid."

"No, she's a woman, man. She's eighteen. How long you gonna stay faithful to a ghost?"

Eamon couldn't pretend she wasn't attractive. He also couldn't ignore her ripe breasts and constantly flushed cheeks, even though he desperately wanted to. Sherry was a kid, too young for him, and an angel for helping Eamon with his baby. It would be wrong of him to take advantage of her in any way. Poppy was only part of it.

"Can we please drop it? Again?"

"You find us some food then let us actually take it and sure, I'll be happy to drop it. Until then, I think it's fair to keep calling you out on the fact that you ain't got nothing to stick your dick into, and that's gonna be a problem."

"You don't have anything to stick your dick into. Why don't you worry about yourself?"

"Sherry don't like dark meat. And I need a woman who knows what she's getting. Reluctant pussy is worse than gummy palms. I'll be a superman to some bitch, and I'm patient until then. Ain't like I got someone willing and wanting and putting her titties in my kid's mouth every fucking day."

"She's feeding him, asshole," Eamon said.

"Bet she'd like to feed you."

Eamon had to put up with it until they found a corner house deep in the neighborhood that was still miraculously untouched. Not that it would be for long. They had to duck a couple of enemy clusters, and one of them was just one block over and coming this way. Eamon welcomed the potential conflict both times — the only two occasions Eamon could get Felony to quit whispering bullshit.

Their bags were stuffed and ready to go. It would be a long way home with all the cans, but the haul was a score and thus a quality problem. Felony had the front door open and was about to step outside when he suddenly slammed it then slapped his back against the wood like a cartoon character.

"The three guys?" Eamon asked.

Felony shook his head, breathing hard. Only one thing could make the big man lose his breath, and it wasn't the humans they'd seen a block away. Eamon knew what it was before his friend said it.

"A drone," he whispered.

Neither spoke, waiting for it to pass, but not really knowing when or if it would. Information on the alien ships was scarce as expected, but the last several months had yielded a few new universal truths. The ships always arrived in a whisper, and in a few different varieties. There were two types of aliens. Big, powder white superhumans called Titans. They were the good guys, or at least the indifferent ones. The other aliens were like dragon insects with chainsaw limbs. Most people who saw them had been turned into bloody hay. The rest shared their stories.

Reports said a hundred percent of attacks on the aliens so far had resulted in zero wins for the humans. Instead, death was immediate. Drones had killed plenty of humans, as had ground troops.

They waited for fifteen minutes, then Felony cracked the door and peered outside.

He turned back, said, "Let's hurry," then ducked out the door.

They moved in silence, and Eamon was sure there wouldn't be any ribbing from Felony for a while. He'd had plenty. Had thought about it all enough. Felony was probably right. Kindness was a luxury they couldn't afford now. At some point, Eamon would have to hurt good people to care for his kid, and the girl he agreed to take in … the woman who was caring for William.

He also had to keep wondering what was keeping Felony around and how long he'd stay. They'd grown close over the last few months, more than Eamon ever thought possible. But they hadn't heard from Liam, or anyone else since the invasion, and no one was paying him to hang around.

Was he waiting to betray them in some way? It was a paranoid thought, but Eamon had seen Felony go from hot to icy in less time than it takes to twist the knob on a faucet.

"Car."

It was the third word Felony had said since leaving the house, the other two being a couple of *ducks*. Eamon followed his lead, backing into the woods and falling to a crouch.

Sure enough, a family passed by in a wagon, relatively slow, probably scouting.

If they saw Felony or Eamon, they showed no indication. Their car didn't change speed. They kept on going, and Eamon kept on hurting, thinking of Poppy and what the two of them could have had. There were three of them in that car. A man, a woman, and a tiny little boy. Same as they could have been. If hell hadn't rained from the sky into his life.

Into everyone's lives.

Felony and Eamon were still watching the wagon coast out of sight. It was nearly gone when it ran over the IED.

Thunder tore through the air. Then the car was a fireball, making a full rotation ten feet in the air before landing back on its roof, already on fire, and burning the dead family inside it.

Eamon cried out. To his surprise, so did Felony.

Then the two of them wept, hurrying to finish, drying their tears before walking home, stepping around the wreckage, averting their eyes, neither man searching for scraps.

Chapter Eighteen

SHERRY READ Eamon's expression the moment he stepped through the door.

"What is it?"

"I'll tell you later," he said, realizing how much he was already looking forward to getting out of his head and into the air.

Sherry was his medicine. The thing that made him whole, or at least feel like he might be one day.

"Okay." She hefted William from the crook of one arm to the other, eying their loads. "What did you guys get?"

Felony raised two giant duffels, one in each arm, then gestured to Eamon's haul. "Lots of cans."

"Great," Sherry laughed. "Feels like home."

She took the cans to the kitchen and started sticking them in the cupboard, even though they would be taking them right back out, and soon enough with it being all they had. Sherry was domestic like that. Eamon didn't know if it was her natural preference or if the girl was trying to pretend that the end of the world wasn't actually here.

They'd come back to the Cottage after the horror show

at the rocks that stole his Poppy. Eamon wanted to find anywhere else to go, said he couldn't stand knowing how much the memories would haunt him if they returned.

It was an argument Felony didn't let him win.

The cabin was a safe house by design. In the middle of nowhere, and nobody knew where it was. Highly secured, and built for a man who lived a lavish life and tolerated only the nicest things.

"Except the people wanting to kill us," Eamon tried, when suggesting they live elsewhere.

"If you think anyone still gives a shit about us, you're crazy," Felony said.

And he was right. The place was safe and far from everywhere else. They hadn't seen a soul outside their scavenging, or actively searching for people to engage.

"Hi," William said.

And still it gave him a start. Eamon had to catch his breath before he said, "Hi," back.

At six months, his newborn wasn't old enough to be talking like the toddler he wasn't.

It was baffling. He looked almost two. Not in size or shape, or even the way he moved his body. It was something in William's eyes. A deep, almost fathomless knowing.

And there was, of course, the unexplainable. More of the magic they all witnessed, starting with Eamon on the night of his birth — the boy's ability to heal himself, and others.

The kid was fearless and had taken several terrible spills. They barely seemed to matter. Even the deepest cut lasted only days. A month ago, he knocked over a wastebasket and dug out the top of a tin can. He was only playing with it for a minute or two before Sherry found him, cursing herself for leaving him feral — those were her words — and crying when she saw how many cuts the little guy had given himself. They were all over his hands. But some of them seemed to disappear as she washed him, and a few days later the whole thing might as well have been a lie.

But there was something else about the boy. And Eamon didn't know what to do about it. He'd brought it up several times to Sherry. Felony, too. But they both kept telling Eamon over and over not to worry. It was nothing. William was just a little different, and in all sorts of ways.

But Eamon had a cousin with special needs. And William, no doubt about it, was a special needs kind of child. More than anyone he'd ever seen, even though he couldn't explain exactly how.

"Hi, hi, hi, hi ..." William continued.

Eamon helped Sherry pack the pantry, pretending he couldn't hear the odd sounds his son was making, convincing himself, or at least trying, that it was only a baby sound and not the actual word *hi*, which Sherry was sure he'd been imitating for a week.

"Really, I got this." Sherry looked down at William. "Go play with him. He wants your attention."

"He doesn't know who I am," Eamon said, still trying to convince himself.

"Of course he knows who you are! Don't be ridiculous. Now go."

He held his hand out for William. Then, like a little boy instead of a baby, he toddled over and planted his tiny mitt inside his father's open palm. Instead of walking, Eamon hefted his son into his arms then carried him out of the room.

Felony was napping, so Eamon and William had the area all to themselves. He sat on the sofa, set his son on the carpet in front of him, then leaned back, pressing his body into a heaven of leather.

Sherry made everything in this post-invasion world possible. She wasn't the leader, that was Felony for sure. Nor did she help on their supply runs, that was all Eamon. But she handled the household duties with a smile. She was energetic. Feisty. Sherry insisted that Felony teach her to shoot. He was happy to instruct her, but bullets were too scarce, and far too loud. Sort of outlawed in an unspoken way no one was willing to breach. Most people had seen the news, with the aliens dropping those judgment cubes, and bullets brought them faster.

So he taught her to aim, when to squeeze the trigger, and what to think the seconds both before and after she did. Sherry also made arrows. It was her favorite chore. She said she'd do it even if they didn't have to. They all collected rocks and sticks and made them. Felony's were only slightly better than hers, and she made more of them. Eamon came in last on both accounts.

He was grateful for Sherry and wondered what would've happened to him if they had never passed her on that bridge. Or William and Felony. He barely remembered anything from the time right after he lost Poppy. To hear his friends tell it, he was comatose for nearly a month. Not robotic like now. Actually catatonic. Sleepwalking.

Dinner came, and they traded quiet for conversation. The mood was always more buoyant after a successful supply run, with everyone home safe and a fire burning. There was one every night, even when it wasn't cold. Sherry insisted, and Felony hadn't argued once. She said it was the one thing to make this giant cabin feel like a home, that a casual fire burning in the hearth was a sign of hope that it wasn't the end of everything. After they'd been burning their fire at night for more than a month, Sherry admitted she'd never seen a real fireplace before, having grown up in a trailer and not having many friends.

Eamon thought of the dozen or so in his family's home and hated himself for the sins of his father.

"Get anything on the TV yet?" Felony asked.

"Still no signal. Not sure if the TVs are all out or if maybe your dad didn't pay the bill."

Eamon laughed. "Leave it to Dad to have this nice ass TV and not pay for the juke."

Felony told the story about Eamon not taking food from the old couple earlier that afternoon, calling him a pussy for not knowing how to care for his family, but Eamon could tell he was framing the narrative to make him look like a hero. Problem was, that wasn't true at all. Eamon just couldn't stand to add any more sins to his tally.

Dessert was rare, but the day's run deserved a shared fruit cocktail. The syrup was gross, but they enjoyed the taste, anyway. Especially Sherry. Besides, the real dessert followed the cocktail.

William's sleep schedule was almost religious. Always down within an hour after dinner. Felony went out scouting, a nightly ritual that left Eamon and Sherry alone for theirs.

The conversation was natural, easy in the way it once was Poppy. Terrific and terrible together. Stuck in a cabin, in the middle of nowhere and at the end of everything, her acting interested in the things he liked to talk about and craving attention, both of them about as lonely as people could get.

"What if Felony was right? Do you think he has a point?" Sherry asked.

"Of course he has a point," Eamon said. "That doesn't make it right. They're gonna run out of food, eventually. But we don't have to help them run out any faster."

"That's exactly Felony's point. They're going to run out, anyway."

"Whose side are you on? Would you like it better if I was willing to murder old people to feed us?"

Sherry laughed. "No. Of course not. I'm just advocating the devil."

"That's *being the devil's advocate*."

"Whatever." Another laugh, and it struck him like a lot of them were starting to.

Eamon had fallen in love before, and this was an echo of that. But he had to be careful. This thing between them was slippery and brittle. Two lonely people coming together, filling in a few of the pieces each of them was missing in a time when the world was gray enough to make a drop of color look like a mural.

But Sherry was always finding reasons to touch him. Not just hugs, which came often enough, but accidental brushes against him that didn't feel so accidental.

It kept him guilty, about Sherry's age, although now that he thought about it, she wasn't all that young. Plus, she had been pregnant before and was already legal, not that it mattered in a world without any legal system left to enforce it. But mostly it was the ghost of Poppy keeping him away, even though Eamon had so far refused to admit it.

He should nip it in the bud, but like his guilt, he continued to stoke it.

Out of nowhere, Sherry got serious. "How come you never asked me anything about my baby?"

The question caught Eamon off guard. He bought himself a moment by giving Sherry a shrug. Then he said, "I don't know … I guess I didn't want to invade your privacy."

"I'm not sure any of us have much of that around here. Or need it."

"Sorry. It's not because I didn't care."

"I know."

And so he asked, "What about the father? Is it that Bickerson guy you were talking about when we picked you up?"

A faraway look found her eyes. Then she laughed. "Bickford. Wow. I almost forgot about him. No, Bickford wasn't the father."

"Then who was?"

"I'm not exactly sure."

"Oh …" Eamon didn't know what to do with that.

"I was raped," Sherry said with no emotion. "There were six guys. They all finished inside me."

"Oh," Eamon repeated, though this second a different breed than the first.

"All of them are probably dead, and I keep thinking the same exact thing about my mother. Both thoughts make me happy. Does that make me a terrible person?"

"No," Eamon said. "Of course not. I think the same thing about my father. All the time."

"Why?"

"I don't want to talk about it … at least not now."

Sherry rested her head on his shoulder and planted a hand on his chest.

Then Eamon finally admitted to himself how very afraid he was to lose her.

Chapter Nineteen

GLEESON WAS HEADING toward Stonefall's town center, where everyone was already waiting.

It was hard not to walk the grounds with pride. Everything was coming together, better and faster than he had imagined. Or had any right to expect. It was all so much more than he deserved.

"Stop telling yourself that," said Roy, talking beside him, keeping his usual pace. "The Lord provided for you because you will continue to provide for him. Shepherds never apologize."

Roy was right. Always was.

Gleeson could see three signs hung on the side of the town hall.

GOD IS WATCHING. ACT ACCORDINGLY.

THE HEAVENS ARE OUR MIRROR.

SHOW HIM WHO YOU ARE.

He paused to admire the well-designed reminders, then started walking again, smiling to himself at the faint twitters of anticipation he could already hear while everyone waited for their leader to arrive.

Stonefall was the first home Gleeson couldn't imagine wanting to leave. Every moment of his life was lived only so he could end up here. The walls were wide, and the architects on hand were smart. They were among the first to appear at the gates seeking solace, at least among the first with something to offer. Gleeson had to be choosy, and Roy helped him choose. So did Percy and Kirk, though the two of them didn't always agree.

Slowly but surely, they built around the old prison's bones. Thanks to the men who were contractors in their former lives, they leveled what they needed to, with bulldozers and everything else, and put up new construction. Everything from barracks to a Main Street fronted by long rows of two and three-bedroom houses.

The small plots of land were thriving. The greenhouses, too. Gleeson had proved he could provide.

But winter was coming, and there was still much to do.

They were just under a hundred and fifty citizens inside Stonefall, so that left only a handful of spots. The gates would be swinging permanently closed after that. His number wasn't random. A hundred and fifty people was what the human mind could effectively track. A number that meant everyone could know everyone else, in the way people once knew each other. Like they did back in Nazareth.

Gleeson had created a self-sufficient sanctuary amid the ruins of a crumbling civilization. Every spot inside Stonefall was coveted. They would be full soon, and there would be crowds beyond the walls dying to get inside.

"You've done so much already," Roy praised him.

"We're just getting started."

Roy stayed silent for a moment, then said, "Judgement is coming."

"What a caterpillar at first believes to be the end of his world, to the Lord is always a butterfly."

"Tell all who will listen, brother."

That's exactly what Gleeson was trying to do. Every day since founding Stonefall, and especially now at their even sermon. His community was grateful for the safety he provided, and willing to work behind his walls. The old ways were essential to surviving in this new world. His Flock knew it and lived it.

The modern world had turned a blind eye to the Lord, but that world was dead, and there wasn't any TV to tell Gleeson's brothers and sisters the lies that their lives weren't good enough.

Keeping everyone in Stonefall unified in these essential beliefs was Gleeson's mission and calling.

Unlike other small havens that were surely cropping up everywhere, Stonefall had been established with intention. They started by gathering supplies from the communities around them. But their radius kept yawning, expanding out over many months, with their methods eventually turning violent, though of course never cruel. Stonefall's ferocity leveled only against those who stood in opposition to their message.

There was another spot, calling itself the Reserve, born from the bones of an old ranger station in Yosemite.

He had to consider them an enemy. Same for everyone else outside of Stonefall. An unfortunate fact that Gleeson could do nothing to change if he was expected to protect his Flock. And as God reminded him with every new sunrise, that was the most important star in his sky. Gleeson was destined to aid God with the help of those in Stonefall. Right now, that meant a lot of assembly and waiting, like when the Good Lord needed Noah to build him that arc. The flood would be coming, and once God provided him with the divine weapon, Gleeson could lead the final battle against Hell and help usher in the Savior's second coming.

"You've been forgiven already, but that would make it absolute." Roy said. "Are you ready?"

"I am."

They walked the rest of the way, stopping in front of Kirk, who was standing at the edge of the crowd, around the fire pit at the start of Main Street. The man had become a loyal servant and bodyguard to Gleeson in the last six months. Important, like Percy.

"Father," Kirk said with a nod.

There was no applause as Gleeson took center stage in front of the crowd. Stonefall was far too humble for that. But he still felt their admiration like sunbeams on his skin as he took the three short steps onto the stage. So many grateful smiles. Gleeson was glad to be of such service.

He stood before them, raising his hands and closing his eyes, leading his Flock in a moment of silent prayer as always. A perpetual exercise instead of a singular event, but still worthy of a collective moment now.

"Welcome, my friends," Gleeson said as he lowered his hands.

A chorus of *Father* rippled through the crowd.

"We have much to discuss this evening. Shall we start with our Sins and Transgressions?"

It felt good to make them feel as though it was a choice.

Heads bobbing up and down. Earnest eyes facing forward. *Yes* and *Please* coming together and separate through the room.

Gleeson smiled, and in a gentle voice said, "Let's form a line."

Citizens of the Flock stood single file to deliver their

sins and transgressions. A total of fifteen for tonight. Eleven of them women. Three of the four men reported sex-related offenses, to no one's surprise. Those sorts of thoughts were hard to control. Gleeson had them every day. It was good for them to purge, remove the splinters from their skin by giving voice to their offenses. He didn't need to because thanks to Gleeson's direct line to God, the Lord already knew.

Adam admitted to intrusive thoughts about some of the women in Stonefall, and masturbating to images of them naked. The other two confessed to ample masturbation but weren't as honest as Adam. Of course they were picturing their seed all over Samantha, or any of one of Stonefall's more attractive women. Still, they were more honest than the rest of the men who remained in their seats. Foster reported he'd stolen a book from his neighbor but had already given it back. He wanted everyone to know so it wouldn't be likely to happen again.

Fiona was hoarding medicine.

Sara stole another woman's hair ribbon.

Alexandra gave her daughter a larger portion of lunch than all the other children.

Harriet wasn't taking her chores seriously and had even reported cleaning the communal restrooms when she hadn't.

The other seven were equally petty, but Gleeson personally forgave every citizen, looking into their eyes as he reminded them that, "Only by following God's example can we find our way into heaven."

Kirk stood in the rear, smiling at Gleeson.

Revelations came next. A time for citizens of the Flock who had felt God to share their experiences.

These mostly came from people who had visited Gleeson's old cell. After being spared by the Good Lord

Himself, the man had turned his prison into a small town, expanded behind its walls to make something big and beautiful out of what was built to house endless rows of lifetime hauntings. Humans like rats, trapped in their torment like bricks in a fire, charred without the mercy of ever turning to ash. His cell was now a shrine where citizens went to pray, meditate on their present, and seek commune with God. That's where it happened. Where the Good Lord spoke directly to him. A new Mt. Sinai.

They didn't have time for them all. But Brother Raymond gave Gleeson regular reports, so he knew who to call on at random. Alice, Romney, and Sara all had stories worth telling, praise God.

Gleeson encouraged everyone to reflect on the shared Revelations as well as their own, then reminded them that even though God was always listening, he listened hardest during prayer.

Roy whispered in his ear, "The earnest prayer of a righteous person has great power and produces wonderful results."

And Gleeson repeated, "The earnest prayer of a righteous person has great power and produces wonderful results."

Each person told how they had experienced the Lord and encouraged those who hadn't yet spoken to Him that their time would come soon. They testified that the holy spot would help them.

The end of revelations folded neatly into his sermon, this time about Ezra and Nehemiah. Jerusalem lay in ruins for decades after its destruction. Judah was exiled, and the people left behind were deemed unworthy of capture. When Ezra and Nehemiah returned, they had no one to rebuild their Temple or city. It lay in scavenged ashes.

But one man was a Bible teacher, and the other a motivator of men. One knew the law, and the other knew people. One knew how to inspire, and the other how to *do*. They had little food, security, or sleep. The stones weighed two tons and more and would have to be moved by hand. The walls would need to be rebuilt by men with a sword in one hand and a trowel in the other. But together, they made it.

Gleeson mostly just repeated what Roy told him to say, then finished with a thought of his own.

"These are the hardest of times, but that makes them the times when we must prove ourselves to the Lord. Now let me hear you!"

The Flock let him hear them. One day, the masses beyond the walls of Stonefall would hear them, too.

Kirk was beaming. Percy, too, though he was waiting for Father to finish, their business on his patient face.

His sermon wound down, then Gleeson asked if there were any more volunteers for Excursions — the small but growing groups that left Stonefall, looking for citizens to join them.

Gleeson waited through another short round of reverence, then stepped away to where Percy was waiting to usher him to the front office, where Kirk was already waiting.

As usual, Gleeson could feel the tension between Kirk and his second in command. Percy clearly couldn't stand him, but that was his history to deal with. Gleeson didn't understand why he was still skeptical of a man who had his offensive tattoos burned off publicly and violently, both acts as a condemnation of the hate he once felt in his blood. The man had been an admirable warrior for them and Stonefall. He was the only one Saved, besides Percy and himself, though Percy told him in private that he thinks that's only because of Kirk's proximity to Gleeson when God unleashed judgment on the prison.

The men were quietly but constantly warring for his approval, and that wasn't necessarily a terrible thing.

"We lost a few men today," Percy said.

That explained his face.

Gleeson sighed. "Tell me what happened."

"Not sure exactly. Nathan's group never came back. But it's been more than nine hours since their last check-in, and the odds that they all lost communication are slim. I think they were robbed, and that the bandits took their truck. Maybe kidnapped them. We should gather a group of volunteers and look for them at first light."

Gleeson glared at Percy, suddenly irritated. "I wish I'd known that during the sermon. We could have rallied the troops and reinforced the message that it isn't safe outside."

Percy was resolute. "You told me to never bother you with business before your sermons, no matter what."

"Agreed on going out in first light. Kirk can gather the troops. Any update on Angel?"

"We've sent Thomas and Leo to look for her in Wyoming," Percy said, looking sorry that he didn't have anything better to report. "Nothing new other than that."

Gleeson nodded, wishing for better news but grateful for anything. Almost everyone in Stonefall was missing someone outside. He was the only person with the luxury of looking for his past.

Finding Angel would heal a lot inside him. Making amends would stitch him together. So would knowing she was safe.

"Sorry there's not more," Percy tried to apologize. "But communication keeps going in and—"

"I understand," he said, clapping the man on his shoulder.

Roy grabbed Gleeson by his arm and demanded his attention. "You need to be leading that run tomorrow."

He turned to his men. "I'll be going with the volunteers in the morning."

"Are you sure?" Kirk asked, clearly surprised.

"Of course I'm sure." But he looked at Roy askance because he actually wasn't.

And Roy said, "The demons are testing you, brother. Tomorrow is a big chance at another hallelujah."

"I go wherever God needs me most," Gleeson said. Then he added, "And right now he needs me to get a good night's sleep."

There was other business, but he had an early day and wanted Percy and Kirk to start working on their differences, anyway. So Gleeson left and went into his room. Poured himself a drink before he followed with another, enjoying one of the luxuries that came with creating something from nothing.

A lot like the Good Lord Himself.

Chapter Twenty

PERCY COULDN'T STAND Kirk and hated that Gleeson left the two of them alone, though he also supposed it sort of made sense. They did need to get along, and it was mostly him feeling animosity. But Kirk burning tattoos off of his body to save his own life didn't erase the fact that he'd had enough hate in him to get all inked up in the first place.

But he was trying, even if it wasn't sincere, and it would be a long apocalypse if Percy didn't learn to relax. He settled their business without any animus, which seemed to surprise Kirk. He didn't try to make any of his idiot jokes like he did around some of the other guys or engage him in small talk, but Kirk had an appreciative smile that struck Percy as unexpectedly genuine, and he held it throughout their exchange.

Percy wasn't sure how he felt about Gleeson going on their morning excursion. Kirk agreed it seemed like an unnecessary risk. But it was one they both accounted for as they polished their plan and determined who they would approach first before asking around for volunteers.

He opened the door and felt a wallop from whatever

Melinda was making in the kitchen. It smelled delicious, and he had his mouth open to tell her so when he suddenly shut it, stepping past the threshold and seeing that she wasn't cooking alone.

"Hey, Ophelia," he said instead.

"Hey there, Percy." Ophelia smiled.

Percy smiled back, happy to see her.

Ophelia lost her parents on Astral Day. Maybe dead, maybe abducted, the girl had no idea. Only that she was sixteen, suddenly alone, and terrified by the sky overhead and the earth underfoot — day or night, the time didn't matter. She started hanging around at their place more than hers, until she was eating dinner with them most nights. Sometimes she would stick around for some long conversations, and every so often it made sense to stay over, rather than making the short walk back to her assigned quarters. They had the extra bedroom, after all.

So soon enough, Ophelia was living with them. By then, Percy and Melinda were already seeing her as their own. God's miracle in an apocalypse where such things were like seeds under sand in the desert. Percy liked her a lot, maybe even more than Melinda did, since the girl was a bit more religious, and into Gleeson's movement more than she felt comfortable with. She'd said so on several occasions, despite also constantly telling Percy that it felt great to have the girl around. She never had to say the second part out loud, even as a hollow echo — it helped make up for their miscarriages and the fact that Melinda could no longer get pregnant.

He stayed in the kitchen, making small talk but not helping with the meal. Not even setting the table, which Percy would have been happy to do. It was better than standing around. But Ophelia insisted, saying it was her duty and pleasure. His discomfort wasn't enough to stop her.

Dinner was delicious. Rice looted from CostCo, and vegetables grown at home. Cleanup was easy, and like the prep, there was nothing for him to do except listen to the women chatter and insert a thought when it seemed fitting or wanted. He caught Melinda's gaze a couple of times and could tell there was something she wanted to talk about.

That made him eager to get her alone and hurry their usual post-dinner conversation, where Ophelia would tell stories about growing up so Percy and Melinda could get to know her better.

He finally said he was exhausted after such a long day and reminded them that he had an early excursion. Melinda feigned a headache. Ophelia took the hint, bid them goodnight, then went off to bed.

"What is it?" Percy asked, the moment he heard her door close.

"I caught Allison stealing from the farm."

"She didn't say anything tonight at Sins and Transgressions."

"Of course she didn't, Percy. Do you know how many people are stealing food? If everyone said what they were doing out loud, the sermon would turn into a riot. I even think Ruth is stealing, and she's like the nicest woman ever. If *she's* stealing, how bad are things getting?"

"How do you know that's happening?"

"Same as I always tell you. I run the farm, and I know what we're producing compared to what winds up in storage."

"Are you going to tell Gleeson?"

"I don't want to." Melinda shook her head. "He'll start banishing people, and winter is pretty much here."

"If people are stealing, then maybe they don't belong here."

"They're taking food because they don't have enough. It's not like they're teenagers taking twenties from the register to buy cigarettes."

"There haven't been twenties in registers for a long time, even before the invasion."

"You don't need to make me feel old, Percy. The point is, this is our community. We need to get production up so that people don't have to steal or live on a dole of nothing. And we can do that if we work together as a community, but we can't do it if we start kicking everybody out."

"Do we have enough to survive the winter?"

The depth of her sigh made it scary. "The greenhouses aren't performing like we need them to. There's an infestation of bugs and we can't do anything about it."

"What kind of bugs?"

"Thrips, mites, aphids, beetles. Whatever. We have everything. They're eating the plants, and we don't have the right pesticide to kill them. Same for the fungus and fungicide."

"What pesticides and fungicides have you tried?"

"All of them. And the problems on the farm aren't getting better, or at least it isn't happening fast enough. There's a gap between harvesting the last of our September crops and when the vegetables we planted in October start producing enough to eat them. We can't plant grains until next year, and the stores are quickly running dry."

"Is that it?" Percy half-smiled.

"I'm serious about the stuff from CostCo. Even if it lasts through winter, that's it. We need systems in place by springtime or everything is going to fall apart. Even the stealing might not be that big of a problem if it wasn't for the roaches and mice."

He shook his head. It was a hard reality to face.

"Is that why you're going out tomorrow? Did you find some food somewhere?"

"I wish. We lost Nathan today."

She gasped, hand over mouth. "Just Nathan?"

"The whole group. We lost communication. We're fearing the worst. We'll head out in the morning to go look for them."

"Oh, my God. Bailey will be devastated. It's getting worse out there, isn't it?"

"Yes," Percy admitted without pause, even though he desperately wanted to lie.

"The rumors are getting around. Might be that everyone's heard them by now. Ophelia told me she heard those eight-year-old twins talking about the crosses and figured if they knew, then everyone did."

"Which rumors?"

"All of them, but mostly about the people nailed upside down."

"How many people do you think actually believe it?"

Melinda shrugged. "I think a lot of people want to believe it's like the bogeyman. I wish I could."

"Would you rather I lied to you?"

"No. But I would love it if you weren't the one always leaving. What happened to Nathan today … that could have happened to you."

"I'm careful."

"I'm sure Nathan was careful." After a beat, she said, "Do you think someone is looking to invade Stonefall and take us over? Or at least take what we have?"

"I wish I didn't."

Maybe he shouldn't have said that. Now her eyes were

more haunted than before. "Do you think we can handle it?"

"I do." He smiled, glad that he was telling the truth.

"The thing about the stealing is that it's isolated now. One person at a time, with most people ashamed to admit what they've done. But folks are starting to talk. Or grumble, more like it. Everyone is worried about the rationing … some people might be starting to doubt their leader's powers … or his plans."

"What are you saying, Melinda? What do you want me to do?"

"Maybe you could assuage some fears without letting Gleeson know about the grumbling. Last thing we need is another witch hunt. Or more banishing. That will only divide us. He can't just say we need community. He has to live it."

"If he finds out that people are stealing, he'll want them gone. And if he finds out I'm helping to cover up, then I don't know what he'll want, but I'm sure that neither of us want to find out."

He gave her a solemn look, then once he felt sure she'd accepted it, he said, "I'll see what I can do."

"Are you gonna ask around? And when?"

"Hopefully tomorrow goes well. We'll find Nathan, or maybe some supplies to turn the mood. Make people believe we can conquer the first winter of this new world, same as folks did for all those thousands of years before us."

"They were built to do it. We've all been watching our jukes."

"Humans learn fast. We're safe here. We just need to remind people, keep their hopes alive."

Melinda cleared her throat, of both phlegm and a

question. "Do you still believe in Gleeson? That he was chosen by God?"

"I do."

"I wish I could."

She didn't say anything else, such as he seemed like little more than a con man. She'd said it enough. Percy didn't have to remind her of what Gleeson did in prison, how he saved his life, twice. He'd said that plenty himself. Same for all the stuff about him maybe being a little crazy, sure, but also no doubt a good man. Same for the reminders about how history's prophets were all considered dangerous by some and lunatics by most.

"Can't you admit that he's doing good here at Stonefall? That we're building a community to keep us safe? That people don't mess with us because they know we're strong?"

"We can agree that he's building something, all right. And yes, I believe the 'Flock' is keeping the shepherd safe."

"What *would* make you believe?"

"I don't know." Melinda shook her head. "I just worry, not even about him so much as some of the men around him. Especially Kirk. You better watch your back around him."

"I'd rather watch your back." Percy held out his hand with a smile.

"I mean it. I really—"

"I don't like him, either." He nudged his hand toward her.

Melinda took it, then she let Percy lead her into the bedroom.

Chapter Twenty-One

EAMON AND FELONY returned to yesterday's hunting grounds.

It was simple enough getting inside the housing development, and as long as they paid attention and stayed away from conversation — shallow or deep, it didn't matter — then the pair could avoid the patrols.

And same as the day before, getting in was a case of the ABCs, but it turned into calculus after that.

The total number of marauders seemed to have doubled over night. There were clusters everywhere inside the neighborhood, many roaming the streets. That should've made them feel safer. New recruits opened the door to confusion and subterfuge. Yet the opposite felt true. Everyone seemed to be on high alert. Weapons out, eyes forward. Masses gathering at the neighborhood entrance.

Eamon and Felony were stuck inside, scouting for supplies in a well-manicured quarter that felt like a prison. They stopped in front of a promising looking house, though Eamon argued against it.

"In and out in five minutes," Felony said. "I promise."

"We need to get out of here before they occupy this place and start guarding the gate."

"Agreed."

"That means an hour ago. We'll find food somewhere else."

"If we could have gone, we would have. Now we're hiding in circles. Fuck that. I'm not even talking about food. Let's hit the garage. See if there's a ladder."

Felony pointed to the wall. They were in the last row of houses, the bricks a block behind them were layered in ten feet of mortar. A ladder made that a leap.

"Even if we're dead in ten minutes, this is still a great idea."

"Thanks," Felony said, as the two of them crept toward the house.

Eamon punched through the kitchen window, then went into the garage and opened the door for Felony.

He looked at the old school gas-driven Camaro, not all that different from the Mustang he drove in Billings, then asked Eamon what he thought the odds were of them gunning the fuck out of that thing, then raging out of the gate.

Eamon pointed out that the bad guys had a few high performing vehicles themselves, and theirs were armored. He and Felony wouldn't stand a chance. And besides, there was that ladder they needed leaning right over there in the corner.

Felony had his hand around the aluminum when a truck pulled up outside.

No idling. Four doors opened and six people piled out, one gal for every two guys. Seven weapons among them, including the guy carrying a crowbar in each hand, but Eamon didn't see a single gun among them.

"We must have been spotted," Felony said.

"For sure. They knew we were here."

"So where do we go?"

Eamon glanced back toward the open kitchen door. "We're dead if we go back inside."

Felony gave him an ugly rattling laugh. "But ain't we just about dead, no matter what?"

"You wanted to take the Camaro, so let's take the Camaro."

"That was a joke." He shook his head. "No keys."

He glanced out the trio of small windows in the top of the garage door. The bandits were halfway to the front door.

Eamon nodded at a set of keys hanging on the wall. "And there we go."

Felony grabbed the keys, opened the garage door, then ran over to the Camaro and climbed behind the wheel. It was manual, and he was by far the better driver between them. Eamon was already sitting shotgun.

The garage door was barely high enough before Felony floored it, scraping the roof as he flew down the driveway, wrenching the wheel hard to the right and barely avoiding the bandits' truck.

Eamon was turned around, watching the bandits. Felony held his eyes to the road.

"They're getting back in their truck!" Eamon shouted.

"Where should I go?" Felony asked. "They have radios. No way we can make it through the front gate. They'll be expecting us."

"Sure as shit they will be." But Felony was laughing, and Eamon could smell the adrenaline.

Felony turned around one corner then another, driving smart, swerving hard enough to ditch their tail.

He picked up a new one immediately.

"Double fuck."

"Exactly." Eamon pointed to an empty lot as they passed it. "There. See that lot with the fence? Lose the car then we run back there and hide."

"They'll find us in five minutes and then we'll be dead."

"They're calling all units. We're gonna be dead in three, unless you got a better idea."

"What makes you think I can't lose this asshole?" Felony glanced in the rearview, watching the truck drifting farther back, but nowhere near lost, and surely with many more on the way.

Eamon looked doubtfully around him.

"Fuck you," Felony said. "We're not dying." He swerved hard, careening into an alley without any fencing between a pair of giant houses.

The truck couldn't make it fast enough. It tried, but ended up fishtailing hard and having to correct before flipping twice, then flying by their pivot in a terrifying weave.

"Impressive," Eamon said.

Felony pulled onto the road a block from the fenced in yard and said, "Ready to roll?"

"As I'm gonna be."

They opened the doors and rolled onto the asphalt. It was the first time Eamon had been grateful for the cold, keeping him in layers and free of the road rash that would have otherwise ripped him apart.

The Camaro kept barreling down the road as they ducked behind the wall, backs planted against the high wood, huffing and puffing, with only one of them laughing.

Eamon this time. "Holy fuck," he said between chortles.

Their victory didn't last, but the few moments were righteous and true. Maybe four minutes total, before the first truck stopped in front of the fence, followed seconds later by another two, then a VW with what looked like an old-fashioned cannon fixed to the top.

Eamon and Felony stared through a narrow slit in the fence.

They were surrounded by twenty bandits or so, including the original six.

But Eamon still didn't see any guns. Plenty of melee weapons. Bats and crowbars and such. Nunchakus, spears, and at least two axes. One guy was holding what looked like a large bag of rocks.

Even in conflict, they rarely saw guns, with this part of Montana apparently scared their strafing might invite the invaders to end them. A single shot probably wasn't a big deal, though no one really knew and people were suspicious.

Felony stood.

Eamon put a hand on his shoulder. "Wait."

He looked back.

Eamon said, "At least give them the chance to let us go."

Felony shook his head and walked away. He had no idea whether Felony would hold his fire or not.

So Eamon stood and walked behind him.

"Hey everyone!" Felony waved his gun in the air. "Looks like you brought some bats to a gun fight."

The mob stopped. The bandits started looking at one another, trading expressions of horror, like Felony was holding a bazooka instead of a Baretta.

One of the bandits stepped toward the front, clearly scared shitless but looking right at Felony anyway. "Are you fucking crazy, man? You need to put that thing away!"

"You're the ones attacking us," Felony said. "We're

happy to leave. Every one of you is holding a weapon that could kill us. Mine's just more efficient."

"Be reasonable. You don't put that thing away, they're gonna come."

If the bandits thought Felony would pull the trigger and invite the worst, then Eamon and Felony might have the upper hand long enough to get out of this situation. But Eamon knew what none of them didn't — Felony wasn't suspicious and didn't believe the aliens gave a shit if humans killed each other off or not.

He aimed the Baretta loosely at the convoy. "Give us one of your trucks."

"Fuck you," said the bandit in front.

Felony pulled the trigger and turned the top of the bandit's head to pulp.

Looks of horror. Not in fear of Felony and his weapon, but of the terror to come.

The bandits abandoned their fallen comrade, and scrambled into their vehicles.

"Bunch of cowards ..."

The first man made it to his truck and was swinging the door open when a drone sloped low, hovering right in front of him. Time froze, then the drone bathed the bandit in fire.

He ran to the grass screaming, then started rolling around while everyone ran and began ducking for cover.

The lawn was sand dry and caught fast, adding the crackle of flames to an already terrible chorus.

"Come on!" Felony grabbed Eamon just above the elbow and hauled him across the street, running diagonally, away from the bandits and toward a hopefully empty house.

The front door was mercifully open.

They ducked inside and waited.

Just in time for a lifetime of nightmares in waiting.

Reptars spilled out of the ships, followed by the sounds of a hundred clacking heels as the aliens' reptilian bodies skittered across the concrete, leaping from one victim to the next, tearing each bandit into bloody ribbons before leaving their carcasses to rot in the sun. Victims, not food.

Eamon had heard about the most vicious and monstrously ugly of the aliens from Felony, who'd come across one while out on a supply run, but this was the first time Eamon had seen them. And they were the stuff of nightmares.

"It'll be okay," Felony dared to whisper.

Eamon nodded, needing to believe him.

They watched as the bandits were shredded, staying silent as the lone drone appeared to survey the scene, almost studying it, hovering in some places longer than others.

It came drifting toward their house, then hovered mere feet from the living room, floating just above their trembling bodies.

This was the end, Eamon was sure of it. He thought of William and felt like a failure. He would be leaving his son an orphan and couldn't do anything about it. Eamon braced for whatever the aliens were about to blast through the roof.

He'd seen fire and light and Lord knew what else.

Eamon closed his eyes and told himself he was ready.

Then, a gunshot in the distance, followed by what sounded like bullets on a battlefield. The drone whispered down onto the lawn, the reptars skittered inside it, and then the ship whistled away.

Eamon finally exhaled. "I hope Sherry isn't too worried."

Chapter Twenty-Two

IT WAS GETTING LATE, and Sherry was starting to worry about the boys.

She was going through her nightly ritual, locking the Cottage down and dimming the interior to make sure that as little light as possible was visible to anyone who might be passing by outside. Not that she expected anyone. As much as the three of them sometimes wished for company, the only sounds in the forest around them belonged to the creek and scampering animals. As winter approached, the second grew a lot quieter.

Still, it was better to be safe than sorry. It only took one pack of bandits to find their cabin, break in, murder every one of them — including William — then take what they were all working to protect. Of course, they also needed to see each other without running into things, so Sherry kept a few candles lit, though never more than necessary.

William continued to toddle behind her, just like he did every night, but now he seemed even more able than normal. She did her best not to act like it was too big a deal around Eamon, but in truth, Sherry was dumbfounded by what she was starting to think of as her son. She couldn't help it, with all the time they spent together and her tending to his every need, it all felt so natural. He was special. More than that, Sweet William was different than anything she'd ever seen. He was growing too fast and seemed too aware.

Sherry would never admit it to Eamon, but she kept hearing the word *mama* in her head, and would've sworn she wasn't imagining it at all. There was a light inside that child, and he was somehow sending it from his soul into hers. She could feel William's heart wanting to be beside hers.

"You ready for bed?"

She looked down at William, half expecting him to nod. Instead he followed her into the bedroom and climbed onto the bed, knowing their routine same as she did.

"Which one?" Sherry pointed to a trio of books at the foot of her bed. Eamon had brought them back from one of his runs a few weeks ago, and Sherry was saving them for a night like this. They finished a picture book version of *Pinocchio* the night before, and these three chapter books were all written for slightly older readers, still little, but not so much that they needed pictures to get through the story. They were ancient, from long before everyone had a Juke. Paper that might have once been cream or white was now yellow and waterlogged.

William pointed to the one in the worst shape. A beat to shit copy of *James and the Giant Peach*. Sherry picked it up, turned it over, and read from the back:

After James Henry Trotter's parents are tragically eaten by a rhinoceros, he goes to live with his two horrible aunts, Spiker and Sponge. Life there is no fun, until James accidentally drops some magic crystals by the old peach tree and strange things start to happen.

The peach at the top of the tree begins to grow, and before long it's as big as a house. Inside, James meets a bunch of oversized friends — Grasshopper, Centipede, Ladybug, and more. With a snip of the stem, the peach starts rolling away, and the great adventure begins!

"That sounds better than I remember," Sherry said, looking down at William. "What do you think."

He giggled and clapped, like no infant should be able to do, then pointed at the book.

Sherry scooped him up and put him in bed. Next to her nighttime conversations with Eamon, this was her favorite part of each day. One usually led into the other. She would miss him at least double, then worry ten times as much.

It was scary how much she was starting to feel for Eamon. Or not starting to — she'd been feeling it the whole time. Ever since he lost his wife and went zombie on her and William and Felony. But she could tell he wasn't ready, so Sherry kept telling herself the same damn thing, over and over. After six months, though, the lie was getting harder to believe.

Yes, the world had turned into a scary place. They were hiding out and scavenging for food. But it was still better than Splendid Oaks, a nice name for the shitty trailer park she'd called home for far too long. A lot more fun, and safe in a different way. Sherry felt more at home than she ever had anywhere, and more loved.

They couldn't stay in the Cottage forever, no matter how nice it was. But Sherry hoped they could stay a while. It was the nicest place she'd ever been, and the most peaceful. No one ever came around. As long as they had food, they could have a life. And there wasn't any reason they couldn't grow their own crops come springtime. She'd never done anything like that before, neither had Eamon or Felony. But they were all fast learners and could work the land, teaching William as he grew. And at his present rate, they could probably give him a hoe for his birthday.

Sherry read from *James and the Giant Peach*, William seeming fixed on her every word.

He fell asleep on schedule. She tucked him tightly under the covers, kissed him on the forehead, then whispered, "*I love you Sweet William,*" before leaving the room, quietly closing the door behind her.

She made the rounds again, checking the windows and doors, trying but failing not to worry.

Sherry went to the old secretary desk in the small sunroom, lowered the lid, and turned on the shortwave radio. Felony came back with that one after trip number twelve. She had never once listened to the broadcasts alone. They were too scary. Audio horror, mostly reporting the atrocities happening out there in the real world, outside of the cabin and far from this forest. It was impossible to know the difference between true and false, but even the best of what everyone seemed to agree on was awful.

There were aliens everywhere, and bandits taking advantage of a humanity dispersed to the breeze. Her fingers trembled as she turned the knob, searching for a broadcast, not wanting to listen but longing for an answer, desperate for news about Eamon and Felony, or any clue as to what could have happened, or where they might be.

She stopped on a preacher talking about Stonefall, how they were rebuilding the world into a "more pure place, a Godlier place."

While Stonefall wasn't too far away and might offer some safety, she'd heard enough false preachers making false promises to ever take one at face value. She laughed at the oily-sounding conman and turned the dial again.

She heard something that sounded almost official — a

man's voice, a more trustworthy voice than that of the preacher, saying something about sanctuary.

Surprised, she accidentally dialed away from the channel then fumbled with the dial until she found it again, the repeat sounding even more like a promise than it had the first time.

Sherry leaned forward and cranked the volume.

"... Sanctuary city called New Hope. We welcome all Montanans. We repeat —The city of ..."

She lost the signal to white noise and it wasn't coming back, but Sherry didn't need it. At least, not tonight. The name was enough. *Hope.* It didn't soothe her worry over the boys, but it made her feel almost inexplicably better about their possible future.

The town's name reminded her of *Star Wars*, and while that lit something inside her, it also made an already hollow spot feel a little more empty. She wanted to picture herself sitting with Eamon next to a little boy version of the baby William she already knew, the three of them watching Star Wars together. But the image felt like a lie.

Star Wars was probably dead, along with everything else Disney ever made. No more fairytales. Not the old ones, nor the new. It was sad to consider, even though she'd never given it thought before, but popular culture was dead — an artifact of a past being quickly forgotten.

Shakespeare was gone, and so were the Brothers Grimm. Spielberg and Rowling. All that stuff from Fable. Eventually every juke would die and all that had ever been printed would fade away. The Internet was probably gone for good. Sitting on the couch, Sherry couldn't help but mourn for the world that would never be again, even though it made her guilty. At least she was safe and warm while it seemed like so much of the world was still in hiding.

She peeled back the curtain and peeked outside. The night was black, and of course she saw nothing.

Maybe things were different in New Hope. Maybe they had power there. And other stuff. Maybe she should tell Eamon and Felony about the place as soon as they got home.

Or not. The cabin was safe, so why leave?

And besides, it could also have been only a joke or a rumor. That's probably the first thing Felony would say.

The Cottage was good, as much as it was going to get. Sherry should be grateful for what she already had instead of wanting more. She should realize that New Hope was probably only offering a promise that was already being delivered to her right here in the cabin.

But a haven like New Hope would have more people, and their resources in the forest were unpredictable. Or so the men kept saying. It was possible—

A loud knock on the door pulled Sherry out of her thoughts.

"Hello?" A female voice preceded another, louder knock. "Is anyone in there?"

Then a second voice, this one male. "We need help."

Sherry's heart was pounding, but instead of opening her mouth, she covered it with her palm.

She tried to shrink into the couch, hoping the intruders would go away, half-certain it was a trick.

If she went to help them, they would burst inside, kill her, then take William away.

And Sherry had to protect him. She and Eamon agreed, there was nothing more important in the world.

The doorknob rattled, and Sherry wanted to scream.

Chapter Twenty-Three

SHERRY RAN TO THE KITCHEN, terrified for her and William.

The front door was still rattling, and the pair of voices outside were now arguing about what to do. They knew she was in the cabin, and they weren't going to stop until they were inside, too. Eamon and Felony weren't home, so that meant protecting their family and space was all up to her.

She grabbed a knife. Even the worst blade in the kitchen was better than anything Sherry had in the trailer. Her mom's knives always hurt her hands if she needed to cut anything for more than a few minutes at a time. That's what you get for spending three dollars at a gas station. Felony taught her the difference, along with all the help he'd been, teaching her to shoot a bow and arrow — not that it would help her in such close quarters.

A good knife should feel like an extension of her hand. Cheap knives were either too heavy or too light, poorly balanced so they never felt right. Sherry looked at the knife in her hand now, bracing herself, hearing Felony's voice in her head.

Check out the bevel grinds. Cheap knives have a small bevel with too much steel at the spine. A good knife like this one has smoother grinds. Fit and finish, that's what you want. No gaps where the handle and blade come together, especially if you'll be plunging into bone. And if you're using this out there, you will be.

She wanted to grab a fighting knife from storage, but there wasn't time. The intruders might get inside by then, find Sherry with her back to them, digging through a weapon's chest instead of standing stolid and ready to fight.

Sherry walked to the living room, holding the weapon tightly in her hand.

She called out, "Go away!"

There was muttering outside, then the man's voice: "Please … we need help. It's starting to snow out here."

Is that true? If so, it feels early.

Her hand tightened on the knife. "Snow won't hurt you!"

"We have a sick child!" The woman sounded frantic.

Sherry didn't believe that their trick. But then she heard the baby crying, all at once and way too loud.

"*Please,*" the woman begged.

Sherry found herself creeping toward the door. The knife was parallel to her waist, her hand on the knob. Before she knew what she was doing, or had the sense to stop herself, the Cottage door swung open and Sherry was inviting the family inside.

They shuffled in and Sherry shut the door behind them.

"Thank you." The woman was clutching a baby tightly to her chest. It looked less than a year old, but much smaller than William. "I'm Angel, and this is our daughter, Sophia. That's my husband, Craig."

She nodded toward a guy who looked a lot sketchier than Sherry would have liked, showing up this late at night outside their secret forest cabin. His hair was shaggy, and surely hadn't seen a pair of scissors since long before Astral Day. Same for his face and a razor. His eyes weren't nearly kind enough, considering they were strangers. The adults could try and kill her if they wanted, and Sherry had let them all inside.

Craig looked hard and unforgiving, the way he was standing made her think that he probably didn't even know the word *gratitude*. He seemed dangerous, but maybe she was being judgmental on account of all her fear.

"Thank you," Craig said, surprising Sherry with a softness she didn't expect. "We've been wandering for days."

"And we haven't eaten," Angel added.

"We didn't believe your place when we saw it." Craig shook his head. "Thought we might be sharing a hallucination."

Angel started to laugh, soft and sad until a tear rolled down her cheek. She again muttered, "*Thank you.*"

"Let me get you something to eat," Sherry offered.

Gratitude found their faces, like baking dough beginning to bronze.

Sophia started to cough. Long and hacking. Their smiles died.

Angel went to the sofa and sat. Started rocking Sophia back and forth. Craig was on the couch a second later, his arms around them both, rocking them harder.

"Is there anything I can do?" Sherry asked.

Neither answered, and both looked scared out of their goddamn minds.

Sherry approached them and said, "May I?"

Angel looked up and nodded. Craig did the same thing a second behind her.

Then Sherry warmed her knuckles on Sophia's burning forehead.

"How long has she had the fever?"

"Two days." Craig had to gulp once he said it.

Sherry could feel sweat on her forehead that wasn't from the fire. This was all so awful. Sophia was going to die unless she did something. She could cook them some soup and give them a warm bed. It would be enough for Angel and Craig. But the baby might not make it without the one thing she couldn't say out loud but Sherry knew in her soul would save that child's life.

For now, Sherry would have to wait it out. Sophia was safe inside now, clutched to her mother's bosom. Maybe that was enough. She would cook. Take care of them. Wait for the boys to come home.

"She'll be okay," Sherry said, giving the couple her very best smile. "Now, who wants soup?"

She started the wood burning stove and a fresh conversation, feeling guilty she wouldn't leave the knife out of quick and easy reach but knowing that such things were necessary, no matter what. Sherry trusted Angel with all of her heart, even though she only just met her, but the jury was still in deliberation on Craig. Maybe it was his beard, or maybe it was just because he was a man and she already had two of those to manage, but Sherry didn't feel sure.

"What's it like out there? You're the first people I've seen. My friends live here with me. They'll be back any minute. They always go out on the supply runs, so I haven't seen anyone since ... you know."

The couple traded a look. Silence was heavy, with it being obvious that neither one of them wanted to discuss it.

"It's bad," Craig finally said.

"The aliens?" Sherry asked.

"Of course," he nodded. "And the people."

Sophia started screaming.

Sherry stirred the soup while waiting for Sophia to quiet.

She finally did, then Sherry asked, "How did you end up in the forest?"

"We were being chased by a bunch of outlaws," Angel said.

"I don't know if they were outlaws, since there's no more law, but they were born killers for sure. It was 'join us or die.' So we joined them until we could run, which we did, right into the forest. We didn't have any food or water, and didn't know where we were going—"

"With a baby to take care of!" Angel added.

"—but it was still better than whatever hell those assholes were headed off to."

"And you just happened to find this place?" That was almost harder for Sherry to believe than the alien attack. This cabin was in the middle of a forest, smack in the center of nowhere.

"Not exactly," Craig said, shaking his head, then tipping it toward Angel. "It was all her. She kept insisting we were headed the right way, for two days straight, even though there was no reason to think we were."

"And you doubted me the whole way," Angel added.

"Maybe half the way." He looked sheepish.

They kissed fast but deep before parting.

"Have you heard about New Hope?" Sherry asked.

"A few times," Craig said. "That's where we're—"

The front door swung open. Eamon and Felony came in. Sherry looked over, surprised by how hard it was snowing, and how much had piled behind them. So winter was early.

Eamon looked confused, and Felony angry, both of them eyeing the strangers on their sofa.

"This is Angel and Craig." Sherry pointed to the couple on the couch. "And their baby, Sophia. She's sick. We're about to have some soup. I'll add another couple of cans and you can tell us about your day. And night apparently. I'm sure you have stories."

"I'm Felony." He approached Craig first, extending his hand and sizing the stranger up. Angel came next, then Eamon took his turn with them both.

Sherry stirred the soup in silence, the rapport she'd been building now bruised and retreating.

She served everyone a small bowl, then they all sat around eating in silence until Sherry reignited the conversation by asking the boys about their day, wanting to know why they were late without saying anything specific.

But Felony didn't want to discuss it, thanks to the strangers she was sure, so he shifted the conversation to comparing encounters with bandits and drones, possible havens and trade routes. Plus a few other subjects that kept Sherry on the outside looking in. Craig mentioned a group of killers calling themselves The Forsaken that Eamon and Felony were obviously hoping she wouldn't find out about.

"Can I talk to you for a minute?" Eamon said, helping Sherry take the soup bowls back into the kitchen.

His anger made her stomach hurt.

"Of course." She put her bowls on the counter to clean later, then turned to Eamon. "What's up?"

Sherry had seen his eyes that mad before, but never directed at her.

"What the hell were you thinking?"

"I'm sorry?"

"Letting strangers into the house." Eamon shook his head, looking like he wanted to spit. "I can't believe that you did that. You could be dead!"

"Like I don't know that!" Sherry was doing a better job at keeping her voice down than Eamon. "If you were here, I never would've had to make the choice. You would've done the same thing, and you can't convince me you wouldn't. I made a judgment call."

"It was the wrong one."

"How can you say that? Those poor people would have died if I hadn't opened the door."

"You could have died because you did. That's what I need you to realize. You and William matter the most. Isn't that what you were trying to tell me? About having to make the hard decisions? That's what it means to be a grownup."

That hurt the worst. Nothing was more awful than being talked down to, or treated like a child. Sherry was eighteen, not that the age meant what it used to, but still she was an adult all the same. But Eamon didn't see her that way. He saw her as a kid, and that made him treat her with less respect than she deserved.

"I am a grownup, Eamon. As much as you. I'd say raising a baby's about as grownup as it gets. And you know what else is adult? Making hard choices, like not letting a nice family freeze to death on my front porch. Would you have really wanted to come home to that? Three frozen bodies, and one of them a baby?"

She stared at him until he softened. It didn't take long.

"I'm sorry. You're right." He took her hands and squeezed them, surprising as much as delighting her.

That gave Sherry the courage to ask what she might not have otherwise. "Sophia is really sick, Eamon."

He looked at her, probably expecting what she was about to say. Or ask. His face was already changing.

"Do you think William could heal him?"

"No, Sherry. Absolutely not."

"But why? Can't we—"

"Because we don't understand how it works. What if the sickness spreads to him and he can't heal himself?"

"He always heals himself."

"He's never been sick like that. Do you really want to take that chance?"

"Do you want to see a baby die in our living room?" Sherry stared into his eyes until he blinked.

"We aren't going to be able to find anyone to help us if William gets sick."

Sherry shook her head, not willing to let this go. "William isn't like other kids. He hasn't been sick because he doesn't get sick. Maybe you don't want to talk about it, but that doesn't mean it isn't a fact. He's different, Eamon. Better. Maybe a little worse in some ways, or maybe that's just stuff we don't understand yet, but your son is a healer."

She was whispering, her words coming hard and fast.

"You can't deny that, and you can't deny the baby who needs his help, who is needlessly suffering out there. Felony came staggering home, bleeding out with three arrows in his body. A couple days later and he was walking around like he'd been hit by a foam dart."

Eamon looked at Sherry, and in his eyes she could see that he wanted to say yes, and that it was breaking something inside him to say no. But he was too protective of his son, and terrified that he might lose William like he'd lost his wife. And so he shook his head. "We can't, Sherry. William comes—"

She spun around and started back into the other room.

"Wait!" Eamon said, coming after her.

She stopped, a step into the living room. As if walking into an invisible wall.

William was standing on the couch, touching Sophia's forehead, both babies laughing, Williams scars bright like light shining through his cheek.

Both parents stared in awe — and likely confusion — at the boy as he spoke.

"Help," William said.

"Your baby is a miracle," Angel said.

Chapter Twenty-Four

EAMON WAS PISSED.

Fuming mad. Totally fucking irate.

The angriest he'd been since the goddamned apocalypse started.

Sweet William's secret had been exposed, and now his son was a target. Because something like that in a world like this ... well, there wasn't anything more valuable.

Sherry had meant well, just like Poppy would have. It was obvious why his heart kept pulling him toward the girl. But she invited this family inside, and now they couldn't leave. Their secret would go with them if they did. Eamon couldn't allow that, but he didn't want — or need — another three mouths to feed.

This was a mess, and as much as Sherry obviously wanted to hash it out, she was the last person he wanted to look at, let alone talk to, right now.

He needed to get Felony alone. The two of them could dribble ideas. He wondered how to do it without being obvious, then decided fuck that, this was his Cottage and he didn't have to tiptoe around anyone.

"Yo, Felony. We need to talk."

Felony looked up, nodded, and followed Eamon out of the room.

Across the cabin and into his bedroom. Eamon shut the door then said, "We can't let them leave."

"Of course we can let them leave. If you think more hands will lighten your load instead of giving you more shit to worry about, you're crazier than—"

"They'll tell people about William."

"*Oh*," Felony said, the truth hitting him like a hammer on his skull. "Then we kill the parents and keep the kid. You and Sherry have an instant family."

"Fuck you, man."

"You think I'm not serious? Don't drag me in here asking for advice if you're not willing to take it. The fuck you think that's gonna accomplish?"

"We're not killing them."

"What? You never killed no one before? That's what you're telling me right here in my bedroom?"

"I'm not a murderer."

"There's a difference?" Felony raised his eyebrows.

"Of course there's a difference."

"You want to keep William a secret, then you better find a way to believe there isn't."

Eamon sighed, shaking his head. "We can't do that."

"Do what?" Felony pressed. "Add an orphan to the family, or let the world know about our treasure and turn the four of us into a target?"

"I can't murder innocent people, especially when they're in my house looking for help … but we also can't let them leave."

"Helluva conundrum," Felony said, in a voice that let Eamon know it wasn't. "Look man, you've gotta make a decision here, and you know what it is. Putting it off until later isn't going to help anyone. It's like naming an animal you're eventually going to eat. Let's take them back out and get this over with."

"You're kidding. Just like that? Fuck you, man. Sherry would never forgive me."

"She would get over it real quick, with another baby to take care of."

Eamon paused, wondering if that might be true.

Felony said, "There's no reason we need to figure this out tonight. It's been a long day, and we should all go to bed. They can stay."

"For how long?"

"I don't know. Not long. Until we figure things out."

The two men shared a long stare, neither of them particularly happy with the exchange, but both knowing it was the best they were going to do, then they returned to the living room together.

"Did you figure out what to do with us?" Craig asked.

The room shared an uncomfortable laugh, then Eamon said, "We'd like for you to stay, at least for the night. We can figure out the rest of it tomorrow."

Relief washed over Craig and Angel. Sophia gurgled in her mother's arms. William clapped in Sherry's lap.

"That's wonderful," Angel said. "Thank you so much."

"You saved our lives," Craig added. "All of them. And don't worry, we don't want to overstay our welcome. Like we were telling Sherry just before you guys came in, we're on our way to New Hope. You're welcome to come with us if you want. Safety in numbers and all that."

Eamon couldn't ignore the way Craig's gaze drifted over to William.

"New Hope?" Felony said.

"You've never heard of it?" Angel asked.

Eamon shook his head. Felony, too.

Craig said, "It's been on the radio for a few days, when you can get it. Might be a prank, who knows, but neither of us has anywhere else to go, so we figured why not? We were following the signals when they found us."

"Who found you?" Felony asked.

"Some sort of bandits," he answered. "They chased us into the forest."

Eamon shook his head, not liking any of this. "And you found this cabin in the middle of the forest?"

"And in the dark?" Felony added.

"Because this is the time for miracles," Sherry said, shutting all of them up. "And New Hope might be exactly that."

Eamon didn't like that Sherry was talking about a place he'd never heard about like it was old news, but there were bigger things to argue about.

"You can have my room," Sherry said to the three of them, Sophia looking up like she could actually understand.

William was doing the same, though Eamon believed he got it fine and knew Sherry was thinking the same thing. Their thoughts felt like bubbles on the same bar of soap.

"Thank you," said Angel.

"You really did save our lives," Craig added.

"I'm glad I wasn't too scared to open the door." Sherry glanced at Eamon then finished. "I'm glad I could trust you enough."

Laughing, Craig said, "Trust in God, but tie your camel."

"I'm sorry?" Sherry looked at Craig, confused. Not getting it.

Still laughing, he said, "Invite them into your house, but keep a giant knife in your hand at all times."

Finally, Sherry laughed along with him. The mood finally exhaled enough for them all to retire.

She fluffed up her room, then showed Angel and Craig into it. The bed was a king, easily big enough for the three of them. Same for the other two bedrooms.

"Can I sleep in your room with you?" Sherry asked Eamon, after the two of them were finally alone. Felony had gone to bed, their guests were in her room, and William was already asleep in his bed, a few feet from Eamon.

"I don't know." Eamon shook his head, uneasy. "I'm not sure that's such a good idea."

"It's not like that, silly." A slap on the shoulder, light and playful. Harmless. "I know you, and you're going to say that you'll sleep out here on the sofa so I'll feel safe, and so I'm comfortable. But I want us both to feel safe and comfortable. No reason we can't share a bed for one night. It's plenty big. People were sleeping in tiny spaces without fucking every five minutes for thousands of years. The pill changed everything, you know."

Eamon didn't know what to say. It was an odd and awkward conversation. Finally, he managed a single weak word. "Okay."

She followed him into his bedroom, then they climbed under the covers, one right after the other. He got in with his back facing her, figuring it would be easier not to be tempted.

It was cold in the room, but better beneath their bundle of blankets. She wormed her way against him. Wiggled a little too much. It was so quiet and still, his heart pounded hard in his ear. He was going to scoot away from her, or tell Sherry he needed some space, but she broke the silence and stole his chance.

"What made you go soft in the kitchen like that? After you were so mad at me and wanting to tear my head off?"

Eamon went back to the moment and found the words. "Because you have a good heart, like Poppy. I wish she'd had the chance to really know you better. She would've loved you."

"And it sounds like I would have loved her."

Then she pushed her body closer against him and wrapped her arms around him.

"Thank you for trusting me with your son."

"Thank you ... for everything."

"I love him just like he was my own."

"I know you do." He shouldn't say it, but ... "You're everything he needs right now. Everything I need."

Her hands were between his legs, and he was hardening inside her palm.

When he turned to Sherry, her lips were parted and ready. He pressed his against them, and the kissing was good, their tongues swimming in something long needed and finally met.

She panted against him, and he panted right back.

But then Eamon pushed her away.

He planted his palms on the mattress and shoved himself farther from her, into a sitting position.

"What is it?" Sherry sounded upset.

Of course she sounded upset. He was rude and hurtful. No way she wouldn't take this personally.

Eamon was sorry for that, but he had no other choice. He couldn't lead her on and wasn't ready for this.

He was drowning in a sea of emotions, clinging to love and guilt like driftwood floating at the top.

If Eamon loved, then he could lose again. And he wouldn't survive it a second time.

Seconds ticked by in silence, yet all he did was stare at her.

"I'm sorry." She turned from him.

"Don't be. I want to hold you."

Then he did, tight like he wanted, and the two of them drifted into sleep, softly crying together.

Chapter Twenty-Five

GLEESON TOOK another shot and clapped Roy on the back, commiserating rather than congratulatory. "I'm concerned my people are losing their fear of God."

"You're right to worry," Roy said.

Gleeson collapsed in his chair, looked at the bottle and figured he might as well empty it, so he got the tall mug he usually used for his coffee — there wasn't much to go around, but enough for him in the mornings for now — and poured every last drop of the whiskey inside it.

He raised the mug to his lips and took a long swallow, turning to Roy as he winced. "Any suggestions."

"Of course." Roy always had suggestions. "You need a show of force. To remind them of God's power. Good news is, it's in play, brother."

"What do you mean?" Gleeson took another swallow.

"You find your missing men, and/or the guilty men responsible."

"Agreed," Gleeson said.

That spilled his liquor-soaked dream into a nightmare where a set of awful things were happening like a split-screen movie in front of him. Hellfire raining with the usual demons, and all of them coming for him beside the giant he was beneath a mountain of blankets, tossing and turning, sweating like a hog in his sleep. A thought cloud appeared above him like an old-fashioned comic strip, and inside the bubble another version of himself, this one drinking hard and yucking it up with Roy, the man he murdered before assigning him to a life as his spiritual guide.

The nightmare softened at the edges, and Gleeson found himself staring at an angel. No, *the* Angel. *His* Angel.

And now the dream was beautiful, because Angel no longer hated him. She had been looking for him too, and she had something to show him.

"Look, Daddy …"

Gleeson turned his gaze to the giggling bundle in the crook of her arms. But then he blinked, and the baby was suddenly no longer so small. Three times bigger, at least. And talking. About what, Gleeson didn't know, but his chatter was constant.

"His name is William," Angel said.

But Gleeson knew that.

He woke up covered in sweat but smiling.

Gleeson didn't remember his dreams, but he knew there were plenty, and they were thick. The sort that sometimes drifted back. Same kind he'd been having since finding himself locked in Stonefall next to a man named Roy that he'd once made the error of mistaking for crazy.

It didn't take Gleeson long to get ready. He didn't need to do much. The modern world scrubbed too much, anyway. The areas in need of tending were obvious. Hands, armpits, feet, teeth, cock, and balls. Plus the asshole, of course, which people should pay extra attention to. The area where waste left the body should be a person's cleanest part. Gleeson's starfish was squeaky clean, a habit he'd had since long before the apocalypse on account of him liking it licked.

He was the last one out, but not by a lot. Perfect really, since these days Gleeson Crowe shouldn't be waiting on anyone.

"Father."

Kirk said it first, and did so with a dip of his head. Reverent kid, his faith was obvious.

"Morning, Father," Percy said. He had a dip too, but not so subservient.

Gleeson nodded at them both, then went to the front of the two trucks and climbed into the passenger seat. Percy followed him to the front but got behind the wheel.

"Where we headed first?" Gleeson asked, having left it to Kirk and Percy to decide so he could get to his drinking.

"Carson's Neck. Might as well start close. We have no idea how far they got."

"You and Kirk get along last night?"

"We got along fine," Percy said without expression.

"Sounds like you had a blast. You two talk about the mysteries of the universe?"

"No, boss. I save that for you."

"Boss? Not Father?"

"Same thing," Percy said, "isn't it?"

"No. It isn't. Let's drive."

He didn't need Percy to kiss his ass like Kirk and everyone else in Stonefall. It was refreshing. Percy had faith, but told him the truth. A leader needed a man like that by his side.

Percy wanted to discuss the state of Stonefall's provisions and some better strategies for their supply runs, but Gleeson wanted to focus on the road. The devil lived in the details, so it was worth paying attention to everything they passed. Especially with the so called Forsaken haunting the lands beyond his walls.

"At least one of us should be paying attention," Gleeson said. "The story of what's happening outside of Stonefall is being told by everything we pass."

"And you don't think any one of the people in this truck or the one behind us can read it?" Percy asked.

"Some of us are better at reading scripture than others."

"I gave you your first Bible, and it wasn't long ago, lest you forget."

"That's why you're driving my truck."

There wasn't much of a reason to speak after that, but there was plenty to say about halfway to Carson's Neck when they came across six people hanging upside down, eyes gouged out and sockets still bloody, lacerated bodies on upside down crosses.

"This is close." Percy coughed.

"Godless savages. Look how far the world has fallen. How much the demons have influenced humanity, dragging them into Hell already. It's been six months …" Gleeson paused, looking at Percy. "What's with that face? And don't tell me you don't have one."

"I'm just having a hard time with the word demons. Aliens are bad enough, and that's exactly what they are."

"You don't think demons come in many forms?"

"I don't know what I believe, but I do know you had a religious experience. I saw that for myself, and my gut says to trust it. I also know old school religion does a lot to keep the peace in a place like Stonefall. Folks behave when they know the Lord is watching. Unless they're afraid for their life, or for their family."

"What's that supposed to mean? Who's afraid in Stonefall?"

"I don't mean like that. But I can see people starting to worry about our stores. Like I was saying before when—"

"If anyone thinks they have a better chance at feeding themselves outside, they're welcome to take their chances."

"That's not what I'm saying. There are things we could be doing to figure it out inside Stonefall, so we're not always having to go hunting for food like this."

"Of course," Gleeson said, agreeing about the food stuff like he always did with Percy. "We need better systems."

"But it isn't enough to agree, we have to actually—"

Percy clammed up for the same reason Gleeson stopped listening. Smoke rising beyond some hills in the distance.

"Tell them to pull over," Gleeson said, though Percy was already squeezing his comm, about to give Kirk the order in the other truck while doing the same thing himself.

"What do you want to do?" Kirk asked Gleeson through the window.

Gleeson surveyed the scene then turned to Roy.

Hide the trucks in the forest, then follow that hill. You'll find what you're looking for there.

"We hide the trucks then follow that hill." Gleeson pointed. "We'll find what we're looking for there."

Then he started walking without waiting for anyone to follow.

Of course they would. A few were running fast to catch up after taking care of the trucks, Kirk and Percy included.

By the time they were all back together, Gleeson was crouched with his men, staring through a pair of binoculars.

"What do you see?" Percy asked.

Gleeson handed him the binoculars. "One of our trucks."

Percy looked into the lenses and his lip curled in fury.

"Someone hand me a pair?" Gleeson held out his hand.

"Me, too," Kirk said, doing the same.

But there were only two pairs. So Gleeson and Percy kept watching as a group of men with machetes, bats, and a single rifle, heading out in one of Stonefall's stolen trucks.

Gleeson turned to Percy and said, "Hand me the radio."

Then he made a call.

Chapter Twenty-Six

GLEESON WAS SITTING cross-legged in a comfortable leather chair, trying to show his gratitude for his whiskey, taking long sips as his heel tapped on concrete in time to Steve Earl's South Nashville Blues.

He stared at the bodies of his fallen men. Nathan and the rest of them. He would sit in this comfortable chair, a curious choice in a filthy garage like this one, and wait for his enemies to return. Then he would gut them, feed their pieces of slop to starving animals, then kill those scavengers for meat and a mighty feast inside Stonefall.

Percy and Kirk were hiding outside with the rest of their men. There were women and children in the compound behind the garage. They'd stay alive if they didn't interfere, at least for now.

His eyes moved from the closed garage door back down to the bodies. The sight made him thirsty for blood.

He took another long swallow of whiskey, glad for the privacy and for his drink. The bandits could take their time. He would be ready whenever they returned. The longer they took, the less forgiving he would be.

Gleeson wiped his mouth and flinched, assaulted by an odd thought of his daughter. Angel holding a baby, it had to be hers, with those gecko green eyes, and another that left him with a jolt of déjà vu.

The garage door began to open. Gleeson could see the tires and feel the rumbling air.

The door slowly rose, faster than the sun but no less beautiful. Retribution was now only seconds away.

Then it was all the way up and an old armored Escalade was pulling inside. It burned gas fast, causing Gleeson to wonder where they were getting their fuel and why they were willing to bother.

The driver and passenger were both out of the car before either spied Gleeson, now standing like a sequoia, holding a red stained strip of rebar and smiling.

The guy on Gleeson's left drew a knife from the sheaf at his waist, but Kirk was standing behind him and ready. He sent a bolt sailing from this crossbow into the back of the bandit's head.

The man fell forward and landed on his mouth, audibly shattering two rows of teeth that he'd never need again.

Percy was behind the driver, gun pressed to the back of his head. "How many more in the truck?"

"Two."

"Okay," Percy said. "That's how many bullets I'll use if you're lying to me. An hour apart, the first one in your dick. Is that your final answer?"

The driver swallowed then nodded.

"You can both come out!" Kirk yelled.

The rear doors opened and two men hopped out of the Escalade, one on each side.

"How many still in the truck?" Percy nodded toward the truck.

"None," they both said.

Gleeson finally spoke, stepping forward and tossing his rebar from one hand to the other for dramatic effect. "Which one of you is Noel?"

The driver stepped forward and without so much as a quiver in his voice he said, "I am."

"Where are you getting your fuel?" Gleeson swung the rebar into his palm.

"Wherever we can."

"Where was the last place?" Gleeson asked. "And be specific."

"A farm about fifty miles from here."

"And when was that?" Another swing into his palm.

"Yesterday."

"Before or after what you did to my men?" Gleeson looked down at the bodies.

"That was their fault," Noel said.

"Oh?" Gleeson raised his eyebrows. "How so?"

"It was us or them, same as now. You're gonna kill us all no matter what, right? Isn't that why you're here?"

"Sounds like you're making assumptions," Gleeson said.

But Noel looked back at him fiercely. "You're from Stonefall. We know who you are."

Gleeson smiled. "If you know about Stonefall, then you won't be surprised that we're taking you back, trying you for your sins. I hope you're ready to face your truth."

Kirk and Percy cuffed their prisoners, then loaded them into one of the newly arrived trucks while the rest of their troop loaded the women and children into the cars.

"It's sick. What you do with those crosses."

"That isn't us," Noel insisted, glaring at Gleeson. "We're only surviving."

"What are you doing here in this house?"

"*Surviving,*" Noel stressed, as though he hadn't been clear. "We don't have nothing, and your men are only dead because they tried to take what didn't belong to them."

"I don't believe you," Gleeson said.

"Well, it don't—"

"But it doesn't matter if I believe you. It only matters if the Lord believes you, and we'll find out if he does, tonight after our sermon, during Sins and Transgressions."

He slammed the door and turned to Kirk, glad Percy wasn't there. He wouldn't like what Gleeson was about to say. He put a hand on Kirk's shoulder and leaned into his ear.

"Stay behind with Beckett and the men you need to take their vehicles and fuel to Stonefall."

"That it?" Kirk asked.

"No," Gleeson said. "Before you leave, I want you to burn this place to the ground."

Chapter Twenty-Seven

EVERYONE WAS present in the town square for the Father of Stonefall's evening sermon.

Gleeson promised an extra special Sins and Transgressions, though Percy heard him reminding everyone who would listen as he and Melinda approached their designated spot off to the side, that they were all special. Sins and Transgressions, he always insisted, was one of those things that helped their community to grow the most.

Sermons would have to be moved into the old chapel now that the weather was changing. To Percy's mind, the shift was overdue. They were now ankle deep in snow, and a roaring fire just wasn't enough.

Gleeson's length of rebar lay next to the fire, a reminder that this was going to get ugly. Melinda probably didn't want to hold Percy's hand or be standing anywhere near that courtyard, but appearances were everything and she was smart enough to know it. Still, looking out at the crowd, it didn't appear that the majority of citizens were there for appearances. The crowd looked eager, thirsty for entertainment or blood. Maybe even both.

Percy didn't want to be there any more than Melinda did, but attendance was mandatory, and his absence would be impossible to miss.

Gleeson began his sermon, preaching about how the citizens of Stonefall must always protect each other, no matter what.

He spoke of their stronghold and the songs that would one day be sung in the land of Judah. "Stonefall is strong!" Gleeson declared with his hands held high. "And behind these walls, we shall see that God destroys what is false and sanctifies what is true. We are the redeemed, and we shall live without fear in this city. We have turned a prison into a fortress, yet manmade walls will never save us from the perils still walking this Earth. Stonefall will open its gates for the righteous, and only the faithful may enter."

Gleeson continued, talking about how no citizen could live inside Stonefall unless God and His Character lived deep in their hearts. Finished, he turned to his adoring crowd, his body like a cross, arms wide and palms out, more than a hundred citizens hanging on his every word, most if not all of them stealing glances at the trio of men on their knees, positioned off to the side of Gleeson, opposite where Percy and Melinda were standing.

Same for the eleven men, women, and children behind him, assembled with Kirk and several more of Gleeson's men.

"It is time for Sins and Transgressions. But tonight we must turn outward, bring the devil here to show him that we are not afraid. Who's with me?"

Gleeson liked to put on a show, but this time it felt different, and Percy was reminded more of the man who had murdered Roy Oversham in his cell than the one who built this town.

A chorus of cheers rippled through the crowd as Gleeson turned and looked down at his prisoners.

"Each of you will have the chance to confess your sins before all of Stonefall, then you may beg for the Good Lord's mercy." Gleeson turned to the families assembled behind the prisoners. "Your fates will be decided by these men. What they're willing to confess, and that which they choose to hide. The Lord knows when men are lying. If they tell the truth, then the eleven of you will have an opportunity to join our community in safety and solace. If not, unfortunately, you will all be forced to join them in hell."

A round of gasps rolled through the press of people as Gleeson called the first man to the stage.

He held his head high, but the man was still trembling. Despite his ferocious eyes, he was Gleeson's puppet, with his family held hostage behind him, out of sight but certainly not out of mind.

"Name your Sins and Transgressions," Gleeson said to his victim, looking out at the crowd.

Then the man opened his mouth to an avalanche of admissions that Percy was certain were mostly lies. He could tell by the way his family was looking at him — this man wasn't a murderer, and of course the former CO had known his share. This was the kind of man who would kill only if it meant keeping his family safe. Same for stealing, or admitting to atrocities that had nothing to do with him.

Percy wondered if Kirk, or someone else, had gotten to these men when Percy was busy, coached them on what they had to say to stay alive. And, if so, did Gleeson know about it? Had he given the instructions?

Gleeson waited for him to finish his false confessions, pleading guilty to murder and worse. The torture of innocents and the kidnapping of children, though there had been no evidence of either so far as Percy knew. Once done, Gleeson moved to the next confessor, asked the man an identical question then waited for a similar answer.

The second man wasn't nearly as prepared, or maybe he just lost it once on his knees in front of a barbarous horde pretending they were just. He spent a few moments sobbing, working to collect his breath and words before fully divulging the breadth of his sins. The second confession took twice as long, but then it finally finished, and Percy watched Gleeson encourage the crowd, promising that the chill would be worth it as he called their leader to the front.

Gleeson paced in front of the man, still speaking to the crowd.

"This man is named Noel, and he is the worst of them. The one who gave the orders. The one who told his men where to go and what to do. The devil and corruptor." Gleeson looked down at his prisoner. "Your friends have faced their demons. Confessed their sins to save their families. Are you now penitent and willing to do the same?"

"That's not what I heard," Noel dared to say.

The crowd gasped.

Percy could feel Melinda wanting to tremble beside him, but still she stood like a statue.

"You know, I had a feeling that this would happen." Gleeson shook his head, eyes now full of mock sorrow. "Sometimes God can pave every brick on the path to Salvation, and still some people are too blinded by His Light to walk in a straight line. Is that what happened to you, Noel?"

Noel made the mistake of spitting at Gleeson's feet. Percy shuddered.

The Father of Stonefall turned to the captives standing in back. "Which one of you is Andrew?"

But Gleeson knew. His gaze was fixed on a lanky kid, maybe fourteen or fifteen, his resemblance to Noel obvious. Percy would have wondered how Gleeson knew his name, if he didn't always seem to know plenty he shouldn't.

"Why don't you come up here, son? Don't worry," Gleeson said with a wolfish smile. "We won't hurt you. No one in Stonefall wants to punish the son for the sins of his father."

Andrew seemed to be forcing one foot in front of the other, slowly approaching what had to feel like an execution in waiting.

Gleeson looked down at Noel. "Don't you want your son to have a chance at entering God's kingdom?"

Noel stared up at the ringmaster of this sickening circus.

"Do you have anything to add to this evening's Sins and Transgressions?" Gleeson smiled and waited.

Noel finally broke, spilling one false confession after another, starting with his thieving and raping, followed by his murdering innocents for fun. No one seemed to care that every word sounded like farce. They wanted to see someone punished, or were at least glad the discipline wasn't falling on them. It was hard to watch so many of Stonefall's citizens either smiling or nodding in what looked like unconscious endorsement.

Percy wished he couldn't hear the twitters of approval, would have given anything to believe that Stonefall wasn't changing for the worse, right in front of his eyes.

Noel finished his false confessions, eyes hopeful that at least he might have saved his son.

Gleeson turned to the transfixed crowd.

"Though we here are safe behind our walls, there is a band of devil worshippers haunting this part of Montana.

They call themselves The Forsaken." Gleeson paused so the congregation could absorb the gravity of his revelation. Then he continued. "These three men were all a part of this savage clan. They are a vicious, ungodly people, taking advantage of the world as it is so they may fashion it more into a world of their liking. They crave a dark planet full of death and decay, where predators can slowly chew their prey without fear of interruption."

Gleeson's eyes were now sad as he looked out at the crowd.

"You've all heard the rumors. Humans skinned alive and hanging upside down on crosses as some sort of warning to those who might defy them." Gleeson raised both his hands and his voice. "We here in Stonefall defy you! We reject The Forsaken and choose to walk only in the Light of Christ, disregarding the devil and his minions."

Gleeson looked down at Noel — the man was withered and quivering.

"Do you confess to being one of The Forsaken?"

Noel shook his head and without hesitation said, "No."

"I'm sorry?" Gleeson walked over to the fire and picked up his strip of rebar from the ground. Then he patiently dipped its tip into the fire, waited for the metal to turn a hateful shade of red, then slowly walked back over to Noel, his eyes fixed on its glowing tip as if studying the color.

Gleeson raised the rebar over his head.

Noel started to sob, suddenly confessing his many atrocities as one of the satellite leaders of The Forsaken, begging the Father of Stonefall to kill him if he must, but to please not to hurt any of the innocent men, women, or children, obviously saying it more for the crowd's benefit than for Gleeson.

"They didn't know," Noel insisted. "It was all my idea!"

"Yeah," added one of the other two men. "Just ours."

The third man tried to agree, but his whimpers were too deep to decipher.

"What was?" Gleeson asked Noel, working to hide a smile that Percy knew him well enough to see anyway.

"Strapping those bodies to the crosses, gouging eyes out. All of it. That was us. Anything you've seen here in Stonefall like that, it was us."

"Thank you for speaking the truth," Gleeson said once Noel finally finished. "That wasn't so hard now, was it?"

"Not at all. Thank you for giving me the opportunity to unburden my soul." Then Noel looked up, hopeful.

But Gleeson walked over to the other two men, still kneeling with their bound hands in front of them, heads down, firelight throwing shadows on their sweaty foreheads. He was solemn, as though taking no delight in the exercise, but by now Percy could see that it was all an act, and one he couldn't do a single thing to stop.

Noel winced as the rebar came down.

It made a precision stop just above his head. Gleeson holding it steady with his gaze still fixed on the crowd. Smiling like Barnum. There was nothing holy in this moment, and few in the crowd seemed to care or even know it. But Melinda was one of them, and her hands were now digging their disgust into Percy's arm.

Gleeson gave his attention to the other two men, turned their heads into chowder with the rebar while the horde leaned forward and the men's families were forced to throttle their wailing, terrified of what might happen to them next if they cried.

He finished and turned to the families as though he'd done them a favor. Smiled and nodded, then swung his body back toward the crowd. "They have paid the price for their sins, and opened the gates of Stonefall for their families."

Gleeson looked back at the newest members of his Flock. "You will be safe here."

It was hard to believe people were cheering.

Noel's expression made Percy want to vomit on his behalf.

"How many children do you have?" Gleeson asked him.

"Just one. Only Andrew."

Gleeson looked over at Andrew, then back down at Noel. He shook his head, looking almost forlorn. "I'm sorry, Noel."

After a terrifying silence he stuttered, "Sorry for what?"

Another glance at Andrew. "We've all seen the movies. Your boy'll grow up and want to avenge his father's death. It's only natural." Gleeson waved him over. "Come over here, son."

Noel said, "You've proven your point. Two men dead. The rest of us will leave and we'll never come back. We'll disappear. No one wants to see any more bloodshed tonight."

"I think you're wrong. I think the good citizens of Stonefall would very much like to see a man such as yourself punished for what he's just admitted to doing."

"We didn't do anything. You've made your point. You don't have to do this, you can still let us all go. Or at least all of them." He dared to glance back at the innocents. "Do what you want with me, but—"

Gleeson shushed him by raising a finger on one hand and his rebar in the other. "But you're the only one I don't want. Sinners aren't welcome in Stonefall. Same for their sons. I meant what I said. Andrew isn't being punished for your sins, But I must do my job as Father of Stonefall, and that means keeping everyone safe. Unfortunately, that includes future revenge-seeking offspring."

Gleeson brought the rebar down on Andrew, several unnecessary strikes before the deathblow rained on his head. All of it so his father had to watch. Percy was stunned. Disgusted. Nearly propelled onto the stage to stop the madness, but it was too late. Melinda held him hard, pulled him back, her eyes wet with knowing that if Percy stepped in now, he might be next.

The crowd was mostly quiet., a suddenly ugly mood now staining the occasion.

A few people started to cheer, and Melinda broke away to comfort a quietly crying Ophelia as the girl came up beside her. Percy caught Kirk looking at him, the hint of a smile lighting the fucker's evil little eyes.

He again wondered how much Kirk had to do with this.

But this horror wasn't just on Kirk. Percy was at least partly to blame. Gleeson was a despot, but Percy had enabled him. Helped bring a violent convict to power, just because he'd pulled his ass out of the fire a couple of times.

Gleeson turned to Stonefall's newest citizens, and welcomed them with wide arms. "Tonight, we feast!"

Percy and Melinda traded a glance. They could barely afford scraps, let alone a feast.

Whatever Gleeson was planning, they could no longer be a part of it.

They needed to get the hell out of Stonefall, the second they could.

Chapter Twenty-Eight

MELINDA AND PERCY spoke in low voices, barely willing to whisper for fear of being overheard, even in their own home.

It was easy to be paranoid after all they just saw, and hard not to be furious with her husband for paving the path that took them there.

"We'll have to be careful," Percy said, putting his hand on top of hers. "*Very* careful."

Melinda yanked her hand away. "You don't have to tell me about being careful. I've been watching myself since long before there were aliens in the sky or some evil man pretending to be righteous down here on the ground."

"I'm just saying that we can't leave yet, even though you want to."

"You think I don't know that?" Melinda looked away from him, disgusted even though she was trying her hardest not to be. "We'll need a while to gather enough supplies without drawing attention. We're lucky I'm in the position to do so, but I still don't think we should give ourselves any less than three or four days, and even that's rushing it."

"Fine," Percy said. "I just thought you would want to get out of here before that."

"I never wanted to come, but that doesn't mean I want to die in front of an audience on my way out."

Percy looked haunted. Not just by what they saw, but because he had begged Melinda to come, promised her miracles after bearing witness himself. Or so he thought. But that was Percy, always wanting to believe in something. Always wanting to do the right thing.

Even if he was wrong, Melinda understood why he'd made the assumptions. She valued herself based on the amount of work she could do and always had. But being good at a thing, or being used to doing it, didn't make that thing a desire. The opposite was often true, and it was a deep disappointment that Percy didn't understand that. He knew she grew up with a father who hit every female in his house and a chore chart that was strictly enforced. Melinda was trained to accept her worth as being equal only to what she provided for others. She wanted to exorcise the lessons, not live them all over.

Percy had pulled Melinda from her shell. Saved her life. Taught her to laugh and to love. Helped her to become the free-spirited woman she tried to be prior to the aliens coming, before her loving husband led her into this hell, turning her back into a worker bee now inside the hive of a highly religious community. Instead of measuring themselves against each other's possessions and fashion sense, the women of Stonefall compared their piety and religious affectations. The Women's Group, led by Lucinda, had gone from providing companionship to breeding contempt for one another.

Who is the most devout?

Melinda didn't care. She wanted to drink away her PTSD, but there wasn't a drop to be had.

"I'll keep you safe," Percy promised, his insistent hand forcing hers to surrender beneath it. "We're going to get through this."

"There he is — Sir Galahad, promising to save the day again."

She called him Sir Galahad often. Sometimes it was a compliment. Other times it was a nod towards his naïveté, at his eagerness to believe in people being generally good, despite the overwhelming evidence otherwise.

"We *will* get through this."

Something cracked, and Melinda finally had to ask. To say it out loud so the question would stop rotting inside her. "Why did you make me come here?"

"I didn't *make* you come. I asked you if you wanted to."

"No, Percy." Melinda shook her head. "You don't get to do that. In every way, you made me come here."

"I—"

"Did you know that the idea made me uncomfortable?"

"I—"

"Yes or no, Percy?"

"Yes."

"I need you to really think about it before you answer this next question."

"Okay."

"Out of all the times we discussed it, did you even once suggest anything other than coming here? Despite my objections, did we ever have a conversation entertaining an alternative to helping Gleeson Crowe build the town of Stonefall? Because I tried, Percy. But you weren't listening. You shut me up. Told me this was what was good for me, even if you never said those words."

"I'm so sorry. I was only trying to keep us safe."

"I know, and you have. It sounds awful out there, and other than right at first, we haven't had to see the aliens. And from the stories, I hope we never do. I know we're safer in here, awful as it is, and I'm willing to survive. Whatever that means. But we can't change, Percy, and right now, we're not telling each other the truth. That I have to act like I believe in this lunatic. It's not—"

"You're right." He squeezed her hand, and for the first time it felt good. "I'm sorry I didn't see his dark side sooner."

"He is a truly evil man."

"I know," he nodded.

"But he's kept us safe, and if it wasn't for New Hope, I'm not sure I'd have the courage to leave." Melinda looked at Percy, hoping he had the answer she wanted. "You still don't think he knows about the place?"

Percy sighed. "He might."

"Do you think he would've told you or asked if you'd heard anything?"

"Unless he's waiting, testing to see if I'm reporting all I know." Percy shook his head. "It's never a straight line with Gleeson."

"Can you find out?"

"I can do my best. But the last thing we want is to draw unnecessary attention. Questions out of the blue are likely to do that."

"Who else has heard about New Hope that you know of?"

"As long as Gleeson keeps the radios out of Stonefall, then everything is secondhand. Kirk and the others could have heard about it the same way I did, from the families we brought with the prisoners. It was a whisper, and only in passing. But it was enough for me to ask Andrew, and he was scared enough to tell me. He said it's all over the radio."

"You're always so sure Gleeson doesn't listen to a radio. Why?"

Percy shrugged. "Hard to say without you thinking I'm drinking the Kool-Aid. But I don't think Gleeson needs the radio, and he doesn't want anyone else to have them. He says it's so the community isn't confused by conflicting sources of information, and that every broadcast could be littered with lies. The only radio he's interested in is broadcasting his sermons."

"But where do you think he's getting his information? Because it's obviously a lot."

"That's the Kool-Aid part. Believe it or not, I still think Gleeson's touched by something. I thought it was light, but now I'm guessing it's dark. Either way, I've seen too many things to doubt something is there."

Melinda didn't ask *what things?* She hated those stories and didn't want to know.

"We need to bring Ophelia with us."

"It's dangerous enough," Percy said. "We can't say anything to anyone, including her."

"We leave Ophelia here and Gleeson takes it out on her. And know I'm right about that, Percy. That man loves to make his examples. We can't just abandon her. At *best*, she'll end up pregnant and in servitude to one of the Brothers."

"Okay," Percy said, not arguing like she expected. "We'll bring Ophelia with us. We can tell her in the morning."

"I promise, she won't say anything."

Percy nodded and stood from the table.

"Where are you going?" Melinda asked.

"To talk with Gleeson."

"Why?"

"Because he'll be expecting me after tonight's performance. He'll know I didn't like it. If I'm not there to talk it out with him, then he's going to think I'm talking it out with someone else."

"You are."

"Exactly. And besides, I want to feel him out about New Hope."

"Be careful," Melinda told him.

"I will be." A kiss on her cheek, then, "You, too."

Chapter Twenty-Nine

EAMON WASN'T ENJOYING his canned breakfast skillet at all.

In the pre-apocalypse days, he would've found it disgusting. But at least it was warm, and he was definitely hungry. Picking at the little he had on his plate served as a distraction, allowing him to pay less visible attention to their guests.

But that didn't mean he wasn't studying them. Eamon couldn't help his suspicions, on his chest like a sweater, itchy and heavy. Clinging to his skin. He wanted to take them off but was trapped in a wooly kind of confusion. Angel and Craig were planning to leave with their daughter, but he couldn't let that happen. Not with their knowing about William. He also didn't want to just take off for this New Hope place without knowing anything more about it, but he and Sherry weren't really seeing eye to eye.

She didn't seem nearly as bothered by Craig as she should be, though Felony was irritated enough for them all. His eyes hadn't moved from the guy. At least Eamon tried to be subtle.

"So, are you coming with us?" Angel asked, the notes in her voice suggesting that this was the final time.

Sherry looked at Eamon and Felony, clearly sensing their uncertainty.

"A lot happened yesterday, and we haven't really had a chance to talk," Eamon said.

"Of course," Angel said.

Craig smirked, though it seemed apropos to nothing, then he stood and held his arms out for their baby — gurgling, giggling, and happy. Not at all like the feverish infant Eamon had seen after finally making it home.

Sherry led them into the kitchen. Eamon was a beat behind her and Felony, falling behind to grab William on his way rather than leaving him out there with people he didn't know, even as happy as he seemed. Once in the kitchen, she shut the door, then turned around and harshly whispered, "What is it with you two?"

Felony said, "I'm not sure we should go with them."

"Why not?" Sherry asked. "Don't you want to know what else is out there?"

"Maybe. But not necessarily with them."

Sherry turned to Eamon. "Do you have a problem with them, too?"

"I'm not sure." Then in an even lower voice than he was already using, Eamon added, "I don't trust Craig."

Sherry sighed. "Fine. I think you're both wrong, but whatever, no New Hope, at least not for now. They can go by themselves. But we should still—"

Eamon shook his head. "They can't leave."

"What?"

"They know about William," Felony explained.

"What does that matter?" Sherry asked.

Eamon looked at her, wishing he didn't have to spell out something so obvious. But Sherry saw the good in people, same as Poppy always had. "Because he's a healer in a world that is dying. People will kill to make him their slave."

"He's right," Felony said.

"Well, we can't keep them prisoners," Sherry whispered.

"Maybe I should go with them," Felony suggested. "If I make it to New Hope and everything seems great, I'll tell the folks making the broadcast to give you a shout-out, then you guys can follow the route and join me. If these people aren't who they say they are, I'll take care of things as I see fit, then come back here. Sound about right?"

"What do you mean *take care of things as you see fit?*" Sherry asked.

"It means that I don't like the way that guy is looking at us," Felony said.

"And how is he looking at us?"

"Like an opportunist standing in the shadows," Eamon answered. "Waiting to grab his chance as it's passing by."

"Isn't that a little dramatic?" Sherry was getting louder. "What do you think he's going to do? Kill you and Felony so he can make me his second wife?"

Felony said, "Murder us for the Cottage and all our supplies."

"Steal William and either use him for his healing powers, or sell him to someone willing to pay whatever it costs to control something like that." Terror flooded his bloodstream as the nightmares fell out of his mouth. Eamon swallowed. "Maybe we shouldn't be talking about any of this in front of him."

They all looked down at William, who appeared to be studying their conversation.

"I love that you're so protective, but I don't think you have anything to worry about. With William knowing what we're talking about, or with Angel and Craig." Sherry laughed, her face softening. "Maybe Felony should go with them and leave us here alone with William until we know better."

"We need to get back out there. I don't want them suspicious if I'm traveling with them, and I've been giving them the stink eye through breakfast."

Felony was right, there would be some bridge building to do. Fortunately, he knew how to pour on the charm when necessary, coming out of the kitchen with a wide smile, a honey-coated voice, and laughter-laced small talk to warm everyone before it was suggested that Felony go ahead with the two of them to New Hope because they couldn't afford to risk taking William on the road.

But then Eamon asked a simple answer and got a complicated response. "What did you do before the invasion?"

Craig looked at him, and even though he could have made anything up, the stranger said, "I don't like to talk about it."

"You don't have to talk about it. I'm just asking what you did. What was your profession?"

"I understood the question, but like I said, I don't want to talk about it."

It was perplexing. Unnecessarily dodgy. Eamon didn't know what to do, but he definitely couldn't just let it go.

"Were you an assassin? A drug dealer? Private chef to the stars and still fiercely protecting their secrets?" Eamon was getting suddenly and perhaps even inexplicably pissed, wanting to know what the guy might be hiding. "I'm not asking for your Dear Diary, just an idea about how you used to spend your days."

"Honey," Angel said, putting her hand on Craig's shoulder.

"You want me to make something up?"

"He doesn't want to talk about it," Angel said.

So Eamon dropped it out loud, but turned it over even more in his head.

"What are you thinking?" Felony asked, the two of them back in the kitchen, apparently the cabin's designated spot for their clandestine affairs.

"I want you to go, but don't kill them."

"Why would I kill them?" Felony asked, acting offended. "I'd never kill a baby. You must think I'm some sort of monster."

"I meant the couple."

"Oh, yeah," Felony smiled. "I'll kill them if they need it. And we both know they probably will."

"No." Eamon shook his head. "They don't deserve it."

"What do you mean *they don't deserve it?* You were just talking about how you didn't trust that guy. We already thought he was dodgy as fuck, now he's talking about being some secret agent and acting like he got PTSD when he probably cleaned windows at the top of some high rise and had to overcome a fear of heights."

Eamon laughed. "You're right. I don't like the guy. But he could have lied and he didn't. That says something."

"Does it say that if I kill them, even if it's the right fucking thing to do and you know it, that Sherry's gonna be pissed at us both, but especially you, since she ain't ever planning to put my black snake moan into her pretty little mouth?"

"Fuck you, Felony."

"You should fuck Sherry."

"Don't kill them. Feel the situation out. If things go bad, then come back here and we'll find somewhere else to go."

"I won't do anything unnecessary, but if things go bad, then that fucker Craig will be the first to go."

"Fair enough," Eamon said.

"Damn right it's fair enough. And just so we're clear, at some point you're going to have to make a difficult decision."

"So you keep telling me."

"I like that you're a good kid, and always appreciated how much it bugged the hell out of your brother and father. But it's a lot less amusing now that I've gotta deal with it all by myself."

"Fuck you twice."

"I'm serious," Felony said. "Eventually your kindness might cost us all our lives."

Chapter Thirty

SHERRY WAS WATCHING William playing with Sophia, laughing as her little boy goaded the baby into a series of giggles and claps. She seemed like a different baby than the one suffering so much just hours before.

"You figure two weeks?" Sherry asked, looking down at the homemade map Craig had laid on the coffee table, comprised of four cocktail napkins. She didn't dare ask where he got it, and didn't want any more of the crazy evasive talk that came whenever anyone asked Craig about his life before Astral Day.

"Looks that way." Craig nodded at the napkins. "But we're all only guessing."

"And everything you've got is from those broadcasts?" Felony asked.

"All of it," Angel confirmed.

"And you're sure about the horses?" Felony pointed to a tiny square with a triangle on top, and a handful of Xs around it.

Craig nodded. "I'm sure."

"Even if you have the right place, how do you know the horses will still be there?" Eamon asked.

"I just have a feeling," Angel answered for him.

Sherry smiled. That was enough for her. Eamon was looking at her like he was wishing it wasn't, but from everything she'd ever heard about Poppy, it would have been enough for her, too.

"Seems to be going around," Felony grumbled.

Then they were pulling the babies apart and three of the seven people were packing what little they had and preparing to go. Eamon made sure that Sherry was genuinely okay, parting with so many cans. She was, of course, and Eamon told himself he'd find a way to replace what was missing, and soon.

Goodbye was harder than Sherry expected, with a weird feeling sitting in her stomach, suddenly and inexplicably certain that she'd never see Angel or Craig or Sophia again. That she'd never see New Hope, and that this was Felony's final goodbye.

"Two weeks," he said, scooping Sherry into his arms and giving her a squeeze. Felony was much gentler with his goodbye to William, then he ushered Eamon away to whisper something in his ear before joining the four of them at the door.

"Maybe you should stay one more night," Sherry suggested. "And get an early start in the morning."

Craig shook his head. "No use wasting half a day and using up more of the food here when we could be getting closer to where we need to go."

Angel left holding Sophia, going first since she would probably have the hardest time leaving last, then Craig followed behind with Felony in the rear.

Sherry shut the door behind them, then turned around and said, "Well, I guess the place is all ours."

"All ours," William repeated to her delight and surprise, despite the shadow of horror on his face.

He sat on the floor and patted the ground beside him.

William toddled over and fell onto his bottom, clapping and smiling, looking up from his father over to what Sherry wanted to believe the little boy was beginning to think of as his mother, if such a concept were possible so young.

She sat, too, then leaned her head on Eamon's shoulder, not really sure if he'd shrug her off or allow her to say. He didn't speak, and Sherry didn't press him, enjoying his silence instead, knowing they had a long couple of weeks and that things would only grow if she let them.

They sat on the floor for a while, but Eamon mostly ignored her, at least in the ways she wished he wouldn't, pretending Sherry wasn't in the same room even when she was and acting like he couldn't feel her brushing by, despite her reaching out and wanting to touch him.

Dinner was quiet, they barely ate, and of course they didn't bother with dessert. Not even for William. Sherry nursed the baby then put him straight to bed.

Eamon didn't want to talk, even though they always did. It was different when Felony wasn't patrolling. He was gone for a while, and maybe for good. This was their house now. They should enjoy it together.

"I'm going to bed," Sherry announced after too long of Eamon not paying attention.

"Okay," he said, sounding too far away.

She went to her room and got undressed, waited naked under a mountain of covers, hoping that Eamon would come into her room and take what she wanted him to. But he didn't, and about an hour after she heard the door to his bedroom closing, cutting the cabin's unearthly quiet — so still that Sherry imagined the whirring of drones just above them — she got out of bed with one of those blankets pulled tightly around her, and scurried out of her room and into Eamon's.

He didn't seem surprised as she slipped into his bed, nor did he push her away.

Eamon was already hard as her hand found his cock, then harder as she tightened her grip and started to stroke it.

"Tell me that feels good," she whispered into his ear.

"It feels good," Eamon admitted.

"Tell me you want me."

"I want you."

"Tell me that right now, you need me more than anything in the world."

Eamon did, just before he rolled Sherry onto her back. Her legs parted on the way, craving his entry.

He slid inside her and started to push, already grunting, fast and hard, falling into a whimper.

He didn't last long, but Sherry didn't want or need him to. Long could come later. Right now, she wanted to feel close — feel the warmth of his body against her skin, his breath like a warm breeze on her neck, and his seed spilling out and running down her leg.

Neither of them spoke. Not that they needed to. Eamon wasn't about to say what he was thinking, but nestled against him, Sherry was sure she knew.

Eamon felt vulnerable. More than at any time since Poppy's death.

Because now he was afraid of losing her, too.

Chapter Thirty-One

PERCY COULD SEE that Gleeson was a mess from the moment he entered his chambers.

His spirits were high, and who knew how many glasses of whiskey he'd already downed. He usually went through the farce of hiding his alcohol. But tonight he had it in plain sight, glass in hand, swirling the amber, both before and after every swallow. Grinning at Percy, he did it again.

He'd been in Gleeson's quarters for more than twenty minutes, but the two of them had so far gotten nowhere. Gleeson seemed stuck in a conversation with someone else. Percy had seen him like this before, plenty of times, though it had never been quite so evident. At times Gleeson was staring right past or even through Percy, laughing at something he never said or responding to a question that hadn't been asked. They hadn't talked about New Hope, even though that was one of the reasons for his being there, nor did they talk about anything of consequence. Only a lot of abstraction that Percy didn't, and maybe couldn't, understand.

Percy tried again. "I thought you might want to talk about tonight."

Gleeson emptied his glass and slammed it onto the nearest counter. "No need to discuss the ugly stuff. It had to happen so we can celebrate."

"And what are we celebrating?" Then to lubricate the situation, Percy added, "Father?"

"I've had a vision." Gleeson was in the midst of what seemed like the rantings and ravings of a lunatic, but Percy had seen this maniac's visions bear fruit a few times before. His skin tingled, and something scratched at his throat. The same thing he always felt when Gleeson was about to say something that would change his life forever.

"Tell me about your vision," Percy said.

"It was about Angel, and how she's going to save us. Any news as to where she might be?"

"No, Father. Not since a few hours ago ... since the last time you asked, just before your sermon."

"Of course," Gleeson said, but then he asked again anyway. "What do you know?"

Percy had no good way to answer that. He didn't know anything, and the subject gave him a stomach ache whenever it came up. How was he supposed to track Gleeson's estranged daughter with aliens patrolling the skies? The Internet was no longer working, the radio couldn't be trusted — Gleeson was right about that — and they didn't have a single lead to follow beyond a few of Angel's social media posts from before Astral Day.

There was also the tidbit Percy had heard from the convoy they encountered a few days ago. They'd apparently spotted Angel, or someone maybe matching her description, but Gleeson wasn't around when that story was told, and Percy found it far too thin for the resources the supposed prophet would likely require.

"Just that she was still in Montana, and traveling with Craig, the father of her baby."

"I know who Craig is." But then Gleeson laughed. "That's enough. Like I said, I had a vision. Angel is a mother."

"Yes. That is what her social media said. She had a baby, a bit before Astral Day."

"No. That isn't the child I'm talking about."

Gleeson mumbled something to the nothing next to him, then said, "It's another child. A weapon in our war against the demons. Do you understand, Percy? This child changes everything."

Now he was back to pacing. "Once we find my Angel, and this very special child, Stonefall will have all she needs to stay safe, no matter how many demons come clawing at our gates."

No point going back and forth when half of their volley was batshit, so Percy simply nodded, wondering what Angel might be thinking now or would be once her estranged father finally got his hands around her.

Maybe she would be happy to see him and willing to bury whatever had been lingering between them since before the apocalypse. Maybe she would be grateful for the high walls and safety. Maybe she would want to raise her baby here, reunited with her father.

But Percy imagined she'd probably want to run screaming, more like Melinda than the brainwashed and faithful. She wouldn't have been there at the building of Stonefall like the most devoted citizens, or inside the prison to see the miracles. Angel had probably only seen her father as the monster he'd always been.

"Tell me about your vision," Percy said. "What have you seen?"

"She's close, brother." Gleeson smiled wider. "And ready to come home."

"What makes you so sure?"

"What makes any of us certain about anything? It's a feeling. But it's been more than two seasons since my instincts have led me wayward, or any of us astray. Would you disagree with me, Percy?"

"No, Father," he bowed, "I would not."

"I dreamed that Angel was in a cabin. Somewhere in the woods. There are others there with her. I had a glimpse of a last name ... Quinn."

"When was this?"

Gleeson didn't like the question, but Percy had to ask. His visions didn't come with timestamps, and even if they were always right, they often arrived out of order.

"Recently," Gleeson said, unsure. "I need you to assemble a team to find her."

"Find her *where*?" He couldn't be serious. "You mean in the forest?"

"All cabins are built on land, and each acre is owned by someone. We have access to every title deed in Montana. Find the cabin, and you'll find Angel. Then you'll bring her home to me, won't you Percy?"

He and Melinda would be gone before Gleeson could reasonably expect any results on such a ludicrous request. So there was no need to argue with him now. "Of course, Father. I'll get started tomorrow.

Then Percy left, without being heard.

But it didn't matter. He was working on his promise already, getting him and Melinda both out of Stonefall.

Chapter Thirty-Two

MAYBE I SHOULDN'T HAVE LEFT.

Eamon kept thinking the same thing, over and over, wondering what the hell he'd been thinking when he left the safety of his family Cottage, abandoning Sherry and William so that he might possibly be able to find more food, when they had already agreed to sit tight and wait for Felony to come back home.

Problem was, Eamon was honest with himself enough to know that even if he tried to block those particular thoughts, their dwindling supplies weren't about to leave his mind. Not only did they not have enough to feed their unexpected guests, they let them leave with Felony, fully stocked for their trip. After taking inventory before the party's departure, it was decided that there was still enough at the cabin if the two of them were careful with their rations.

But the *what ifs* weren't going anywhere, and Eamon kept imagining having to go out and scare up some food once there was nothing left, with him feeling weak and all of them deeper into winter.

He couldn't relax until he left, but Sherry couldn't settle while he was gone — she told him so until her voice started going hoarse, but here he was, hating that he'd left while knowing she was back at the cabin wishing he hadn't.

The only way to make any of this okay was to return victorious, with enough food to keep them fed until Felony sent word on the radio or came back home. Eamon didn't even want to consider the other possibilities.

That was hard, after a half-day spent tromping through the forest to reach the crumbling streets, headed for The Oaks, the neighborhood where he and Felony had been picking at. It had become overrun by bandits and aliens the last time he was there. Felony would be furious with Eamon for going in alone. But he kept getting one foot in front of the other by telling himself he had no other choice.

Eamon was walking for fifteen minutes or so after emerging from the woods by the bright blue water tower, before finding what might be his salvation. A car sitting off to the side of the road. It had been recently driven. It didn't have the caked-dirt-on-crusted-metal look the abandoned vehicles all had. Plus, he and Felony had walked this road plenty, and had never seen that car before.

It was an older model PriusX, and that in itself was a godsend. The thing made less noise than an exhale and barely needed a few drops of gas to get going and stay there. He'd have to manage the guilt of stealing a vehicle that clearly belonged to someone, but …

Up close, Eamon could see why the car was just sitting there on the side of the road. Its driver was asleep behind the wheel, her head lolled to the side.

He wouldn't steal the car, but they could compare notes, and maybe he could get a ride to The Oaks.

Eamon knocked on the window, but the woman kept sleeping.

He rapped his knuckles harder against the glass, shifting from one foot to the other. Eamon was bundled in layers, but it was just above freezing and patience was harder when standing still.

A terrible truth was dawning on Eamon, as he slowly realized what he was seeing. He tried the door and was only half-surprised that the PriusX opened right up.

And sure enough, the driver was dead. It hadn't been long, but the body was already cold and stiff, enough that Eamon wondered why he didn't see it immediately. The wishful thinking, probably.

There weren't any words, and Eamon tried not to feel like a monster as he pulled the woman's body out of the Prius, then rolled it off the side of the road and into the forest before returning to claim her vehicle. He wasn't sure if it would start — maybe a dead car was what made her want to empty the plastic bottle on the floormat — but the engine turned and the dashboard went bright, showing Eamon he had enough fuel to make it to Billings and back without any worry.

Eamon drove, heading to The Oaks as planned but teasing himself with the idea that he might hit Billings. Felony wanted to stay out of the city, but the neighborhood had been emptied by bandits and ravaged by aliens. Eamon found it hard to believe there'd be anything else inside. But it was so much closer. And really, Billings might be even worse. Felony sure seemed to think so.

They had talked about going to Yellowstone. Sherry thought there might be people there. But Eamon wasn't sure there were people anywhere, and Felony even less so. They all liked the idea of plentiful game, but it was hard to argue with the Cottage, comfortable as it was, and hidden away from everyone and everything. Felony also said the park would likely be patrolled if there were still people there, with ex-rangers and the like. People who knew the land better than them. And because it was an obvious spot, the hunting would dwindle faster than the two of them were imagining.

Eamon passed a mile marker for Carson's Neck and felt a chill. He and Felony had heard a tale on the road about a town being built on the bones of the old prison. The place was built to keep the kind of prisoners who knew how to escape, with walls like concrete mountains. The story was first told to them by a woman who had clearly lost her mind. It was simple to dismiss every word out of her mouth, seeing as she drooled through them all.

In between all the mumbling and nonsense, and what for a few scattered minutes sounded like the woman speaking in tongues, she told them about living in Carson's Neck forever, one of only a few hundred, and how the prison was poison from foundation to gate. Toxic inside, from soil to garrets. The aliens hit the prison hard and immediately. Like it was their first stop after Jupiter. They killed every prisoner except for a man they now called the Father of Stonefall, and the two men he decided to save.

They heard similar stories another few times, including on the radio. Even the most fortified place around wouldn't do dick to protect the place from aliens, but neither would a nuclear bomb. It sure as hell hadn't helped Russia. Still, high walls would keep intruders away, and the place had space for crops.

Two miles after the marker, Eamon arrived at The Oaks to find the human convoy was gone. But the aliens weren't. A pair of drones made an X in the sky, each ship cutting an opposite diagonal through the heavens.

He swallowed hard and wanted to turn the Prius

around, but instead he pulled into the neighborhood. He felt drawn, as if something was calling, telling him to stop here instead of heading for Billings. Maybe it was the giant boulders sticking out of the ground. They hadn't been there the last time when Eamon and Felony had been there, but now he could almost feel their warmth.

He drove into The Oaks, turned a corner, and nearly crashed, audibly gasping as he slammed on the brakes.

A hulking mammoth of a man was slowly crossing the street. Humanoid, yet not. Alien, but nothing like the creatures who tore through humans like scissors through paper, throats crackling in sparking bolts of cobalt. He was huge, maybe seven feet, though that might've been Eamon's imagination adding to the majesty. His skin was the color of snow, like white chalk on dark black asphalt, and Eamon didn't see a hair on his body.

Of course he'd heard about titans, but this was the first one he'd ever seen for himself. It either had no idea Eamon was there, which seemed impossible, or didn't care.

He waited for the alien to pass. Its clothes appeared to be part of him, or her — it almost could have been either, despite its size — but Eamon didn't understand how any of that was possible. He passed another three titans before losing his nerve and turning around, heading back toward the exit.

The aliens walked as if in a daze, or deep in observation. Of what, he had no idea. The place was a graveyard. Maybe that was the point. Maybe the titans were somehow reading the emotional echoes people left behind. Maybe one day he'd be torn to pieces by one of these giant alien's demented pets, ripping him to shreds so the big guy could read the dear diary inside his dead brain.

Eamon shuddered, wondering if the old couple was

still alive. Maybe the aliens hadn't spared them like Eamon had.

He pulled out of The Oaks and headed back toward Billings, realizing with another sickening twist that he had no idea where he was going. A general direction, sure, and there would be signs, but he had no GPS or Felony to guide him. He also left early in the morning, promising Sherry he'd be back before dark.

Felony didn't need GPS. He could read a map, same as a trail. He actively encouraged Eamon to learn and ridiculed the pace at which he got through his lessons. It wasn't native to Eamon. Felony explained that it was because his dad was an asshole and had dropped him a lot, but also it was because GPS rotted the mind.

Billings was a straight shot. He followed the signs and arrived to a wasteland.

More of the aliens, hulking white beasts, all looking the same but not then the same again, clothes showing in their skin even though that didn't make any sense.

He drove through the abandoned streets, seeing nothing, until he passed three reptars ripping into a dozen or so humans. One had a screeching woman impaled on the end of its leg, looking like a speared piece of meat, except thrashing. It flung her off of its gleaming limb like a booger. Her head hit the concrete hard enough to grate her scalp to the brain. A purple current rippled across the reptar's shiny black body before it skittered away, oblivious to Eamon.

It all happened so fast. He tried to see nothing and told himself to keep driving.

He had failed. Left Sherry alone all day with William, for nothing.

It was eating him up, wondering what they would do for food, the truth chewing at him, knowing winter was coming and Montana always made them long. Now it was late, and he had to race back with nothing.

The road was icy, and Eamon was afraid of driving too fast. But he wanted to go home. Felony liked to walk in the dark, but Eamon thought it was like inhaling a nightmare. Plus, he'd made that promise to Sherry.

He was almost home, water tower in sight and a sliver of light still in the sky, when Eamon saw someone suffering on the side of the road.

A woman lying in a pool of blood, crying and waving for him to slow down.

Eamon pulled up beside her and practically jumped out of the car, leaving his door open with the engine running.

"Are you okay?" Eamon asked, falling to his knees beside her.

But the woman stood. "I told you he'd come back."

She wasn't talking to him.

A group of kids emerged from the shadows. Five of them. The oldest maybe seventeen and a boy, the youngest a girl a decade behind him. All were armed with either a bat or a spear and wearing garish makeup, painted like whorish warriors.

The youngest girl hurled her spear. She was fast and accurate; it landed deep in his knee.

Eamon fell to the ground wailing, pain like acid eating its way through his body.

"Finish him off," said the woman, "then get your sister's car."

Chapter Thirty-Three

SHERRY WAS GOING out of her goddamned mind.

Eamon still wasn't home, and it was getting harder to pretend there wasn't something terribly wrong.

She begged him not to go, on her knees and everything. Though she didn't get down to plead with him, Sherry was on the floor playing with William at the time, but still staring up into his eyes and trying not to cry while he insisted on leaving her.

"Why do you have to go? Felony just left and told us to stay here!"

But then he went on and on about not having enough food and how it was his job to keep them safe. Eamon was a duty-bound man for sure, but it didn't seem to Sherry that his obligations were always in the right place. He wouldn't promise not to go, but he did give her his word — three times — that he'd be back after dark.

Now her nightly rituals were like déjà vu. The last time she'd felt like this, just last night, visitors came knocking on her door. That seemed like forever ago, now she was back to trembling at every sound and wondering when creatures from outer space might descend from the sky to tear her apart.

"Daddy's gone."

Her heart stopped. Sherry couldn't have heard what she was sure William just said.

"Daddy's gone," he repeated.

William climbed up onto the couch, clapped both palms on the cushions and said it again, this time even more emphatic. "*Daddy's gone.*"

She couldn't believe what their little boy was saying, three times in a row.

Their little boy.

She tried not to feel guilty, but the thought was so loud it was practically screaming.

And why not? Why shouldn't she take ownership of her feelings, of wanting the child?

Sherry knew what it was like to not be wanted, to be the dead skin of another person's life.

"Yes," Sherry finally answered. "Daddy's gone. But he'll be home soon. And then we can go to bed."

"Bedtime."

"Yes. Bedtime." She ruffled his hair and stood. "Wanna help me clean? It takes my mind off of Daddy not being here."

"Cleaning time."

"Right."

He followed Sherry around the cabin as she cleaned things that didn't need to be cleaned, barely keeping her mind from clawing into countless *what ifs* like a clarinet making scales.

Sherry wished she didn't keep thinking about her mother. But the woman was a constant thought, anyway. Cleaning was her solace from the worry, but it came with the yolk of memory — her mom and the misery she dragged into their trailer at the end of every shift while Sherry was always somehow sure that if she could get the place clean enough this time, her mom wouldn't fly into a rage.

But even when the trailer was all picked up, she still had plenty to bitch about. It wasn't Sherry's fault the place was ancient, old even when it was new to them. That's why it was so damned cheap. Mom only had it because she was shacking up with the guy who died inside it. No one claimed the place, so they stayed. Less for rent meant more for booze. But it still reeked, no matter how much elbow Sherry put into cleaning it.

She taught herself to stay in the shallows and managed to do so more often than not. But with all the cleaning and thinking about her mom, in a dark cabin with only three candles burning, and Eamon yet to come home, the worst of her worries were born. Like a dark army marching, relentless and unyielding, taking over, shoving her into remembrance.

Blackout drunk and high on GHB. She shouldn't have any memories of that night, so Sherry was forced to make new ones, waking up hungover and in pain, the video of what had been done to her fresh on her newsfeed.

She recognized a few voices and some of the clothes. But it wasn't enough.

Her mother had spent a lifetime being awful, but it was never worse than the night when she kept calling Sherry a whore, spittle flying and no reprieve, stopping only to try and elevate the exchange with a word like *harlot* or *trollop*. She even used the word *strumpet* once. Sherry had to look it up, and when she did, she became convinced her mom must've done the same thing, just to have more awful things to call her. And that felt like the worst thing of all.

All the yelling, and none of it was because she gave a

shit about Sherry. She was obviously working something out that had nothing and everything to do with her daughter. But she was rarely ever loving, and when she was, it didn't last. There was never any acceptance or guidance. No relationship. No—

"Daddy trouble."

"What did you say?"

"Daddy trouble." William was looking up at Sherry with wide eyes. His expression was still years more knowing than it should have been, or could possibly be, but his gaze wasn't playful like usual. It was adamant and insistent instead. His eyes said *Listen to me*, and Sherry knew she had no other choice.

"How is Daddy in trouble?"

He shook his head, frustrated, reaching for vocabulary that he didn't have. "Bad."

The singular word seemed to take a lot out of him. He wobbled, unsteady on his fat little legs.

"Bad people?" Sherry asked.

William smiled and clapped, suddenly looking very much like a baby.

"Did bad people hurt him?" Sherry felt like she was standing several feet away, watching it all happen, staring at herself having a conversation with a six-month old baby in utter disbelief.

"Yes," he said, emphatic.

Sherry was terrified for Eamon, and their son knew it. He was desperate to help, and her head kept on hurting, throbbing like something was trying to get inside it.

"Where is he? Do you know?"

A long moment passed with William's eyes squinting and his face looking like he was filling his cloth diaper. Then he said, "*Big.*" And following like a giant exhale behind it, "*Blue.*"

Something scratched at her brain. It was almost painful, tugging at the thought without managing to free it, and that knocking at her mind still insistent and screaming.

She looked down at William and somehow the water in his eyes told her the truth — it was him at that mental door, her sweet baby boy wanting to show his mommy the things with pictures he couldn't yet tell her in words.

The realization dragged her black canvas into brilliant color. Suddenly, Sherry saw it all. The big blue water tower that wasn't too far from the Cottage, straight through the forest and onto the highway.

Except, it was dark, and Sherry had never traveled alone. She didn't know what had happened to Eamon, or if she had enough time to help him. Her heart was already pounding, standing paralyzed on her living room floor.

"The water tower …"

"Help," William said.

And there was nothing she wanted to do more.

Sherry wasn't sure she could even reach the water tower, or what she would do once there. It was a few miles through the forest to the highway. She was a strong woman, but that might mean nothing to whatever had brought Eamon down. He was a brutal fighter. Felony delighted in telling stories that embarrassed him but aroused her.

No, Eamon wouldn't have gone down easy.

She couldn't take their baby into a situation like that, or leave William alone in the cabin. Who knows what he might do if left by himself. Maybe they were—

"Help," he repeated.

"I know. I want to help, too. But I don't know how. I can't leave you or take you, and I don't know my way in the dark. But your daddy needs me, and we need him."

Sherry trailed off and started laughing to herself. It was better than crying.

"We can't go," she said. "It isn't safe."

"Knife."

"A lot of good that will do if I'm holding you."

"Walk."

"Can you see in the dark?"

William shook his head. "Light."

"Light?"

He nodded. "*Light.*"

Then Sherry felt suddenly warm — not just her skin, but her bones — and she saw the world through William's eyes. It was for less than a second, because she couldn't take more than that, but it was like seeing hellfire burning in Heaven.

The world for her William was brilliant. A gleaming star inside him, and his glowing star like a compass.

"Go."

"I think you're readier for this adventure than I am," Sherry admitted in a whisper, mostly to herself.

"Ready."

"Okay, then." She went to the kitchen and got the knife.

"Knife." William clapped.

She donned her layers and did the same for William, putting on some socks and shoes that Eamon had picked up on a run a few months ago.

"Clothes," he said.

She grabbed one of their seven flashlights from a box by the door.

"Flashlight."

"You're very good at this." Sherry swallowed as she shut the door behind them, hoping she wasn't making a big mistake and costing both her and William their lives.

"Good."

Sherry walked into the still falling snow, holding a knife at her side, William toddling behind her, as they walked through the woods on the way to save his father. She'd let him walk a bit, then she'd insist on carrying him. While he walked extremely well for his age, he was still small and slow. They needed to find Eamon fast.

Like usual, William seemed to be reading her mind.

"Save," he said.

Chapter Thirty-Four

THERE WERE about a thousand things Percy needed to do in the next couple of days before he and Melinda could get the hell out of Stonefall, trading the place for New Hope and whatever future they could carve for themselves away from the former — and one might argue, present day — prison.

But Percy wasn't getting any of those things done. It was almost comedic, the line of bullshit standing in his way. Religious arbitration was becoming an ever-increasing part of his job. Since Percy was a CO in Stonefall, the job had fallen to him. He didn't want to be judge or jury, even if executions were left to someone else, but Percy wasn't given a choice. He was forced to involve himself in matters that didn't concern him — petty disputes between women Melinda was always bitching about, marital affairs, and the frequency with which women in Stonefall were heeding their marital duties.

Percy would love to put a *Gone Fishing* sign in his window, but Gleeson was a naturally suspicious man and these days always on edge. Firsthand, secondhand, third-hand — it didn't matter. If Gleeson caught a whiff of his indifference, the vice would tighten and Percy would be stuck, unable to ferret Melinda away.

So he cleared the decks of every complaint or concern coming his way or catching his attention, keeping busy but intentionally overlooking Gleeson's ridiculous directive to locate his daughter almost entirely. It stayed in the back of his mind as something he couldn't afford to forget, but kept on a back burner like water left to boil.

Until Kirk reminded him.

"Hey, boy," he said, catching Percy on his way home, going to check-in with Melinda since he'd been out all morning and had yet to finish even one of the things she'd asked him to do. "Father wants to know how the search for Angel is coming."

"I guess as well as can be expected, considering how little we have to go on."

"Father had a vision." Kirk was standing in the way, holding his body so Percy couldn't pass without engaging him first. "He says we're supposed to start there."

"I'm afraid his vision wasn't very specific." Percy gave Kirk a knowing smile, hoping that might be enough.

It wasn't, of course.

"Father had a feeling you might see things that way, so he asked me to organize a search party and make sure you came along with us."

"Okay." Percy went cold but tried not to show it. "When are we leaving?"

"We've been waiting for you. We can head out of here as soon as we have your maps."

"Of course. I'll go get them, then say my goodbyes and grab my bag at home." Then, like it was no big deal, Percy added, "How long do you expect we'll be gone? Melinda will want to know."

"Of course," Kirk nodded. A day or two. Three at most."

"Where should I meet you?"

"We'll be waiting at the gates. Take your time."

But he could hear it in the Nazi's voice — Kirk only meant the first part.

Percy didn't want to go. Leaving Stonefall with Kirk seemed like the worst possible idea. Knowing he didn't have a choice, and that Melinda was in mortal danger the second he stepped out of line, he returned a friendly smile to his face.

"I'll be there, soon as I can." Percy gave Kirk a nod then walked to his quarters without so much as a glance behind him.

Melinda looked up from the kitchen counter where she was mincing some sort of dried root. She didn't seem happy to see him. "You have to do what?"

"I'm sorry. There's no way out of it. Gleeson got one of his visions, so suddenly nothing else is more important."

"So even if I can have all of our food, you're not going to be ready to go?"

"No," Percy shook his head. "I promise we'll go, soon as I get back. In a couple of days. I'll figure it out, just do your best to stay invisible until then. Don't do anything that will make Gleeson wonder or look your way. Don't do anything to invite attention from any of the Brothers. Be agreeable with—"

"I'll be a good little girl, Percy. Now tell me how that's supposed to keep *you* safe!"

"I'm not worried about myself. I've been out there plenty."

Melinda narrowed her eyes, shaking her head and looking upset. "Is Kirk going with you?"

"Yes," Percy said, wishing he could lie. "He put the crew together."

"And that doesn't make you worry?"

"Why would that make me worry? Unless Gleeson knows what we're planning to do, we're protected. Kirk can't touch me, no matter what he thinks about the color of my skin or anything else."

"Do you think Gleeson knows? Maybe had one of his *visions?*" Melinda asked, making the little leap from upset to scared.

Percy shook his head. "I don't think he has any idea. He's focused on finding his daughter, and right now I don't think he cares about anything else."

They stopped talking, staring into each other's eyes, both more frightened than they wanted or were willing to admit.

"Be careful, Galahad."

"I will be."

Percy left their small kitchen to find Ophelia sitting in the living room, looking at him with curious eyes and a tiny open mouth, as if pregnant with something vital to say. But nothing came out. He wondered what she might've heard. They had been talking in low voices like always, but he didn't know that Ophelia was there, and despite their agreeing that they'd take the girl, and tell her the plan, they hadn't. And now probably wasn't the time.

"Is everything okay?" Ophelia finally managed.

Percy could see the fear in her eyes, so he smiled. "Of course. Everything is fine."

The lie forced him to confront the truth. To consider the stakes and wonder what Gleeson would do to punish them if he found out. They weren't friends, not exactly, and the Father of Stonefall couldn't just let Percy and his woman leave without the community seeing it as some sort of betrayal. People were sent out, they didn't ask to go. Especially not his second in command.

But Percy could no longer pretend Gleeson wasn't batshit. Not to Melinda or to himself.

"What were the two of you talking about in there?"

It was such a direct question, Percy wasn't sure how to answer. Maybe he should call Melinda into the living room. But then, he didn't want to make a big deal out of it. Really, he wanted this to go away so he could get away. But Percy could hear Melinda in his head, telling him to trust the girl. Bring Ophelia to their side and prepare her for their flight.

She and Melinda would be alone for a couple of days until he returned. Percy supposed there wasn't any reason he couldn't get the conversation started now. It might even make Melinda happy to know he'd taken the initiative.

Percy remembered all the times his parents had lied to him, even when he could clearly hear what they were talking about. He knew how much that eroded his trust. So he told her a version of the truth. "We were talking about leaving Stonefall."

She didn't look completely surprised, making him wonder if she'd overheard them talking. She did, however, look thoroughly afraid. "You and Melinda?"

"All of us. We want you to come."

"But why would we want to leave? Don't we already have everything we need here?"

"There are a few reasons, and you can talk about them with Melinda while I'm away."

"Where are you going?"

"Out on the road. I'll be gone for a couple of days, three at the most. We'll leave Stonefall as soon as I get back."

"Okay." She sounded defeated and didn't look like she wanted to leave in the least.

Percy gave her a hug, which he'd never done before, then promised that everything would be fine. Two or three days would fly by, then he would take care of them, ushering them away to someplace safe. It sounded a bit like a fairy tale as he said it, but Percy didn't know what else to do and wished he hadn't been caught by Ophelia on his way out.

He went to his office, a makeshift space next to Gleeson's, rather than the actual prison offices that had been torn down in the rebuild, and took the few assets that might help him on this quest. Maps, property records, and some things he didn't necessarily believe would help but would be nice to have handy in case Gleeson requested a status report. He gathered the assorted papers and folders and stuffed them into a bag, his heart beating with an odd sense of finality, as though he was standing in this office for the final time.

Percy was six steps outside when he turned back and decided to check in with Gleeson. It was terrifying, thinking he might be onto them, but the only way to appease the part his brain wouldn't stop ruminating on was to look the giant in his unblinking eyes and see for himself.

He knocked once.

"Come in!" He sounded almost jovial.

Percy opened the door, stepped inside, then walked directly to Gleeson. He had his back to Percy and was studying a map of Yellowstone, his gaze on The Reserve.

"I just wanted to say goodbye before leaving."

Gleeson turned from the map to Percy, smiling. "And when I see you next, my Angel will be in your company."

Percy nodded. "That's what we're hoping."

Gleeson straightened his body, his face losing some of

its humor. "Faith isn't always easy, brother, but it is necessary for all we are doing."

"Of course. And I don't doubt our success."

"We are fortunate to have Heaven's Light shining inside our hearts. Do you feel Him, Percy?"

"Yes, of course." Still not blinking.

"Good." Gleeson clapped Percy on the shoulder, turned back to his map, and finished with his back turned to the door. "If you fail to see the favor God has given us, then He will no longer bless us with abundance."

"Faith is the first step, even when you can't see the staircase." Percy bowed even though Gleeson couldn't see him. The man always seemed to feel plenty.

He approached the waiting truck with his two packs, one in his hand and the other over his shoulder.

"You ready?" Kirk was standing outside of the truck instead of sitting inside it like everyone else.

Percy was raw more than ready, but even tenderized by life and abraded by a creeping panic within an ever-darkening hope, he was unwilling to let himself wither into something less than what he was.

"Dead or alive," he answered, then got in the truck and left it at that.

Chapter Thirty-Five

HOLDING William and protecting his body meant Sherry's face was getting scratched up pretty badly as they passed through thick branches.

She stopped walking and put a hand to her cheek, then shined the flashlight to see how much blood was coating her fingers. Seeing the dark red against her white flesh under such a wicked beam of light made her cheek hurt a lot more than it would probably have otherwise.

"Okay?" he said, the scars of light on his cheek brighter as if responding to the darkness.

"Yeah, sweetie, I'm okay. Let's keep walking."

It wasn't easy to keep from panicking, since Sherry was living right on the edge of utter hysteria, certain she was insane for tromping through the forest clutching a kitchen knife while holding the infant.

Her infant.

Maybe that's where all the crazy was coming from. If she wasn't nuts enough to think the baby belonged to her, then she probably wouldn't also think Sweet William was walking and talking at only six months. His single word answers might as well have been monologues with all the thought behind them, his knowing eyes dilating whenever he squeezed out the words.

They were going as fast as they could, but it wasn't enough. Her heart kept beating harder and harder, both because Sherry could feel how much they were running out of time, but also thanks to the overwhelming sense that something was after her. Hunting William. And she couldn't tell if it was before or behind them.

Her back was killing her. She wasn't sure how long she could keep carrying William. And while she'd put him down to walk a few times, it was very slow going. His little legs couldn't keep up.

Maybe they should stop. Turn around. Cut their losses and get back to the Cottage. This mission was clearly crazy, feeding delusion and putting her son in harm's way. It was time to shelve this absurdity, head back while they still could. They'd been walking for more than an hour.

But then William put his hands on her face and a warmth spread over her cuts.

"Heal!" he said.

Sherry felt the scratches. Blood was still there, but the cuts were smooth, if not healed completely.

They kept walking. Finally, they broke through the forest and stepped onto the road, right where she expected the water tower to be, thanks to the uncanny compass waddling next to her leg.

She saw Eamon immediately. Spilled on the ground like liquid from a kicked over bucket. Obviously dying.

They ran across the street in a second. Sherry dropped to her knees. Touched his face and stroked his cheek. Dripped tears as though that would help anything.

She set William down in front of his father, wondering what to do. They never *had* him heal anyone. They didn't know how to do that. It always just happened. But it wasn't happening now. Instead, the baby was staring down at his father, confused.

Eamon's face was ashen. She'd never seen someone looking so close to dead yet still alive.

"Baby, can you heal him?" she asked William, tears running down her cheeks.

It was bad. Maybe too bad. Their son probably didn't know where to start. Or maybe if he could.

What if William couldn't heal him?

What if Sherry had made it all the way out here just to watch Eamon die? And give his son a front row seat to the show?

A baby who was walking and talking — and healing — at six months would probably never forget what he saw.

Eamon stirred, a twitch of his body and a groan that sounded like it was born somewhere murky and shallow.

William put a palm on his father and winced. His hand glowed bright, surrounded in radiant white light, and his baby face twisted like he was tasting a sour apple. He was losing color fast. Knees without kneecaps were starting to wobble.

He shouldn't continue … this could very well be killing them both.

Sherry put out a tentative hand toward her son, maybe to stop him. But William looked up at her and shook his head twice before returning attention to Eamon, moving his small hands in tiny circles across his father's body, a Lilliputian rumble humming steadily from his throat.

She was watching a miracle in real time. Eamon was healing. His pallor had warmed, his frame had straightened. He seemed stronger already. Less withered, like the water was back in his body.

But William looked terrible, the tax for healing Eamon too high.

Sherry reached out again, and again he looked up while shaking his head.

He was almost finished. Soon they could rest.

But the light changed as shadows appeared from nowhere. The three of them were suddenly surrounded by eight figures. It took Sherry three heartbeats to count them. It looked like a mom and her very dangerous children. They held bats and spears. The smallest among them was only a child — a little girl who looked like she might be in first grade if the world wasn't already over.

The first grader raised her spear in the air and said, "See, I told you!"

Sherry followed her gaze to William. Only then did she realize just how much her boy was glowing — his entire being.

"Fight," William said, without looking up, his eyes and efforts stayed with his father.

She wondered where he heard the word and again marveled at her boy. So did the family preparing to attack them.

The mom yelled, "Get that child!"

And the young warriors fanned out around her.

Sherry caught a flash, maybe from William though it could've been from somewhere else, showing her what might have been a visual echo of something from before — the girl surprising Eamon by chucking her spear into his knee before he could think or react or do a goddamned thing about it.

Imagination or not, Sherry managed to duck the spear being hurled at her. Then the little girl snarled and charged.

But it wasn't like Sherry was going to carve up a kid,

even if she just tried to jab her, so she kicked the girl in her face and sent her to the ground.

She dodged another long swipe from a spear, held by a girl a couple of years younger than she was, but then her older brother brought his bat down onto Sherry's shin, swinging it more like a stick to a puck than a bat to a ball.

William's glow was fading. But Sherry wasn't sure what that meant, and the blows were already raining.

Something punctured her in the side, and that was probably it.

They were outnumbered and overwhelmed. Sherry didn't have the guts to use her knife like she should have.

But she couldn't just lie down and let this happen.

Sherry rolled over and away from the blows. She leapt to her feet and staggered back, swiping her knife in wild arcs to keep the children at bay. It was cruel, making her fight people so much younger than her. She would have been fine driving the knife right into their mother's face, but the woman stood behind them all, goading the kids like a coward, unwilling to face the danger herself.

Sherry stood between her family and the psychos. She would open the first one who got close enough to allow it. Make sure that—

The little girl pulled her trick again, but this time it worked. The spear hit Sherry in the thigh and she went down like a kettle screaming for tea.

Then they were on her, all of them now laughing, their monster of a mother the loudest.

This was it. The end for all of them. Sherry had tried, but there were too many and she wasn't enough.

She hated to die like this, failing two babies, the one in the womb and the one she'd loved with everything inside her for the best six months of her life, even full of loneliness and sorrow as they were.

Now that time was over, and her approaching death had put a gleam in her attacker's eyes.

But then something whistled through the air and struck the oldest boy in his shoulder.

He fell back, gasping. Crying out. Reaching up for the thing now jutting out of his body.

"There's more where that came from."

There was an old man holding a crossbow, aimed loosely at the family, another bolt already loaded.

The eldest child regained his composure. "Go ahead. You'll get one shot before we finish you off."

The man shrugged. "Seems about right. I'm old enough. Hell, I've already lived long enough to see an alien invasion. If it's my time to go, it's my time to go. But I'd like to leave this Earth better off before I go, and you're all scars on this planet, so I'll be taking the youngest one with me, at least."

He aimed his crossbow right at the little girl while his dog continued to growl.

"Fuck off," said one of the middle kids.

The old man smiled, drawing a shotgun from a holster on his back. "Stay or go, it's up to you. But decide to stick around and it'll be alien city. I will pull this trigger, and that will be the end of everyone here."

The mother finally spoke. "Why would you do that?"

"Because if you don't back off, these folks are dead anyway. And you all deserve to die. So why not take the grace of my letting you live by turning around and getting the hell out of here while you still have the chance?"

Sherry wondered if the old man had a death wish.

Or did he really want to save them?

But maybe it was something worse … did he want the same thing as the mother and her kids? Was William a magnet who had drawn him to this spot, same as it had drawn them?

The mother and the man stared at one another long enough for neither one to truly lose face, then she blew a gust of air through her nose and said, "Come on, then. Let's go. There's nothing more for us here."

They made it a handful of steps up the road before the woman turned back around to find a crossbow still aimed at her skull.

"I hope we meet again," she said, falling back and letting her children take the lead.

Then the moment broke, and Sherry could finally collect her breath.

Eamon was sitting up, holding a shriveled William in his arms.

"He'll be okay. He's already getting better, just—" Sherry was trying to talk but started hacking instead. A wad of blood flew from her mouth. More began to drip from her lips. "I'm sorry." She started to cry, everything she'd been holding in now pouring right out of her.

Everything was dizzy, her world already fading away.

"It'll be okay," Eamon said, though there was no way to promise. He looked up at the old man as if seeing him for the first time. Then he looked at William, surely knowing his son was too faded to save her. "What do we do?"

"We take her home," the old man said.

Chapter Thirty-Six

THE LAST HOUR felt like a dream.

Pulling over to the side of the road, getting attacked by the damsel in distress, going down, then slowly bleeding to death as his brain and body filled with memories and emotions, only some of which were rightfully his. Eamon couldn't be sure he wasn't dreaming the whole thing, but he felt certain that there had been a drone hovering above his body for a while now. Odd since they usually whistled by faster than he could really see them.

This one swayed in the sky, pulsing. Almost felt to Eamon like it was keeping him warm until help arrived.

And help came — the woman he was afraid to love and their miracle of a child.

Eamon flinched at the stab of pain as he thought of Poppy.

Then his thoughts turned to the present. Sherry had somehow left the safety of their cabin and come through the woods with William to find him. His son had performed yet another impossible feat of healing. Even after all that, the three of them would still be dead if it wasn't for this old man, somehow familiar yet no one Eamon knew.

He was finally back to steady breaths, and William was quickly recovering, but Sherry was coughing blood and could very well die.

It was a short walk to the old man's vehicle, just past the bend in the road.

"This is yours?" Eamon asked, trying to figure out exactly what he was looking at. It didn't look like anything you could buy off a lot. Sturdy, but it appeared almost homemade. "What kind of car is this? Some sort of Jeep?"

"I call her Olive. Can't see it in the dark, but that's her color. Uglier than you're probably imagining."

The man loaded them into Olive, Eamon in the back with William. Once they were driving, he introduced himself as Jefferson then tried to take their minds off the dying woman in the passenger seat by talking more about his almost car on their way to wherever they were going.

"I printed her myself. Cheaper this way, and who needs navigation or auto-drive? I was driving long before they had any of that, and the world was smarter when we all had to think a little harder. The body panels were printed in carbon-fiber-reinforced plastic on a decade old printer. I did it all, from designing Olive to giving her that pretty resin coat to programming her to only start for the code I gave her. Prevents anyone from taking her."

"How fast does she go?" Eamon asked, rubbing Sherry's arm while trying not to think of her dying.

"Thirty-five miles an hour, but I don't ever need to go faster than that. I've a feeling the speed of light wouldn't be enough to outrun them." Jefferson glanced at the sky.

Eamon kept turning it over in his mind, the places where he might have seen the old man before. There weren't many choices. He'd never been this far out before

Astral Day, and most encounters since then had been a daze of conversation. It was probably nothing. Maybe he looked like someone that Eamon and Felony had talked to, or a body he'd had to step across without vomiting. But then Eamon finally got tired of asking.

"Do I seem familiar to you? Have we met?"

Jefferson laughed, though it stayed in the shallows with a dying angel beside him. "We have."

"Where?" The certainty didn't surprise him, but the mystery did.

"That hurts … you not remembering me." But there was no pain in his voice.

Eamon thought, but it went nowhere.

"Want a hint?"

"Yes, please," Eamon said, feeling like a child.

"Last time we met, you were convincing your partner not to kill me and my wife and take us for all we had."

"Oh," Eamon said, the truth dawning. His driver was one half of the old couple from The Oaks he couldn't bring himself to rob, or allow Felony to.

"You made the right choice," Jefferson said.

"I can see that now." Eamon laughed, low and uncomfortable, realizing he and Felony had probably been spared, rather than it being the other way around. "Why did you let us go?"

"Jolie wasn't about to let me kill two people who were scrounging for food."

"Even though one of us wanted to kill you?"

"I'm with you. I would have gladly shot you both then thrown your bodies out the window. But I don't argue with Jolie, seeing as she always wins."

"Kill." William giggled. It was the first word he'd spoken since healing Eamon, and he seemed to know that the devil lived in the syllable.

Jefferson looked into the rearview, his surprised eyes settling on William.

Sherry groaned in her seat.

"Where are we going?" Eamon asked.

"Home. Like I said. And now you know where that is … seeing as you tried to rob it."

"How did you know where we were? Or how to find us?"

"I was out for a walk and came across the three of you getting beat to shit in the middle of the road."

"Seriously?" Eamon said in disbelief. "You just *happened* to be out walking?"

"Of course not," Jefferson shook his head. Even without seeing the old man's face, Eamon could feel his disappointment. "Please tell me I didn't rescue an idiot."

Eamon was still leaning forward between the two front seats with one hand around William, sitting in his lap, and the other on Sherry. "Maybe so, but it isn't her. So thank you for finding us."

He wasn't going to push it and figured he'd have to be content with the mystery, but Jefferson answered, anyway.

"I was making the final rounds, not that there's much to protect. The Oaks has been emptied and the aliens have it under some sort of surveillance, so humans have been staying away. Jolie and I have plenty ourselves and can stay in our place for a long while it seems, so that's what we're planning to do. But something wasn't sitting right. There are some rocks out in front of The Oaks. They weren't there a couple of days ago but now they are, and I swear they're responsible for some of the things I've been seeing."

"What have you been seeing?"

"Things like tonight when I'm getting ready for bed, taking one last circle outside the house. It felt like my mind was bleeding. I had to close my eyes to kill the pain, then I saw you getting attacked. I opened them up again to see the moon telling me exactly where to go. I went in and told Jolie I had to go. She wasn't too happy to hear it but also not all that surprised, knowing me and the way the world had been turning out. I explained it was the young man who thought to spare our lives. She said it sounded like karma trying to have a one-on-one conversation and I couldn't afford not to go. So here we are."

And there they were. Not five minutes later they were pulling into The Oaks, passing four hulking aliens before pulling into Jefferson's garage. Sherry looked almost transparent, making the blood soaking her seat even darker than the night already made it.

She must have been reading his expression. "You don't think I'm going to make it."

"I do," Eamon lied.

William said, "Survive."

The word lit something inside him. Sherry, too, it seemed. Hope brightened her eyes, gave her the strength to let Eamon take her into his arms and out of the car.

He would have told William he'd be right back, but the baby was already out of the car and toddling toward the house, looking like he'd grown an inch in the car ride.

Jefferson had him lay her on the couch, clearly not concerned with a stained sofa when the planet itself was tainted, and looked at William in expectation and awe. He'd spent an entire drive behind the wheel without asking about the miracle he'd witnessed, but he'd seen it all the same and now stood back to see it again.

But nothing happened. Eamon was hoping his son only needed some time to recharge, and that a drive from the water tower to The Oaks might do the trick, but it didn't.

There was no light around William, and his features were waxen. He looked sick and in pain.

"Are you okay?" Eamon asked.

"Help," William said, hands on his mother.

Sherry whimpered. "It's okay if I die … don't hurt him to save me."

William coughed.

"Maybe that Sophia made him sick," Eamon caught himself wondering out loud.

"Who's Sophia?" Jefferson asked.

"A baby. She had a fever, and he healed her. But maybe she passed it on. Or, I don't know …" Eamon shook his head. "Maybe he's just empty after spending all of his energy on me."

Jefferson looked right into Eamon's eyes. "Mind if I ask you something and expect an honest answer?"

"Of course," Eamon said.

He looked down at the baby and then over to Sherry. His voice fell to an apologetic whisper. "That baby one of them?"

Eamon laughed, suddenly seeing things from Jefferson's perspective. "No. But he was born right underneath one of the ships on Astral Day. In the forest, not all that far from here. I think it made him special."

"Obviously." Jefferson wiped his sweaty brow then yelled, "It's okay, Jolie. You can come out now."

The old woman Eamon had seen — and probably imagined — cowering with her husband upstairs was suddenly in the living room. "I was a nurse for twenty-three years," she said. "I'll do everything I can to save your friend."

Chapter Thirty-Seven

IT WAS NEVER easy being around Kirk, but it was even worse trying to get the guy to talk when he didn't want to, which was pretty much all the time unless there was a chance to be homophobic, racist, misogynist, or in any other way loudly offensive, though he never pulled that shit anywhere near Gleeson, of course.

He was the kind of racist who delighted in his ignorance. Kirk couldn't blame it on bad parenting, an erosion of culture, or anything else. Even if those other things were true, Kirk was racist because the man was a monster. He hated because it was fun. He was sadistic, and deserved to die with all of the other inmates at Stonefall.

"I have the maps," Percy said, finally breaking the silence. "Do you want to pull over and look at them?"

They had been driving for a while, flying by a whole lot of nothing. With winter just a sneeze away, the world was looking like death on its way to a wedding. Kirk didn't like to be told anything and always wanted to see everything for himself. So if they were to discuss any coordinates, they'd need to pull over soon. Percy didn't want to be standing outside in the icy air with Kirk, but anything was better than the misery circulating inside the cabin among the three of them. Even a brief reprieve from the tension would be welcome.

From the passenger seat. Kirk said, "We won't be needing your maps."

Beckett was driving, the two of them making Percy feel almost like a prisoner, sitting in the back by himself with neither of the assholes in front willing to turn around.

His gun at his side begged him to use it, to kill them both. But he knew the danger of using a gun, even in a truck, the aliens might hear the shot go off. He also had a knife, but he doubted he could kill both of them before one of them used one of their guns, even if it meant the aliens would kill them all. Psychopaths didn't care if they ended the world with them.

"But you asked me to get them," Percy said.

"That's because I wanted to see if you would fetch like a good boy." Then he laughed.

"Why don't you need them? Do you know where we're going?"

Kirk nodded at Beckett. "Our directions are pretty specific."

Percy realized that he was no longer in control. Or second in command. "How long until we get there?"

"Oh, not long," Kirk said, and Percy imagined his smile.

They were barreling down the frozen highway. Even if he was brave enough to open the door and roll out onto the road, and even if Percy could survive the fall, he wouldn't last long. The truck would flip a bitch and come back. Kirk would climb out of the cabin, put a bullet in Percy's face both before and after calling him a nigger, then get back in the truck, grateful for both his excuse and the witness.

There was nothing Percy could do but put his faith in God.

Percy waited about fifteen minutes, then broke the silence again. "What about Angel?"

"What about her?" Kirk finally turned to look at Percy in the backseat. "You want to know if she's hot?"

"No. Of course not." He'd seen a picture and knew exactly how good-looking Gleeson's daughter was, but that was still the last thing on his mind. "I'm asking if you really think that we're going to find her."

Kirk laughed again, his back to Percy. "What do you think?"

"Montana is big. Plenty of places to hide. Maybe it seems like a stretch."

"Gleeson said you had it narrowed it down."

"I did, enough for a decent size task force, given a month and zero movement from the fugitive."

"So now she's a fugitive?" Kirk said.

"She's a wanted woman, isn't she?" Percy argued. "That makes her a fugitive, especially when there isn't any law."

"Oh, I wouldn't say that. There's plenty of law these days."

Beckett started laughing before Kirk finished his sentence.

"You said we didn't need maps or coordinates. So, you wanna tell me what you know that I don't?"

"Are you going to whine the entire time until I tell you?" Kirk was still turned, staring at Percy, trying to make him shrink into the seat like a magic trick, using only his eyes.

"I just might," Percy said.

Kirk turned back so he was facing front. He slapped the dashboard and pointed out the window. "That looks like a good spot. Pull over there."

Percy followed his finger, but he had no idea what Kirk was pointing at. There was only a barren stretch of nothing looming ahead, save for a pickup truck with a bunch of wood in the back of it.

Beckett pulled over, killed the engine, then opened his door. Kirk followed a beat behind, but looking almost rushed, like the two of them were late for some sort of secret rendezvous.

Percy wouldn't have gotten out of the truck if given a choice, but there was a loud rapping at the window, and he looked over to see Kirk grinning wide while banging his gun against the glass. So he opened the door then dropped into the snow. Kirk and Beckett were both armed, Kirk aiming his gun at him, and Beckett a baseball bat riddled with spikes.

"Gimme your gun and knife," Kirk demanded, putting the gun to Percy's head.

Percy let out a defeated sigh. "Why?"

"Do it. Or things will get ugly for you and Melinda."

Percy gritted his teeth as he handed over his weapons.

"Any idea why we're out here?" Kirk asked.

"I'm assuming it has something to do with you being a psychopath."

He expected Kirk to start laughing again, giving Percy one of his over the top guffaws then telling him how funny he was for a nigger. But instead he looked solemn and spoke in a speechifying voice.

"You're a nigger, right Percy?"

He said nothing, not knowing how to answer that.

"Well, of course you are," Kirk continued as Beckett quietly chuckled beside him. "So, seeing as you're a nigger and everything, you probably know the history of cross burning. Is that a safe assumption?"

"I know things." Percy eyed Beckett and his idly swinging bat.

"I'm sure you got it wrong, thinking it was the Klan, but people were burning crosses back in the Middle Ages, and for all the right reasons. Back in Scotland, it was a declaration of war. Here in America, crosses were used to mobilize militia. Did you know that?"

Kirk gave Percy a second to answer, then went on talking. "Most niggers don't. Because they think burning crosses is all about them." He turned to Beckett. "You got this one by yourself while I keep talking to our friend, or you gonna need help?"

Beckett looked like he was freezing and would love some extra hands for whatever evil Kirk was enlisting him to do. But he knew his role and played it as cast.

"I'm on it."

That stuff about talking to their friend must've all been for show, because Kirk didn't say another word while he and Percy stood watching Beckett construct a wooden cross from the rough wooden planks in the back of the pickup truck.

"I'll need you to put that thing upside down," Kirk said, for Percy's benefit.

Beckett knew exactly which way the cross went. He'd clearly done this before.

So Kirk was behind The Forsaken, the supposed group of bandits erecting these upside down crosses and filling them with bodies. He wondered if Gleeson knew, then decided that no, the man was a despot and a brute, maybe even a sham and a charlatan like Melinda had insisted from the first second she saw him, but this felt nothing like him. He saw this as the devil's work and would want to stop it. Percy still had a chance at escape.

A man like Kirk was surely driven by greed. Percy might be able to reason with him, though the odds were against him, and he didn't want to die giving Lucifer the satisfaction of his sniveling pleas.

It was bold, coming out here with just the two of them. Even with both men armed, Percy had a reasonable chance of taking one or both down. He was fast, and even if they were faster, fighting was still better than waiting to die.

But the show was over. Kirk drew a gun from his waistband and showed it to Percy, smiling. Its silencer made all the difference. Proved that Kirk was holding Kings when his enemy had only twos.

"You don't have to do this, Kirk!" Percy cried out, more hysterical than he wanted to sound.

"You need to calm the fuck down," Kirk said. "Don't you see that Stonefall needed an outside threat to keep its citizens in line? People were getting restless, but once they had something to rally around, the community came together. You saw it for yourself."

Percy shook his head. "Gleeson will never allow this."

Beckett laughed.

And Kirk said, "Gleeson will never know."

"This is sick." The words caught in Percy's throat.

"Probably." Kirk shrugged, but was smiling. The monster might as well have been licking his lips.

"I'd like to take credit," Kirk laughed, "But I've had plenty of help. Some people say the aliens came out of nowhere to change the way we think. But that's not true. See, I think they're more like liquor, or too much money, showing us who we really all are. So Gleeson's a little crazier, and all the people who are afraid will pretend all the wrong things are right if it means having a roof over their head. Same for all the Uncle Toms and their whore wives."

Beckett must have seen Percy flinch toward Kirk because his bat came whistling down into Percy's leg, just above his ankle. Beckett yanked the bat back out of his flesh as Percy screamed.

"Quiet," Kirk said. "You'll wake the neighbors."

Percy wanted to double over, fall into the snow and clutch his leg, but instead he stood, denying his tormenters the satisfaction. Kirk looked down at him, actually did lick his lips that time before he continued.

"Sometimes the Lord really does provide, Percy. Especially when you need it most."

The psychopath stood there, smiling at him.

"Everything can serve a purpose, you know. Even niggers. You'll see, because you're gonna serve a purpose too."

Kirk wanted him to ask what that was supposed to mean, but Percy wouldn't give him the satisfaction.

So after another several seconds of silence, the butt of Kirk's gun came down on the back of his head, and Percy saw only darkness.

Chapter Thirty-Eight

Felony had been on the road with Angel, Craig, and their giggling little girl, Sophia, for half a day, a harrowing night in an abandoned warehouse, and well into the following morning. The mood was surprisingly buoyant, considering their lack of decent sleep and the fact that the baby had been on death's door just two days before. The day was a bust, after the horses they were so sure would be there turned out to be gone, with only three bags of feed left behind by whoever had taken them.

The night was better, after having found the perfect place to spend the night — a storage shed outside of an old diner that had already been stripped of food but still had a surprising number of chairs. There were more in the shed than there were in the diner, and in such a motley selection. All the different sizes and shapes prevented them from being stacked, so they littered the floor.

Felony, like the rest of the group, was grateful to be indoors, but every noise seemed amplified inside that shed. Maybe it was the aluminum roof sending violent echoes through the building's thin walls — far too insubstantial for

Montana winters, assuming the shed was designed to house someone rather than storing unused or unwanted objects, which it absolutely was not.

They were scared of bandits, but the night was filled with the more horrifying sounds of alien ships whistling through the sky, short and high-pitched, way too close.

They were all too frightened to go outside and look up to the heavens so they could see for themselves, including Felony, who was used to patrolling the dark. The night was twice as long, with open eyes and pounding hearts, but the ships stopped whistling just before first light, then the group loaded up and left the many chairs behind.

But there was good news. Early on the second day they began to see signs for New Hope, and the place was much closer than any of them had thought, maybe by as much as three days. Not having the horses mattered a lot less after they managed to hitch a ride with a middle-aged couple in a restored VW bus. The man drove while the woman held a taser on the four of them, including Sophia, as if the baby might launch an attack. They traded a hundred miles for ten cans of food — the old couple wanted twenty — then were dropped off the second the odometer rolled over on that final mile, despite them still all heading in the same direction.

"We're heavier and using more gas with all of you," the man explained.

"You got more than you paid for," said the woman, waving her taser and obviously still bitter about Felony's bargaining being harder than sheetrock.

The couple never shared their names and weren't much for idle conversation, but they compared some essential notes and learned more of what Felony already knew. Like the alien presence seemed to have a higher concentration in and around Montana, more than most places in what was left of America. Probably the first time his state had ever been a focus for anything beyond the blue sky itself.

It had been another long while since they were unceremoniously dropped off on the side of the road, and Felony was getting tired of counting the hours.

He was also trying to figure out what it was about Craig that bothered him so much. The feeling had both dimmed and worsened since leaving the Cottage. Felony was surprised to find himself liking the guy, but couldn't dismiss his nagging gut, triggered every time Craig would get evasive instead of answering a goddamned question about his past. The guy was a talker, so long as conversation was kept to speculation on alien whereabouts or possible activities. But pre-invasion exchanges were limited to one- or three-word answers. Never anything longer than a sentence.

Eventually, Angel couldn't take it. "Just tell him."

But Craig said nothing.

"Tell me what?" Felony asked, hoping he already knew.

Sophia gurgled in Angel's arms. "He doesn't want to tell you what he used to do for a living because he's embarrassed."

"I'm not embarrassed."

"Why is he embarrassed?" Felony felt a smile tugging at his mouth.

"Just tell him."

Craig looked at his wife, sighed, and said, "I was an entertainer."

"What kind of entertainer?" That smile tugged harder.

Angel broke a long silence. "Oh, my gawd. If you don't say it, *I will.*"

"Fine." Through gritted teeth. "I was a street entertainer."

Felony laughed out loud, but immediately corrected. "What the hell, man? You were acting like you were a professional child molester or something. Who gives a shit if you were dancing for your cash?"

"How do you know I danced?"

Felony shrugged, still laughing. "You move with a natural grace. Was it dancing? Or magic? Please tell me it was magic. Or dancing magic. I'll give you all the food if you can pull out something from behind my ear in the next five seconds."

"Yes, I danced."

"To music he made."

He shot Angel a look.

"It was really good," she added.

Clearly humiliated, he kept walking in silence.

"Can I see you dance?" Felony asked after another few minutes of crunching snow.

Craig said nothing.

"What kind of dancing?"

But still, Craig refused the bait.

Felony persisted. "Waltz, mambo, a cha-cha-cha?"

"Whatever went with the music," Craig said.

"It was 80s style breakdancing," Angel added, "and better than it sounds."

"It would have to be." But then Felony laughed and both of them joined him. Sophia sort of did, too.

The mood stayed buoyant until their world stopped turning.

"Get down!" Felony whisper-shouted the second he saw them.

They all crouched, following Felony's lead as he crept toward the thickest group of trees and hid behind the widest trunk.

He pointed, not that he needed to.

Three bad guys ahead — or so he assumed since the trio was armed with one sword and a pair of crowbars.

"You wanna come with me, Moonwalker? Just the three of them, with your moves and my size? I'm sure we can get them to listen." Felony smiled even though he was moments from maybe killing someone. "You up for it?"

Craig nodded, clearly wanting to match Felony's bravado, but his windburned face was haggard under the late afternoon sun, lines drawn by fear and fatigue tearing into his expression. He turned to Angel and his baby. Kissed them each on the forehead, then stood next to his new friend.

Felony looked behind him. "Our sleepy asses just fucked up. It's a trap." Five bandits were walking toward them. He glanced back over his shoulder, and sure enough, the original three were approaching as well.

They were armed with the usual hand-to-hand weapons, and the nearer they got, the more Felony could smell their desperation. "Stay back!"

But of course, they ignored him.

Sophia squeaked, Angel pulled the child to her chest.

Craig whispered, "What now? Like we talked about?"

They were coming faster, all of them with death etched into their expressions.

Felony knew what he had to do but couldn't help hearing Eamon's voice in his head. So, he let some of him out. "Last chance to talk!"

And when they kept walking, Felony turned to his companions and confirmed what Craig had wanted to know. "*Like we talked about.*"

Felony drew his gun and held it high in the air, displaying his doomsday device.

The bandits stopped walking. Felony glanced behind him to make sure.

"Everyone drops their weapons, and the skies stay empty." Again hearing Eamon in his head, and seeing Angel looking up at him with a baby in her arms, he added, "We're just passing through. No need to get ugly."

The men in front of him were following the order, and Felony assumed the same would be true for the bandits behind him. Craig faced that way to make sure. Felony was about to ask when he heard the crunching of boots pounding snowy ground.

Craig yelled, "Look out!"

Felony spun around and saw one of the bandits running right toward him, already close enough to see his red eyes and foaming mouth. No hesitation, he squeezed the trigger and sent a bullet through the bandit's nose and out the back of his head. His body flew back into the snow, crimson already drowning the white underneath it.

The bandits scattered.

Felony screamed, "Run!"

Angel ran toward the forest, clutching a crying Sophia, with Felony a couple of steps behind, and Craig behind him.

Drones dropped from the sky, firing into the bandits.

Screams and chaos behind erupted them, but Felony dared not look back. He pressed himself to move faster in the snow, praying the drones hadn't spotted them.

As Felony, Angel, and Sophia reached the tree line, he realized that Craig wasn't with them.

He turned to see the man sprawled on the ground, struggling to get up. Had he been shot or taken a fall and injured himself?

More drones and ships descended on the bandits. Reptars dropped from them, kicking up a flurry of power snow and blood as the beasts tore through the remaining bandits.

Craig was thirty feet away.

They'd not spotted him yet.

Angel lurched toward him, as if she were going to go get him, throw him on her back, and carry him back.

Felony grabbed her.

She let out a scream.

Two Reptars turned, then spotting Craig, raced toward him.

There was nothing anyone could do.

Felony clapped his hand hard over Angel's mouth to throttle her screams. He covered her eyes with his other hand, pulling her against him as she consciously or unconsciously did the same thing to Sophia, quieting the child and clutching her against her chest, then holding her tight as her father's screaming finally fell silent, his last few seconds spent getting turned into what looked like an unwashed slaughter room floor.

Felony held the woman and her daughter in the cover of trees as snow began to fall harder. He felt his blade at his side. If the reptars came, there was no way he could protect them.

He could only hope to stop them for a moment before the fucking insects eviscerated him on their way to Angel and Sophia.

Please don't see us.

Please don't see us.

As two of the Reptars turned away from Craig's body, a third one turned, staring right at Felony and the girls.

Felony had no idea how good their eyesight was.

But it sure felt like it had to see them. There wasn't enough cover to completely conceal them.

He watched, his heart racing, his gut churning, whispering over and over to Angel and Sophia, "Shhh, don't say a word."

The reptar stared for so long, Felony thought it might be toying with him like a cat would toy with its prey before killing it.

Finally, it turned away, then scampered back onto one of the alien ships from whence they'd come.

Felony held Angel and Sophia for what felt like forever, waiting for the aliens and the drones to leave. When he was certain it was safe, he released them, telling Angel, "Don't look."

But she did.

And her scream cut him deeper than any weapon had ever.

Chapter Thirty-Nine

FELONY TOLD them to sit tight as he gathered some weapons and supplies from the corpses. Then he returned.

"I need to see him," Angel said, handing her daughter to Felony to hold.

Felony watched as she grieved at her husband's corpse. The only good thing was that Craig was so unrecognizable, even if Sophia had seen anything, she wouldn't know it was her father's body on the ground.

When Angel returned, they made their way to where they'd originally spotted the bandits and saw the first good thing in forever — a big industrial van. Sure enough, the thing was electric and half-full, both with gas and food.

Felony was afraid he'd have to coax Angel into the van, that she'd want to stay or bury her husband. But she was terrified to stay, afraid those things would come and finish them.

So they got in the van. Then he drove.

They followed the signs to New Hope, seeing a new one every twenty miles or so, until they ended the day at the edge of a small settlement that had been reduced to ashes.

A sign that had read "New Hope" had been crossed out with what looked to be blood.

Another sign stood next to it, made of plywood. Red spray paint lettering read, "Looking for Salvation? Hope is here in Stonefall."

"Stonefall," Angel whispered, her fingers brushing the map nailed to the bottom. It wasn't too far from where they were. "I think it's a sign."

"Well, obviously," Felony said, pointing at the sign in front of them.

"I meant the other kind of sign. Stonefall used to be a prison. My father was doing time there when this happened."

"I'm sorry."

"Don't be. We barely knew each other. But I think I should go there."

"No way." Felony shook his head. "We're going back to the cabin. For all we know, the folks at Stonefall erased New Hope from existence, torched this place, then left a sign to say not to fuck with them."

"Or the people of Stonefall came and helped these people regroup after someone else attacked them. I can't go back to your Cottage." Her face was resolute. "There's nothing for me there."

Felony couldn't believe he was arguing for human baggage and more mouths to feed, but there it was.

"You'll be safe with us."

Angel started to cry. "I don't think there's anywhere safe in the world."

The girl had a point.

So Felony filled his belly, packed as much food as he could possibly carry, armed himself from paring knife to katana blade, then gave the van and everything in it to the mother and her child.

It was an odd goodbye, seeing as Felony wasn't used to them and was thus not especially good at them. He embraced Angel while she was hugging Sophia, then told the girls that if life was lucky enough, they'd see each other again.

Then they drove into the distance as Felony turned around and started his very long walk back to the Cottage.

Chapter Forty

EAMON LOOKED OVER AT SHERRY, overwhelmed with gratitude that she was still alive.

Though William wasn't able to help her — something that had the baby in a rare fit of tears — Jolie was a godsend. She put them immediately at ease, telling them the bleeding wasn't too severe, though Eamon suspected it was a lie.

"Are you sure?" He didn't want to doubt the woman, especially out loud, but the words were just sort of there.

"I'm sure," she said, her voice firm as she worked. "The wound isn't in her chest or abdomen, and the bleeding's mostly stopped thanks to Sherry being such a great patient and already applying so much pressure."

Jolie applied more until the bleeding stopped. Eamon put the gauze where she told him and left it on Sherry's skin even after it was soaked in blood.

"Do you want me to get any peroxide?"

"Absolutely not," Jolie said. "That can damage tissue. After we protect the wound, we'll apply some antibiotic cream."

Even after Sherry's wound was all dressed, Eamon still felt uncertain. But Jolie assured him she would be fine and got ever more specific as he pressed. The wound wasn't too deep or jagged, and there was nothing gaping open; it was clear of all dirt and debris; there were no signs of infection, and if she kept it clean, there shouldn't be. Sherry wasn't running a fever, and her last tetanus shot was only four years behind her. She would be fine.

"Thanks again," Eamon said. "For saving us, and for dinner."

"Our pleasure." Jolie slid a plate of peppers and sausage across the table as if to prove the post-apocalyptic feast wasn't his imagination. "It's great having people to share with."

"Delicious," William said.

It was probably his most complicated word so far, though Sherry would know better than Eamon. The couple was in awe, but they weren't much more surprised by *delicious* than they had been with *go*. A talking infant was plenty enough to wow them, regardless of the word.

"It's amazing how much you have here," Eamon said, trying not to sound disrespectful.

"You don't have to talk around it." Jolie gave him a smile. "You can ask where it all came from if you want to know the story. Gives Jefferson a chance to brag. It's one of his favorite things to do."

"Is not," Jefferson said.

"He used to be more humble, when everyone was always singing his praises. But now without any neighbors or relatives to tell him how wonderful he is, my husband's like a senile old man, talking about himself out loud."

"It ain't bragging if it's a statement of fact." Jefferson shook his head, like the room didn't understand him, then filled his mouth with a carrot. The sausage and peppers were apparently only for the guests.

"So," Eamon finally got to it. "Where does all the stuff come from?"

And he meant *all of the stuff.* It was laughable that he and Felony had ever thought to rob them. When Eamon suggested they spare the couple, he figured he was saving some old people from starving, but they could have stuffed their packs, and each rolled a pair of stuffed suitcases behind them, and it wouldn't have made a ding in their stores.

"I've never stolen a thing!" Jefferson announced instead of telling a story.

"No one accused you," Jolie said. "Now will you please satisfy our poor guests' curiosity?"

Jefferson smiled, apparently as happy in the spotlight as Jolie promised he would be.

"You want to know the secret about how we got all of this stuff?" Jefferson asked.

Eamon and Sherry nodded.

William said, "Yes."

Jefferson laughed, still shaking his head in disbelief, squeezing Jolie's hand as she looked over at him proudly.

"It was all just there. Because we needed it to be."

He stopped. Emphatic. As if that alone explained it.

Eamon waited through a few moments of silence, then said, "I don't understand."

"Most people don't," Jefferson told them.

"And he likes that," Jolie said, "because then he gets to explain it."

"Damn right, and it's an explanation worth hearing."

Jefferson then expounded upon a life philosophy that was ludicrous and simple, though a lot less nonsensical now that the old man was fully stocked for the apocalypse. Essentially, he surrendered to life and fully embraced wherever that might take him, whether that meant sitting in the house and waiting everything out, or getting in his 3D printed car to head out and save the day.

"We live untethered, so the universe comes to us."

It didn't make sense to Eamon, even after ten minutes of clarification, but it seemed crystal clear to Sherry.

"So, you don't hear any of that jabber in your head?"

"Right," Jefferson said. "And when everything's blank, the truth is always more obvious. Believing *you* are your thoughts means you're likely to blindly follow them. Whether that means running into or away from the aliens or waging war with your fellow man. I'm not living much differently than I did a year ago, despite it all."

"It's true," Jolie confirmed.

"How is that possible?" Eamon asked.

"I wake up around four like I always have."

Sherry blinked. "In the morning?"

Jefferson chuckled. "Of course."

William said, "Early."

Then the old man continued. "I wake up, meditate until breakfast, then go out for a walk. It's during my walks when I've found all our stuff. It was awful, coming across so many slain families, but I'd always gather whatever I could, loading it into Olive and making a few trips if necessary. It seemed smart to keep all our stores in one place. But we'll never use it all, and it seems like everyone's gone from The Oaks. Killed by bad guys or aliens."

"Why do you think they spared you?" Eamon asked.

Jefferson shrugged.

"Probably because they're nicer than the rest of them," Sherry suggested.

Jolie smiled. "What she said."

William clapped. "Nicer!"

"Maybe it's because we weren't surprised," Jefferson added, the thought seeming to surprise him. "We've always said we were sitting on a tiny rock, spinning in space, waiting to see what the universe might bring us."

"I don't understand," Eamon said, sincerely trying to get it. "What did you do for a living?"

"Whatever I wanted." Jefferson laughed.

"What does that mean?"

"That he always had enough, right?" Sherry asked Jefferson, seeming to get it all fine. And long before Eamon.

"That's exactly right."

"This is a nice house, and it's filled with nice things." Eamon pointed randomly to a print on the wall. It could have cost a fortune or come from IKEA. But either way, it came from somewhere. "How can you afford it?"

"Oh, I would never have wanted a house like this. It's too much for us," Jefferson said.

Jolie wrinkled her nose in agreement.

Eamon shook his head. "I don't understand."

"Someone left the house to us."

"In their will," Jolie added.

"Right, in their will." Jefferson smiled as if it all made perfect sense.

"How long ago was that?" Eamon asked.

The couple looked at each other, then together said, "About two weeks before Astral Day."

Eamon leaned forward, enraptured. "Where were you living before that?"

"Around," Jefferson said.

"Right before that, we were living in a tent. We'd been doing that for about six months. But we were living in a much bigger house than that before our time in the tent."

"But I thought this house was too big," Eamon said.

"Oh, it is." Jolie nodded.

"We didn't actually live in the main house. We lived in one of the smaller guest houses."

"That's because Jefferson wouldn't accept payment for his work, and so Mr. Wyatt, the man who owned the house, needed some way to pay him, anyway. Jefferson pretended the house wasn't any sort of a wage since we needed a place to live, and that made the work easier."

"What kind of work?"

"I helped with his medicines," Jefferson said.

"Like a doctor?"

Jolie laughed. "No. Nothing like a doctor. More like a shaman."

"I don't like that word." Then Jefferson gave his wife a look that was the closest thing to irritation that Eamon had seen on his face so far, though it was still an orbit away from anger or anything like it.

"So, you don't have any money?" Eamon was still trying to understand. It wasn't just that this was the opposite of what he'd grown up with, where everyone was always clawing to get a dollar more than everyone else. The world ran on money. You couldn't just circumvent that because you *decided* to.

"Not that we need it now, but we used to have more than we could spend, despite trying our hardest to get rid of it," Jolie said.

"HOW?" Eamon was losing his shit.

Sherry was apparently amused, and the couple indifferent.

"How?" William echoed.

"You ever hear of the Surrender App?"

No one had.

Jolie explained. "Jefferson knew this woman, January Saint. She asked him if he could distill his life philosophy further. So, he said that everything in life came down to a simple *yes* or *no*. Will you surrender, or won't you? Impossible to believe that an idea like that could be worth anything, but January's app had more than a million downloads on the first day. Of course, her company had all sorts of things they were trying to sell the user after they got the free app, which was the opposite of everything we'd told her. It made us not want the money."

Jolie laughed. "But the money kept landing in our account, anyway. Even when we were living in the tent. Jefferson wanted to give it all away at once, but he listened to reason and we've been doing it a little at a time ever since."

"Or we were," Jefferson said, sorrow turning him husky. "No more Secret Thanksgiving this year, and probably not ever again."

"Secret Thanksgiving?" Sherry repeated.

Jolie sighed. "Go ahead."

"It's actually called Secret Shopping. I just like doing it best at Thanksgiving. We start with a long drive. None of the McMansions around here, we go to where people are hurting. We'd arrange the details with the manager ahead of time, then show up with an envelope full of cash. Jolie and I would spend the day peeking into people's shopping carts, seeing who needed help the most."

"We like families. Big ones."

"In a good day, we can hit three grocery stores before coming back home."

No one knew what to say. Except for William.

"Give!"

Jefferson grinned. "That's right. At least more than you

get. A life lived in surrender, knowing wherever it takes you is where you're supposed to go, is a life worth living no matter how long it lasts."

That hadn't given Eamon much clarity. From what he could understand, the man's philosophy and business model were both to *roll with it.* It was absurd ... and impossible to argue with how well it had all worked out for them both.

Jolie was asking Sherry where in the house she thought her family would be most comfortable staying when Sherry shocked the hell out of Eamon.

"Oh, we'll be leaving in the morning. We have to get back to our cabin. But thank you so much for everything."

"Why would you want to go?" Jolie asked. "We have everything here."

"Home," William said.

Sherry looked down at her boy and said, "That's why."

"You can—" Jolie started.

But William made her stop. "Go Home. To Cabin."

Eamon wanted to get her alone so he could argue his point, make sure Sherry understood that she was talking insanity. This couple had everything, including karma, and would surely keep them safe.

"I'm going to surrender and see where that takes me."

Jolie gave Sherry a knowing smile, said, "Fair enough," then helped them all to pack up with plenty of food and medicine.

But they had everything they needed here, including a radio to listen for Felony. Going back to the Cottage was foolish at best and suicide at worst. The seconds felt painful until Eamon could finally say it.

"We need to stay here," Eamon whispered, once Jolie and Jefferson were both out of earshot.

"No, Eamon. We need to go." Sherry was insistent, more than he'd ever heard her.

"It's safe here."

"It's safe wherever William is."

"Home," the baby confirmed. "Cabin."

And to his surprise, Eamon found that he couldn't argue with that.

Chapter Forty-One

PERCY WOKE UP SCREAMING.

It wasn't like rising from a nightmare, with his heart beating too hard and sweat making beads on his brow, a lingering sheen of surreality to remind him of his passing from one plane to another.

This was pain, pure and simple — blunt and brutal, sharp yet unforgiving, beyond agonizing.

He was upside down, getting nailed to a cross. The first spike was through his wrists already, and the pain was excruciating. His forehead was wet, making him realize he was crying. Uncontrollable sobs, belching from his mouth as the second spike exploded through his left hand.

Agony broke him. Torture, marrow-deep. He was upside down, but also inside out, his faith in God the only thing keeping him from breaking into pieces.

"You can keep screaming," Kirk said. "I like it."

You're a monster. The aliens will feast on you first, savoring you, keeping you alive to finish last when they finally take Stonefall.

He could only think it, and Percy realized that he would probably never be able to make any words again.

Then he wondered if he was thinking the right thing, since he was getting nailed to a cross and those weren't the sort of thoughts Jesus would have had, even — or especially — just inches from His end.

Percy bit his lip and filled his mouth with the last blood he'd ever swallow.

The newest suffering was a distraction, if anything. A trifle compared to the profusion of pain pounding down on his body. The metallic taste better than yelling, crying out, or in any way giving Kirk a cell of satisfaction.

He thought of Christ, His last temptation, the final supper at the end. Dwindling minutes spent clinging to life on the cross, waiting for his Father to call him home.

Father, forgive them, for they know not what they do.

The pain was great, the icy air fierce. Percy began to numb out.

And that was good, the torment becoming more like a tickle, mean and insistent but a constant hum he could almost lean into. That didn't stop either of the spikes piercing his ankles and splitting the wood from making his bones feel like they were boiling in acid.

Father, forgive them, for they know not what they do.

"It's not personal, you know. We just couldn't have you leaving Stonefall and putting our town in jeopardy."

How could Kirk possibly know he and Melinda were planning to leave? Had he been spying on them? Were their quarters bugged? Or was this one of those things Gleeson just *knew* and had ordered his third in command — now his second — to stop him?

Percy squeezed his eyes tight to stave off the pain and repeated the mantra in his mind, over and over to keep all of his screaming inside.

Father, forgive them, for they know not what they do.
Father, forgive them, for they know not what they do.

Father, forgive them, for they know not what they do.

He was fully on the cross, dressed for their next round of torture, whatever that might mean. Percy couldn't stop thinking about Melinda, certain she was in more danger than ever, and he was hanging upside down, powerless to help her. He needed more information, so he could know what to pray for, because the time for God to listen and grant his prayers was now.

Take me. I'll go willingly if you spare her.

Like Percy had any other choice.

Finally, even though each syllable was like a spike through his throat, Percy said, "How did you know?"

"About your leaving?" Kirk laughed. "That was easy. Believe it or not, Ophelia was worried about the two of you. She actually thought *you* were in danger. Probably easier than wrestling with the truth that she'd fallen in with a couple of no good niggers."

The predator took a moment to study his prey, narrowing his eyes at Percy on the cross. He smiled like a serpent and licked his dry lips in the bitter wind. Then Kirk shrugged with faux indifference and said, "I guess you get what you pay for — her pussy wouldn't be nearly as sweet if she was old enough to know better."

And then he laughed.

It is finished.

"Ophelia never realized she was living with a couple of traitors. Now she knows, and everything serves a purpose in the end. Your death at the hands of The Forsaken will bring our community together and make Stonefall stronger than ever."

Percy shouldn't have been able to speak, but the words were there in his throat, desperate to leave his mouth, giving him faith that maybe the Good Lord was still listening.

"Please, Kirk," Percy hated himself for begging, "be a man. Whatever your beef, it's between me and you. Leave Melinda out of it."

Kirk scrunched his face, as if considering a very strange idea. Then after a long pause — every one of which felt like an hour — he said, "Why would I want to do that?"

"Because if you believe in God, then you know he's watching, and—"

"God doesn't like niggers any more than I do."

"Gleeson will have your head."

That got Beckett laughing, but the seriousness on Kirk's face shut him back up.

"Gleeson will never know shit. You're just another victim of The Forsaken, a martyr for the sheep to rally around."

"No." Percy shook his head, insistent. Kirk wasn't getting it, and that would be a good thing if he wasn't howling inside, wondering what would happen to Melinda after his passing. "He *sees* things. He will know what you've done here today, and then he'll make you pay."

But Kirk only smiled. "We'll see."

Percy thought it couldn't get any worse than that, but then it did.

"Are you ready?" Kirk asked.

Beckett smiled, grinning like an idiot, then drew a large carving knife from a sheath at his side.

"You can get started," Kirk told him, as though giving Beckett a gift. "Take your time and give it to me once you're done."

Then Kirk stood to the side, watching as Beckett ripped open Percy's shirt then slowly carved an upside cross onto his chest.

Keeping the screams inside was impossible. He

bellowed and yelled, shrieked and screeched, cried and called out, hollered and wailed — all to mocking laughter falling like hail around him.

Father, forgive them, for they know not what they do.

Beckett said nothing, pouring all his concentration into his work, but Kirk continued to taunt Percy. "The blood burns, doesn't it? Don't worry, it won't last too much longer, and at least you won't have to look at this ugly world anymore."

Beckett handed him the knife.

And Kirk carved out Percy's eyes, one at a time.

The pain was too much. Percy was on his final few seconds.

It is finished.

Father, into thy hands I commend my spirit.

Chapter Forty-Two

"Do you think we made a mistake?" Eamon asked.

Sherry looked at him for a while before answering, taking her time, almost as though she was tasting the answer on her tongue before allowing it to leave her mouth. "No," she finally said. "Even though it feels like it."

"I'm not sure it does." Eamon shook his head. "I know what mistakes feel like. Believe me, I've made plenty. But this isn't like that ... it's something else."

"I know. It's a feeling, right?"

"Seems more like a *knowing* to me."

Sherry nodded. "Do you think we hurt their feelings?"

Eamon laughed. "No. I don't think either of them even knows how to get their feelings hurt, and I'm sure they're both familiar with following whatever it is their guts are guiding them to do."

"Do you think they'll be okay?"

As ludicrous as it seemed, Eamon didn't doubt it at all. "I think they'll be great."

Sherry changed the subject. "How long do you think he'll stay sleeping?"

Eamon shrugged. He truly had no idea. William had been down for eighteen hours, and they both agreed it looked like he might have grown another inch in his crib. The poor child was totally empty when they put him to bed, almost a shell. He had been wide awake for the entire trip back to the cabin, refusing to sleep despite Sherry pressing his head to her chest, patting his hair, or doing any of the other things she thought might help comfort and calm him. But he was almost overly alert. Punchy, giggling a lot, his vocabulary growing, sentences stretching to four and even five words at a time.

Once home, he crashed.

"Do you think we should have let them drive us?"

Sherry had already asked Eamon that question twice. He said no both times, but she was clearly still feeling guilty. "It was the right thing to do. William is special, and we need to protect him. That means keeping the Cottage a secret."

"But if they wanted to take him, they could've already done it. And without saving my life."

"It isn't them I'm worried about."

The argument was full of déjà vu, but Eamon understood Sherry was trying to process.

"How long do you think we can stay here … before we have to go?"

"Depends if we have enough to get through winter, then how well we can plant in the spring. If Felony comes back, whatever happens in the rest of the world …"

Eamon trailed off. They'd been talking a lot about that, too. Worrying, even though it was the last thing they should be doing, both of them taking a page out of Jefferson's book — wanting to surrender and wishing for the best.

It was silent for a while. Comfortable, not awkward.

Then Sherry said, "What made you leave them alone? I mean, the first time, when you were with Felony. It's not like you knew them, and you went all the way out there to get food. So why leave The Oaks empty handed?"

"I couldn't do it." Eamon shook his head. "Not ever again."

"What do you mean, robbing old people?"

"Making the wrong decision when the right one was in front of me. My family... they're not good people, Sherry. My father's a monster. He's either murdered or had men murdered on his behalf. All my life, and more than I can count."

Sherry was obviously trying not to let her emotions show, but they were rippling onto her face anyway. And Eamon could feel her in his head. At least he thought so, same as they could feel William.

He wondered if she could see what was in his mind now. His father's bloody knuckles, marching into the house, leaving bloody footprints on the white marble again.

The unforgettable screams coming from their backyard when Eamon was only seven. He asked Liam what they were later, after he finally felt brave enough to leave his room. Casually, his brother said, "Dad was running over some guy with a lawnmower."

Eamon had no memory of his family's business being a secret, or even once being told that he couldn't talk about it at school. Because what the fuck was anyone going to do?

And the only thing Liam was ever ashamed about was having a yellow-bellied brother. In the early days, before Poppy, and before Eamon learned to listen more to who he might be instead of what his father told him he was, the youngest Quinn used his brawn plenty.

"I know I don't talk about Poppy much. It's just ..."

"I know ..." Sherry put her hand on his, squeezing his fingers. "It's okay."

"You were so similar in a couple of ways. And both of you always brought out the best in me. You make me want to do the right thing. Even when it's hard, or I guess especially when it is."

Eamon had to stop talking, breathing in and out to keep himself from losing it.

"I made Poppy a promise that I'd never work for my father, no matter what. But once she was pregnant with William, I felt like I didn't have any other choice. Of course, deep down I knew better, but it was easy to accept payment upfront and put off the tax of hating myself for later."

Sherry squeezed harder.

"That's why we had to run. I'm glad we did, because we found you on the bridge, and who knows what would've happened to you if we hadn't. But Poppy was the first woman I ever loved, and she died knowing I let her down."

Eamon needed another minute, but Sherry had nowhere to go.

"The first time I was at Jefferson's place, I couldn't stand the thought of robbing them because even if you didn't know what I did, it would still be letting you down. And William. The only family I have now."

The first tear fell, but that was fine. Eamon wiped it away and kept going.

"My wife died because of me, and I can never be that man again. I—"

"You were never that man, Eamon. Every day, I can't wait until Felony is gone on his rounds and the cabin is finally quiet so it can be just you and me, talking again. And every morning when I wake up, my first thought is how grateful I am to have you. I don't care about the aliens. I've never been happier, here in this cabin with you."

Everything about Sherry's face said she meant it.

Eamon couldn't make a lot of words and might have otherwise worried about perhaps sounding dumb, but William had shown them that one or two could be plenty.

"I need you," he said.

"I need you, too."

They went to the bedroom without another word. Fell asleep spent, then were roused several hours later by the sweet sounds of their William waking up.

"Hello!

"Well, good morning," Sherry said.

William clapped. "Night!"

"He's right." Eamon nodded toward the window.

"You must be starving," Sherry said on her way to the crib. William hadn't eaten in a day.

Eamon didn't know how that was possible for a baby, at least not without a lot of screaming and crying, but that was true for most things about his son.

Sherry took care of William while Eamon made breakfast for himself and Sherry. Cinnamon Toast Crunch. There was a giant bag of the stuff. Generic, rather than the real thing, but it still made Sherry happy. She told Eamon her mom had only let her buy it twice in her whole entire life. And she didn't care that they didn't have any milk, because she liked the cereal without it better, anyway.

He poured a bowl and set it between them. They'd done this once already, right when they got back from The Oaks. Taking turns, each of them picking up a square, popping it into their mouths, and slowly chewing, one bite at a time, both of them probably knowing they were falling a little more in love by the swallow.

The bowl was still half full when they heard the sound

of crunching snow, immediately followed by a friendly bellow. "Don't shoot, it's just me!"

Felony couldn't believe how much William had grown in his time away, both physically and with the short sentences he was now bundling into ever larger packages. Felony was also awed by their story of Jefferson, Jolie, and the psychic bridges Eamon and Sherry felt almost too shy to mention, though it felt blasphemous to keep it from Felony.

But then Felony took his turn, and his story was horrible. Fire in the sky and insects on earth, ripping some people who deserved it to pieces — and one who didn't. A street performer named Craig. A good man, according to Felony.

He had certainty in his eyes as he looked from Eamon to Sherry and made them a promise to soothe their obvious concern. "You have nothing to worry about with Angel. That girl means your William no harm."

Then Felony told them about New Hope and the irony of its old name. He told them about his trip home, how he had to murder a man and woman with his bare hands, but this time he did it with a shudder, not bragging at all, but bowing his head and declaring that he'd finally enough.

Life had never been more precious, and still death was like snow kicked into a storm all around them.

They put away the cereal and made themselves a feast to celebrate Felony's return. Surprisingly, or maybe not surprising at all, William was ready for bed when they were.

They all slept through the night, then Eamon woke to William tugging at his sleeve.

And in his most insistent voice so far, the baby said, "Good morning, Daddy."

Chapter Forty-Three

"Is HE ALL-KNOWING?" Gleeson asked.

Roy didn't need any thinking time for that question, same as he hadn't needed it for any of the ones before it. They'd been at this for a while. Today. The two of them had also been having the same conversation through every stolen hour of every day for months now. Their exchange was like rubbing a baby blanket between his fingers.

"Depends what you mean by *all-knowing*."

"Does God know everything there is to know?"

"Of course not." Roy shook his head. "That's impossible."

"Does He know the future and the past? Does He know my innermost thoughts?"

"God has shaped our past so He can create our present and fashion a better future so that we may one day ascend."

"When?" Gleeson asked what he wanted to know most.

"When it is time," Roy said like always. "When we are worthy."

"Will we ever be worthy in Stonefall?"

"That I cannot say."

"Tell me what you *think*."

"What do *you* think, Father Crowe? Are you worthy to lead them?"

"If Noah had not been a good man, then the Lord would never have chosen him. Same for Moses or Daniel or anyone else. The Light is shining in me. I feel it even if I cannot explain it. That Gift has helped me to see Heaven and Earth as one, and humans as the stars in between them."

"Hallelujah," Roy said, glad to see Gleeson was finally getting it.

There was a knock on his door, loud and insistent, almost demanding, as if a fist had been pounding on the wood for a while. He turned and said, "Come in."

The door swung open and Kirk walked inside, his face grave and his eyes serious.

Gleeson glanced at Roy, wanting to gauge his expression. His friend seemed worried, as well. "What is it?"

It's Percy.

"It's Percy," Kirk said, as if reading his mind. "He's … dead."

Gleeson had no trouble believing it, felt the truth in his heart and could almost see it behind a billowing black curtain inside his mind. A few words croaked from his closing throat. "Tell me what happened."

"It was The Forsaken, Father. They left Percy as an example."

"No …" Gleeson shook his head.

"It's okay, brother." Roy put a hand on his shoulder.

"Are you okay?" Kirk asked.

No, he wasn't. Percy was the only person in the world who had seen inside Gleeson's soul, both before and after the skies filled with the promise of eternity. Losing him was like losing a piece of himself.

"How do you know it was them?"

Kirk showed Gleeson a Polaroid. Percy fixed to an upside down cross, the eyes gone from his blood-soaked body, his skin like a mixed bowl of mashed berries — raspberry and black.

"I thought you went to find Angel together?" Gleeson worked to control his voice, keep it measured without losing his temper or flying into a rage like he used to. Like Roy warned him he could never do again. "How could this have happened?"

Kirk looked into his eyes without blinking, unafraid, despite Gleeson needing someone to blame.

"Percy wanted to go out on his own. Said he saw something in his head, maybe a vision like yours, Father." Kirk bowed. "Me and Beckett tried to convince him not to go, but he insisted."

"Why didn't *you insist* on going with him?" Gleeson stared at Kirk with accusation in his eyes.

"We couldn't," Kirk shook his head. "Percy wouldn't allow it. He pulled rank and insisted he go alone."

Clenching his fists, overcome with grief, Gleeson flew into a rage. "WHERE ARE THEY?"

Still shaking his head, Kirk said, "I have no idea, Father. But I'm happy to load up some men and follow whatever leads we can find. Percy was an important man. A good man. And we'll need to celebrate his life and mourn his passing here in Stonefall, while also learning as much as we can about the threat, so we can protect ourselves."

Yes, Percy was an important man in Stonefall, and a good one, but Gleeson wasn't a fool and knew that there was no love lost between he and Percy.

Calmer, but still a far cry from cool or collected, he shook his head and said, "Maybe the last sermon was too much."

"No," Kirk shook his head. "Better to end an enemy than exile them. You were protecting Stonefall."

"Sometimes mercy is the loudest," Gleeson said, repeating what Roy had been trying to tell him for a while. The rage was subsiding, with something murkier and sadder seeping into its place. "Where is his body now?"

"I've brought it home to bury."

It was too much. Gleeson pressed four fingers into his temple, two per side, working overtime to ignore Kirk referring to Percy's body as *it*.

"I need to be alone."

"Of course, Father."

Kirk closed the door behind him and left Gleeson alone with his grief.

Or almost alone.

"I'm sorry, brother, this is terrible news." After giving Gleeson a moment, Roy added, "Did you think there was anything off about Kirk's story?"

Gleeson looked at Roy, too distraught for critical thought. Full of rage and yet otherwise empty.

He stood and walked toward the door, wiping his eyes on the way, not wanting to have another conversation with Roy about Kirk.

"Where are you going?"

"To tell Percy's wife," Gleeson said. "I must give her the good news that her husband has gone home to God."

Chapter Forty-Four

MELINDA WASN'T JUST WORRIED. Something was eating everything inside her.

"Are you okay?" Ophelia asked.

It might have been easier to remove the crow's feet from her eyes than it was pasting the smile on her face, but Melinda managed it anyway. "Of course."

It was the fifth time Ophelia had asked the same question, regardless of her answer. Melinda was obviously doing an awful job of hiding her anxiety. But she felt *certain* something had happened to Percy. She couldn't explain it and really wanted Ophelia to stop asking. It wasn't that he'd been gone all morning, or even that he was out with Kirk, the man she trusted least in all of Stonefall. Something awful crept inside Melinda about an hour after her husband left, then another hour was gone and that something awful morphed into a radioactive certainty.

Something was very, *very* wrong. Percy might have been taken away from her, and this life, forever.

"Just let me know if you need anything," Ophelia reminded Melinda again.

"I actually do."

Ophelia brightened. The girl loved to be of service and obviously hated that there was nothing she could do to buoy her friend's drooping mood. "Anything!"

"Could you please take the laundry to Ginnifer?"

"Of course!" Ophelia then scampered off to be of service.

The laundry was light, and Melinda had been looking forward to walking it over herself a bit later. But it would take Ophelia five minutes in each direction, and she would spend at least ten minutes there talking to Ginnifer because the girl liked to talk and wasn't getting a lot of conversation at home.

That gave her twenty minutes of being alone with whatever this was. It should be enough to—

A knock on the door, without so much as a minute behind Ophelia's departure.

Melinda marched over, controlling her breath on the way. The girl wouldn't knock, and if she was doing so to be overly polite, then she was missing the point and pissing Melinda off.

Maybe it was Percy. He wasn't supposed to be back for a couple of days, but …

Of course, her husband would never knock.

She opened the door and immediately started to choke.

"Are you okay?" Gleeson asked.

It took her a moment, then, "Yeah, you just surprised me. I thought you were Ophelia."

"I just ran into her a moment ago. A blithe child."

"Yes," Melinda agreed. "She is."

Gleeson looked solemn. Or, if she let the thought bubble up to the surface, *grave*.

"What is it?"

He looked past Melinda and into her quarters. "May I come in?"

"Of course." She stepped aside to make way for his entry, then turned and closed the door. "What is it?"

The imposing expression still haunted his face. "It's Percy. I'm sorry, but … he was a victim of The Forsaken."

Melinda gasped. "What do you mean?"

She knew exactly what he meant, but asking the question kept the acid from eating her alive.

"Percy is no longer with us." Gleeson bowed his head. "God has called him home."

"No." Her knees went weak, but she forced them not to wobble.

Maybe it wasn't true. Gleeson could be here trying to read her. Percy was trying to make a move, secure something for them. Maybe he had somehow let it slip what the two of them were up to. Now Gleeson was here to ruin her. Fuck with her head before splitting it open. His lost eyes were only an act.

"It isn't true. You're lying."

But then Gleeson spoke, and his sorrow hit her like a tornado tearing through a barn, his voice heavy, like an ancient wooden door. "Love and death bear the best men to heaven. You've always given Percy the first, and today the second has found him. I am sorry, Melinda."

She could tell he was, but that didn't keep her legs from feeling soft enough to spread across a loaf of bread, nor her soul from catching fire.

"I don't believe you." Same thought, different landscaping.

"It's true."

"I want to see the body."

Gleeson shook his head, his bold eyes somehow beautiful despite their constant darkness. Like silver light around an angry cloud. "Percy is with Brother Randall, being prepared for his burial."

"No ..." Shaking her head, tears down both cheeks.

His attention was pulled off to the side like it sometimes seemed to be, then Gleeson turned back to Melinda and with obvious hesitation said, "I have a picture if you insist on seeing for yourself, but I would strongly suggest that you not."

"I have to."

Gleeson reached into his pocket, pulled out a Polaroid, then handed it to Melinda.

Her Percy was hanging upside down. Shirt open, an upside down cross carved onto his chest. Hard to see with all the blood caked across his freezing body — enough blue to look like a bruise — but it was clear enough.

And there was something much worse. Something Melinda was certain would be stealing her sleep for decades to come — two hollow sockets that were once the windows to her husband's soul, now vacant portals to hell.

She dropped the photo and screamed, totally broken, so suddenly alone that the thought of death and converging with Percy was a pinprick of light in the black.

Gleeson hugged Melinda as she sobbed. It didn't matter that she didn't trust him. Her body didn't care that he was a madman. She could feel his grief as her head pressed against him. Her brain didn't care that he was cancerous, because now so was she.

Anything to feel less desperate and lost, even knowing escape might last only an exhale.

"You have my vow that this will be made right. I will turn over Heaven and Earth to avenge him. You have nothing to worry about, not ever again."

But Melinda kept crying.

"We take care of our own, and I will honor Percy by providing for you."

Gleeson kept promising that everything would be okay, and Melinda continued to let him.

Chapter Forty-Five

THE STRING of random events and atrocities finally died.

Despite the drones apparently multiplying, shooting like meteors over the forest, life felt almost normal. Felony was a guard dog, and Eamon and Sherry were both downright domestic. William looked like a one year old and was speaking with shocking clarity. It had been long enough now that Eamon was no longer doing double takes, same for Sherry, but Felony was still having a hell of a time believing his eyes.

Winter sunlight streamed through the window. Sherry was still sleeping. Eamon looked down, wanting to kiss her, nibble on her ear, then turn her around and relieve his morning stiffness.

But he didn't want to wake her yet. It wasn't fair. Raising William took a lot, especially from Sherry because the boy was a beast and always hungry. So, each day she woke up empty and went to bed even emptier. William had been eating solids for a while, but he still wanted his milk, as much as he could get. Two grown men — one with bowling ball shoulders — ate less than a skinny girl and her baby.

Eamon got out of bed. Willam was sleeping.

He wanted to kiss his son on the head, but as with Sherry, Eamon preferred not to wake him. So, he quietly went to the bathroom, then crept out into the living room.

The cabin was eerily silent. Same as the last few mornings, Sherry would probably wake up with William, both of them about an hour before Felony, who stayed out late every night, patrolling the forest and pretending it wasn't a ludicrous task. Eamon liked this new routine. He could exercise in private, without Sherry making him feel self-conscious.

Wall sits, pushups and pull-ups, jumping jacks, planks. They even had a jump rope, and Eamon used it every day.

But something stopped Eamon on the way to his designated workout area. A large note stuck to the fridge. Even without any food inside it, the appliance was still an attention getter.

Eamon walked toward the note, his heart beating harder by the time he pulled it off the fridge. After a quick scan, he hoped his brain was playing games and that he'd read it wrong the first time.

Yo. Needed to fly. Ran into someone last night and found out Liam is still alive. I know where he is, so I need to go and get him. Be back fast.

EAMON WAS glad that Sherry was still asleep. Grateful that while still in bed, she wouldn't be able to see the rage on his face. He wanted to kill Felony. Why would he do something like that? It wasn't just that Eamon felt betrayed by

Felony leaving them alone in the woods without any warning and going back for his piece of shit brother, who deserved to die alongside his father, with or without an alien invasion. And even if he had to go, couldn't he have told them more than he did? The note said practically nothing.

Who did he run into?

How did that person know Liam was still alive?

Where was Liam, and how was Felony planning to get there?

And — this was the hardest one, it ripped out his insides and fried them in bile — why did he choose saving Liam over living happily ever after with the three of them?

It wasn't—

A knock dragged Eamon away from his thoughts.

It had better be Felony.

But something told him it wasn't, and that filled Eamon with dread, every step on his way to the door.

He was probably safe. If someone wanted to kill him, why knock?

To disarm him, of course. The sounds of someone breaking in would put them more on guard than a polite rapping upon their door. Only Felony knew where this place was. They had kept the location a secret even from Jefferson and Jolie, a couple with whom they had otherwise trusted their lives.

Eamon peeked out the window and saw the old man standing outside.

He opened the door, but before Eamon could ask Jefferson how he found the place, or what he was doing there, a panicked missive was leaving his lips.

"You can't stay here," Jefferson said. "We have to go."

"Why?" Then, before he could answer, "We can't leave. We're not even all here."

"Where is William?"

"Sleeping."

"And Sherry?"

"Same."

"So only your friend is missing?"

"Why do we have to go?" Eamon asked.

"That woman and her children are looking for you, and they will find you."

"Why are they looking, and what makes you think they'll find me? They can't possibly be that thirsty for revenge. Surely—"

"It isn't you they want, I'm afraid. It's—"

"No," Eamon said, understanding like a slap across the face.

"Please, may I come in?"

Eamon opened the door the rest of the way and let Jefferson inside. He heard the shuffling of feet behind him then turned to see Sherry entering the room.

"Jefferson …" Surprise was alive in her greeting. Same for fear and foreboding. "What are you doing here … and how did you find us?"

Sherry had an easier time with getting that obvious pair of questions out of her mouth than Eamon had.

Jefferson explained what Eamon already knew, then said something that chilled him.

"Your boy is a beacon for those who can hear his signal."

Sherry spun around and headed for her bedroom, as though she needed William in her arms that second.

Eamon and Jefferson traded a glance then followed.

She was already at the crib, staring down at their son in bewilderment.

"What is it?" Eamon asked, circling around to the side and gauging Sherry's dazed expression.

Then he heard it. William mumbling.

But it wasn't in English.

"Is that Russian?" Sherry asked.

"It was," Jefferson said, as the baby's muttering shifted direction. "But now it sounds like Chinese."

Chapter Forty-Six

"Percy was a Godly man," Gleeson said to the crowd. "Like Abraham, he was a man of faith. He heard the call, was tested and declared righteous. A brother of Abraham."

The crowd — eyes red, cheeks wet and stinging in the bitter wind, shawls pulled tight around sad shoulders — muttered their agreement on the black occasion.

"Abraham lived two-thousand years before Christ," Roy reminded him. "He could not have known Salvation would happen only through death and resurrection."

So Gleeson told his flock, "Abraham could not know what our brother knew, that God would wash his sins way. Our brother is no longer with us, but Percy died a righteous man."

It was time for the service to change its tone, once more before he lifted the curtain on his newest revelation.

"God forgives so we don't have to. Because forgiveness in a time like this is an unnatural act. Let us pray for release, and the freedom from knowing that such an injustice as this has been leveled against us."

Gleeson waited for the crowd to agree. Once they did, he added fuel to their fire.

"We must not allow The Forsaken to live. Every one of their kind must be found, and their seed wiped from the sanctity of God's flawless planet. We will have our vengeance."

Gleeson looked over at Melinda. He wanted to ask if she had any words because her soul was radiating and of course she *had* them. They would be a sickness inside her until she got them all out. But she wouldn't be able to vent them, at least not now, and probably not for a while. She was a specter, trapped in a glass bottom boat drifting down the River Styx, an unwilling witness to the specters and grotesqueries that haunted the rotting floor of hell.

He asked anyway, partly for show. "Melinda, would you care to say any words on behalf of our Brother Percy?"

Already sobbing, the invitation made her wail.

And the people wept with her.

What was awful for Gleeson and Melinda might eventually be good for Stonefall. Bring them together. Unify their intentions so they may continue to stand.

The young woman, Ophelia, sat in the front pew beside Melinda, arms around her, not exactly giving her comfort since such a thing was presently impossible, but perhaps helping her cling to the fraying edges of sanity.

Gleeson turned to his new second in command. "Brother Kirk, do you have any words to say about our Brother Percy?"

Kirk took his place in front of the crowd. Cleared his throat and clenched his fists. A righteous anger had found him, which made Roy appear nervous, though Gleeson was pleased to see it. Kirk's thirst for vengeance would surely serve Stonefall well. Keep them protected. And keep anger away from the Father of Stonefall.

"Brother Percy was a brave, God-fearing man. I'm sure that even in his death, he never lost his faith. I can imagine a prayer on his lips as he perished. He would want the same from us. Demand it, even. We have lost one of Stonefall's founders. Together we will mourn him, then claim the justice on Earth that Jesus has already given our brother in His Kingdom."

The Flock made noises — the closest noises to applause they could make during a service such as this one — then Gleeson resumed his spot, now with the hint of a smile.

There was no glee in Percy's passing, but as Roy kept reminding him, the Good Lord had opened a window.

Gleeson said, "Here in Stonefall, our Savior has delivered."

He looked out past the Flock, to the angel in back.

His Angel. Gleeson's first and only born. A holy child, who delivered unto him a treasure worthy of heaven.

"All hope is not lost!" Gleeson continued. "The Lord has blessed me with visions of someone special. A child that will lead us through the dark days in waiting. A miraculous babe, who will be joining us soon."

He waved his hand, inviting Angel to the stage.

"Meet my daughter, Mother Angel, who shall help lead us to the boy who shall be our salvation. And God damn anyone who try to come between us and this child."

～

FIND OUT
WHAT HAPPENS
NEXT

Get your copy of
Snowfall,
book 2 in the series

The Story Continues...

Gleeson Crowe has found his prize: the miraculous child who can heal the sick and build his ministry to protect the righteous and judge the wicked, and he's not about to give the child up, even to Eamon who has come for his son.

GET SNOWFALL TODAY

A Note from the Authors

Thanks for reading *Stonefall*

If you enjoyed this book, please consider writing a review of it on your favorite bookseller so other readers can enjoy it too. Just a couple of sentences. That would mean a lot to me.

Thank you!

Avery & Dave

About the Authors

Avery Blake doesn't want you to know where she lives, or what she does. She travels the world, moving from place to place quickly to ensure she can't be tracked. It's safer that way.

When she's not looking over her shoulder, you can find her in the corner of a cafe, facing the exit, typing as fast as she can.

David W. Wright is the co-author of edge-of-your seat thrillers including the best-selling post-apocalyptic series *Yesterday's Gone*, the paranoid sci-fi *WhiteSpace* series, and the vigilante series, *No Justice*, as well as standalone thrillers *12*, and *Crash* which was recently optioned for a movie.

David is an accomplished, though intermittent, cartoonist who lives in [LOCATION REDACTED] with his wife and son [NAMES REDACTED.]

He is not at all paranoid.

He is "the grumpy one" on the *The Story Studio Podcast* with fellow Sterling and Stone founders, Sean Platt and Johnny B. Truant.

David writes about books, TV shows, movies, and video games he enjoys; his struggles with anxiety and OCD; writing; and posts the occasional drawing at his personal blog at davidwwright.com

You can email him at david@sterlingandstone.net

We swear, he almost never bites. Unless you feed him after midnight.

For a full list of his most recent books visit sterlingandstone.net.

~

Please join the Invasion Universe Facebook group for the latest news and discussions, including excerpts of upcoming books.

If you'd just like to be told about new releases each week, join our new release mailing list.

Thanks for reading!

Also By Avery Blake

The Invasion Series

Longshot

Invasion

Contact

Colonization

Annihilation

Judgment

Extinction

Resurrection

Save The City Series

Save The City

Save The Girl

Save The World

Stonefall Series

Alienation

Stonefall

Snowfall

Downfall

The Taken Saga

The Taken

The Changed

The Hidden

The Saved

The Next Evolution

Transition

Convergence

Evolution

Stand-Alone Novels

Analog Heart

Family Royale

Ruthless Positivity

Vicarious Joe

Also By David W. Wright

Cold Vengeance

Cold Vengeance

Cold Reckoning

Hidden Justice

Hidden Justice

Hidden Honor

Hidden Shame

Hidden Virtue

No Justice

No Justice

No Escape

No Hope

No Return

No Stopping

No Fear

Karma Police

Jumper

Karma Police

The Collectors

Deviant

The Fall

Homecoming

Yesterday's Gone

October's Gone

Yesterday's Gone Season One

Yesterday's Gone Season Two

Yesterday's Gone Season Three

Yesterday's Gone Season Four

Yesterday's Gone Season Five

Yesterday's Gone Season Six

Tomorrow's Gone

Tomorrow's Gone Season One

Tomorrow's Gone Season Two

Tomorrow's Gone Season Three

Available Darkness

Darkness Itself

Available Darkness Book One

Available Darkness Book Two

Available Darkness Book Three

WhiteSpace

WhiteSpace Season One

WhiteSpace Season Two

WhiteSpace Season Three

Stand Alone Novels

Crash

Emily's List

Threshold

The Secret Within